GET LUCKY

Ballantine Books · New York

GET LUCKY

A Novel

Katherine Center

A Ballantine Books Trade Paperback Original

Copyright © 2010 by Katherine Pannill Center

Published in the United States by Ballantine Books,
an imprint of The Random House Publishing Group,
a division of Random House, Inc., New York.

BALLANTINE and colophon are registered
trademarks of Random House, Inc.

Title-page photograph copyright © iStockphoto.com

ISBN 978-0-345-50791-4
eBook ISBN 978-0-345-51922-1

Printed in the United States of America

www.ballantinebooks.com

1 2 3 4 5 6 7 8 9

Book design by Dana Leigh Blanchette

For my amazing sisters:
Elizabeth Ann Pannill
and Shelley Pannill Stein.
I don't know who I'd be without you.

GET LUCKY

Chapter One

First: I got fired. For emailing a website with hundreds of pictures of breasts to every single person in our company. Even the CEO and chairman of the board. Even the summer interns.

Looking back, I may have been ready to leave my job. I'd like to give myself the benefit of the doubt. Sometimes the crazy things I do are actually very sensible. And sometimes, of course, they're just crazy.

I knew the company had just lost a high-profile sexual harassment lawsuit for some very big money. I knew we were now enforcing our zero-tolerance policy. I knew somebody somewhere in the chain of command was looking to make an example. But I didn't think about all that at the time. Here's another thing I didn't think about: I'd just nailed the ad campaign of a lifetime, and I was finally about to get promoted.

In my defense, it wasn't like these people had never seen a breast before. In fact, our whole agency had been awash in them for months. We'd just finished a national campaign for a major bra company, and I'd led the creative team. I'd even come up with the concept—ads directing women to do all sorts of crazy things with their chests while wearing one of these bras.

"Dip 'em," one ad read, while our push-up-clad model leaned into a swimming pool, dunking her boobs in the water. "Scoop 'em," read another, while she pushed her boobs up toward her chin with two enormous ice cream cones. "Launch 'em," ordered a third, as she arched her back up to the sky. And on and on: "Smack 'em," "Mug 'em," "Wash 'em," "Flush 'em," "Flash 'em," "Love 'em," "Lick 'em," "Leave 'em." I'd spent innumerable hours with those boobs—weekends, nights—working my butt off to turn them into the most famous cleavage in America. Which, by January, they'd become. No small feat.

The model for the campaign was nineteen years old and profoundly anorexic with the most enormous augmented chest you can imagine. I didn't even know her name, actually. We just called her "the Tits." She was a petulant teen who spent all her time between shots wearing earbuds and drinking lattes and then asking people for gum. The question "Do you have any gum?" will forever take me back to that summer. She was a pretty girl, though the freckles, bumpy nose, and squinty eyes would have required retouching. If we'd used her face. In the end, we zoomed in so close that her face didn't even come into the shots. When it came to bras, who needed a face?

That's really how I used to think. I'm not exaggerating at all.

If I sound crass here, that's because I was. If I sound unlikable, that's probably true, too. I was, at this point in my life, after six years in advertising, a person who needed a serious spanking from the universe.

And don't worry. I was about to get it.

I was proud of the ads. They were saturated with color, eye-catching, naughty, and delightful. Everybody was ecstatic, and I was strutting around the office like a diva. The Boob Diva. That was me.

But something was off. Being the Boob Diva wasn't as great as I'd expected. I'd been so underappreciated at that job for so long that when appreciation finally came, it felt false. Maybe I'd built up too many expectations. Maybe all the pep talks I'd given myself about my coworkers being idiots were finally kicking in. Or maybe external validation is always a little disappointing, no matter what.

The books I'd been reading weren't helping, either. I had a whole stack by my bed that chronicled the ways advertising was making us all miserable. Who knows why I kept buying them? It's a chicken-egg question. Did I hate my job because I was reading the books? Or was I reading the books because I hated my job? Either way, I couldn't get around what they had to say: That an economy based on buying stuff needed to keep us all dissatisfied and miserable, needed to keep us focused on what we didn't have instead of what we did, and needed to convince us that things like happiness and peace and beauty could be bought.

Not the greatest watercooler chitchat.

Later, it would occur to me to wonder if advertising in general was screwing over the entire world or if my firm in particular was screwing over just me. I certainly wasn't paid enough. Or recognized enough. Or appreciated. But questions like that are a long time in the making. First, I had to have a little thing we might call a break-down. Or an epiphany. Neither of which was my intention.

Here's what happened, to the best of my recollection: The night before our big final presentation, my sister happened to send me an email link with the subject line "Boob-a-palooza!" Because I was too wired about the next day to go to bed, I clicked on it. And there, I found miles and miles of mug shots of anonymous breasts belonging to real women. No faces, no bodies, just breasts. Breasts au naturel. Breasts in the wild. Breasts as Mother Nature intended.

My sister just thought it was funny. But I had a different reaction: I could not stop scrolling through. I'd seen a lot of breasts on TV and in movies and on magazine covers in my life. Who hasn't? But I'd never seen anything like these real things. The variety was spellbinding. High ones, low ones, flat ones, full ones. Close together, far apart. Lopsided. Droopy. Walleyed. Googly-eyed. Water balloons. Bags of sand. Jellyfish. Cactuses. Bananas, prunes, and pickles. And this was the eighteen-to-thirty-two-year-old category. These were boobs in their prime.

Under each photo there was a caption written by the owner of the breasts. And each caption read something like this: "These are my breasts. They're pretty droopy (or lopsided or small or dimpled or ugly or embarrassing or pickle-shaped). Wish I could fix them." The comments ranged from vehement hatred to mild distaste, but nobody, absolutely nobody, said: "Here are my boobs. Aren't they great? I find them delightful, and hallelujah!" Nobody.

I was slated to hit the office at nine the next morning in my stilettos to present the "Boob 'em!" campaign to everybody who mattered. But instead of getting to bed early, as I'd planned, I stayed up until three in the morning browsing the photos. Something about the realness of the pictures on the site underscored the fakeness of the boobs in our ads. Something about the dignity of the real things made our hyped-up things seem ridiculous. The whole campaign suddenly seemed brash and loud and stupid and just plain rude in a way that I couldn't ignore. How had I never thought about this before? We were about to put a picture of a woman's cleavage getting branded on every bus in America, for Pete's sake.

I thought about all the normal women who had taken off their bras for the cameras. I thought about the bravery of stepping forward with your own imperfections to help others feel better about theirs. And all at once I felt ashamed of being part of the problem. I scanned the site until the images and the words bouncing in my brain became a cacophony of women's dissatisfaction and despair, building louder and louder to a crescendo that I could not shush. That is, until four A.M., when I clicked Forward on my sister's email, selected the company-wide distribution list, and hit Send.

I sat back and nodded a little so-there nod.

Then, in the quiet that followed, I realized what I'd done, sat straight up, choked in a little breath of panic, and started looking for a way to unsend that email. Knowing all the while that there wasn't one. That's the truth about emails: You can't take them back.

In effect, I fired myself. Though the guy who actually did the firing—discreetly and several hours after our slam-dunk presentation—was a VP named J.J. who everybody called "Kid Dy-no-mite." Even though he wasn't dynamite at all, just another ad guy at Marston & Minx. A guy I'd started with six years earlier. A guy who'd been promoted over me based on work we'd done together. A guy I'd slept with back in the beginning until he called me a workaholic and broke things off. Now he was married to a girl who wore pink Bermuda shorts when she brought him lunches in a picnic basket at the office. But I guess I was even less dy-no-mite than he was, because I wasn't married to anyone, nobody ever brought me lunches, and now I was out of a job.

J.J. said, "I'm sure you know that email was inappropriate."

"Was it?" I said.

He gave a short sigh. "People were pretty offended. Yeah."

We were standing in the now-empty meeting room where our "Boob 'em!" campaign would later win promotions for seven people on our team. We were surrounded by enormous blowups of bra-clad breasts in every direction. Breasts larger than our bodies, in full color. Valleys of cleavage the size of La-Z-Boys. The "Steer 'em" ad showed boobs wrapped in barbed wire. "Munch 'em" showed them resting on a giant sub sandwich. And "Whip 'em" had a close-up of a whip just before impact.

"J.J.," I said. "Look around."

He looked around.

I said, "What does stuff like this do to real women?"

"Real women?" he said, cocking his head. "Real women are over-rated."

Then he gave me a flirty smile, patted me on the shoulder, and told me the case was closed. It was lunchtime. He had a meeting. "Be graceful about it," he advised as we headed out. "And if you up-load your own photo to that site"—he opened the door with one hand and pressed the small of my back with the other—"shoot me an email." Then he added, "You'd totally win that contest."

"It's not a contest," I said.

"Everything's a contest," he told me, and then he walked away.

Next: I went out drinking with my team to celebrate our success. I wasn't a big drinker, but it seemed like the thing to do. I didn't tell anyone that night that I'd been fired, and pretended instead, all the while, even to myself, that I was still their boss. They teased me about the website and insisted that it would blow over, and in some small way, I let myself believe them.

Because I didn't want to be by myself. I didn't want to walk back to my apartment quiet and lonesome and fired. The ride down in the elevator alone had been bad enough, as I'd watched the doors close on the last six years of my life. I knew where I'd been, but I had no idea where I was going, and as the elevator started to move down, I felt that drop in my stomach that you feel when you're falling. Except

I couldn't even tell myself that I wasn't falling. Because really, actually, I was.

Here's a trick I've discovered for those moments when your life changes too suddenly to handle: Just ignore it. Ignore it for as long as you can. That was what I decided to do. I'd go home to Texas for Thanksgiving and not think even for one second about being fired until I was back in the city on Monday morning, scrolling through the want ads. Ignoring things doesn't fix anything, but it can buy you some time.

At some point, on the town that night, we all pulled out the last of several samples of gift bras the client had sent us and fastened them on over our clothes. Even the guys. After three glasses of wine and a mixed drink the bartender invented for us called a Double D, I felt relaxed in a way that I never, ever had—and optimistic about my new "freedom," like I was on the verge of a great adventure. As I shared bedroom trivia about Kid Dy-no-mite with our entire table—the Roller Derby fantasy, the Cagney and Lacey fixation, Elton John on continuous play—I found myself thinking, *I should go out drinking more often.*

Though at six the next morning, as I rode in the cab to Newark with my forehead pressed against the window glass, there was nothing about that night I didn't regret.

For the flight home, I had upgraded to first class using frequent flyer miles, and as we lurched through the Holland Tunnel, I clung to the idea of dozing off in one of those wide seats, a glass of Perrier on my tray table. The day before seemed almost like a bad dream, and I was ready to get as far away from it as possible. Home—always a tricky place for me—seemed like a refuge. And since I didn't have another one, I ran with it.

But when I got to the airport, they didn't have a record of the upgrade. And the seat I'd been assigned was in the very last row.

I said, "But I have a confirmation number!"

The airline lady clicked around on her computer, shaking her head. "Nope," she said. "Nothing." And then, as if that settled it, she said, "This confirmation number's not valid."

I was not feeling well. My head hurt, I was nauseated, I was unemployed. But I didn't complain. My roommate, Bekka, was a flight attendant. "Do you know what we do to the rude passengers?" she asked me once. "We reroute their bags to France."

In the end, I wound up thanking the lady for her help and proceeding to what was clearly the worst seat on the plane—one right against the bulkhead that didn't recline. I was also the very last person to board, and by the time I neared my seat, I was starting to sink. All I wanted was to fold myself into my little upright corner and snooze, but first I had to get past the people in my row. I was muscling my carry-on into the overhead bin as they unbuckled, stood up, stepped into the aisle, and waited. Then, just as I was scooting past and almost home, one of my rowmates spoke to me. We were belly-to-belly as I moved past him, and here's what he said: My name.

"Sarah," he said—and not like a question. Not like, *Is that you?* But more like: *Sarah. Of course.* When I paused to look up, there, inches away, was my high school boyfriend, Everett Thompson.

I had broken his heart. I had dumped him for an idiot soccer captain with beautiful calves. The last time I'd spoken to Everett, he'd been seventeen with a hoarse voice from crying. I could still almost hear it if I thought back. He had snuck over and camped outside my window that night, something that seemed sweet now, though at the time it had prompted me to call him a "freakazoid" the next day in the girls' bathroom.

But he'd bounced back. He went off to Stanford and NYU Law. He became a hotshot lawyer out in L.A. There was a rumor at one point that he was dating Mary-Louise Parker. My sister had called me about it and said, "Bet you feel pretty stupid for dumping him, huh?"

"Yep," I'd said.

"You could be Mary-Louise Parker right now," she'd said.

"Is that how it works?"

Here, on the plane, I could see how the Mary-Louise Parker rumor got started. Now, suddenly, Everett had star quality. He looked so different from the boy I'd known in high school, when he'd been six one and maybe ninety pounds. It shouldn't have surprised me that he'd grown up. We all had. But I was surprised. He'd filled out—and clearly joined a gym. He looked like a man. Everything about him was broader and stronger. Though he still had that slightly crooked nose, and one ear that stuck out a little, and the white scar on his chin from when his cousin hit him with a spatula. I felt a quick urge to touch it.

Then I realized I was holding my breath. He had every reason to hate me, and I found myself wondering if he still did. Surely not, right? Not after so many years.

"Wow," he said then, running his eyes all over my face. "You got old."

A jab. I wouldn't have expected a jab. In all my memories, he was just sweet and lovestruck. And anyway, aren't people who haven't seen each other for years supposed to be nice to each other? Out of respect for the passage of time, if nothing else?

But now he'd started it. And I was too stunned to jab back. I'd have given anything for a witty retort, but all I had was a sigh. Plus all I could think about was his mouth, right there, just inches from mine. A mouth I'd kissed before, though I didn't recognize it, exactly. I couldn't have picked it out of a lineup.

I took a second to wonder if that was his true opinion or if he was just being mean before I realized it didn't matter either way. This was, apparently, how it was going to be. I wasn't forgiven. We were enemies for life.

It wasn't really my call, so I decided to take the high road. I said, "It's a pleasure to see you, Everett. I'm glad your acne cleared up."

Then I moved in and got settled while, next to me, Everett put his headphones on and pulled out a laptop. I'd made it to my seat at last, but then I couldn't relax. His elbow was touching my hip, and every time the plane shook, it rubbed against me.

So much for sleeping.

I kept thinking we'd turn to each other eventually and chuckle about how stupid high school kids are, about youth being wasted on the young. It had been more than twelve years since we'd seen each other, after all. We were thirty now. Surely, time had muffled the insults and injuries. New York to Texas was a long flight, and it seemed possible we could even make up. I got my apology ready—or tried to, at least. I wasn't really sure how to account for my behavior back then. I was just stupid. I was just seventeen. I was just flattered by that soccer player. I didn't know who I was. I thought love was easy. I thought life was going to be a whole lot different than it had turned out to be.

My sister, Mackie, was picking me up at the Houston airport, and when she pulled up in her car, not three feet away, I was so busy trying not to look like I was scanning for a last glimpse of Everett Thompson that I didn't even see her.

Finally, she honked.

I hugged her when I got in. She was wearing the earrings I'd given her last Christmas and had a tiny barrette holding her bangs off to the side. "You just keep getting gorgeouser and gorgeouser," I said.

She gave me a kiss on the cheek. "Not as gorgeouser as you, babe."

We zipped out and onto the freeway and I leaned back into my seat. I wanted to comb through the details of the past twenty-four hours with her, and possibly even make her get my job back for me, but she had a topic of her own. As soon as I clicked my seatbelt, she said, "I just want you to know: I'm done."

I was still nauseated from the "speck of turbulence" we'd hit on the way down. "Done with what?" I asked, rolling down the window.

"Done."

"Done with knitting? Done with antiquing? Done with late-night snacks?" I could still feel Everett Thompson's elbow if I thought about it. So I didn't think about it.

"Done with trying," she said.

I got it. I turned to face her. "Done with the baby?" I asked.

Mackie nodded. She'd been to the doctor the day before, and this one had said the exact same thing the others had—about her endometriosis and her attempts to have a baby—though in more poetic words: Her uterus was tied tight by ropy knots of scar tissue. It could not stretch at all, it had no room for a baby, and there was nothing to be done.

This wasn't news, of course. We'd all known this since they started trying. But we had thought Mackie could overcome it with enough optimism and zeal. All the other miracles that it took to make a baby were in place—Mackie could get pregnant just fine. She just couldn't seem to stay pregnant. I think we'd all assumed if she could just stick with it long enough, we'd figure something out. But, as of tonight, she was not going to stick with it. She'd been trying to have a baby for six years, and today, in the car on the tollway, as if anything were ever that easy, she quit.

"What are you going to do?" I asked.

"You mean instead? Instead of becoming a mother?"

"Instead."

"I've been thinking about that," she said. "I'm going to go to graduate school. I need a more interesting job."

I could see why quitting altogether might appeal to her right now. Maybe someday, when she had a little distance, she would think about adopting. But sometimes you just want exactly what you want.

"But I know," she went on. "I'm going to start collecting Blue Willow china. I'm going to learn to quilt and play chess. I'm going to get a better haircut and find a personal trainer and volunteer at the women's shelter and glue that carrot-shaped salt shaker back together. I'm going to read that book everybody's been reading about the rooster."

"Cockatiel."

"Whatever."

"That all sounds great!" I said, aware that my voice was trying too hard.

"And take modern dance," she added. "Maybe. If they don't make me wear a leotard."

"You're an adult," I told her. "Nobody can make you wear a leotard."

We were on the highway now, windows up, zooming toward the heart of Houston, back into the neighborhood we'd grown up in together, where Mackie and her husband, Clive, now lived, just a few blocks over, in a house they'd built themselves.

Mackie was actually Mary Katherine, a name that didn't suit her at all, and I was Sarah Jane. I'd been the one—at age two—to invent "Mackie," for which Mackie still thanked me from time to time.

She was only one year older. We looked a lot alike—in an Olsen twins, you-know-they-aren't-the-same-but-you-can't-tell-them-apart way. We were the same height, same weight, same freckles and red hair. Same bra size. We even had the same curls—except Mackie got up every morning and straightened hers out with a flatiron.

If we'd had the same hair, people would have thought we were twins. Although the truth is, Mackie's nose was quite a bit straighter, and her canine teeth came down much farther, and I had a longer neck and a pointier chin. My eyes were hazel and hers were a cast-iron blue. Also, she had those toes where the second one was longer than the big one—much longer, kind of freaky longer. All her toes were long, actually, and when we were growing up I always made a point of calling them her "worms."

Mackie had been straightening her hair for as long as I could remember—with varied levels of success—and I think for that reason alone people never confused us. I was the Harper sister with the big hair—even though, technically, she was the Harper sister with the *small* hair, since all the women in our family had corkscrew curls, except for my mother, whose silky straightness had always been Mackie's gold standard. Mackie even kept a long lock of it in a keepsake box.

I should mention that my sister and I were close. We weren't best friends exactly, though—because a best friend is a person you choose. A best friend, in most cases, is a temporary person, too, until she moves away, or gets a promotion and starts working too hard, or just drifts off. Friends depend on a certain amount of convenience. With friends, you have to have their number handy, or work in the same office, or live in the same city. With sisters, none of that matters. And in the end, for me, that would be a lucky thing.

I don't mean to say that my sister didn't drive me crazy. She absolutely did. Even though we both knew all the words to every song in *The Music Man,* had a strange affection for hot-air balloons, and had crushes on all the same actors, we were less alike than we looked. I was always late, and she was always on time. She was a neat freak, and I was a total mess. She was pro-cilantro, and I was anti-. And, of course, whenever we had a fight, we went from arguing to screaming in about ten seconds—the express checkout of a lifetime of fighting and making up.

But I felt a connection to her I didn't feel with anyone else in the world. Maybe this is true of all sisters; I don't know. When good things happened to her, it felt a little bit like they were happening to me—and the same with bad things. Which is why I didn't want her to pretend to be okay about giving up on the baby. I knew she wasn't okay, because I certainly wasn't okay, and I wanted us to at least not be okay together.

Now, in the car, I accidentally started arguing with Mackie. I never should have let myself do that. If I hadn't been hungover, jobless, motion-sick, and newly old, I wouldn't have. But I had a moment when I felt irritated with her, as if she had just made an enormous decision that affected my life without consulting me. Which, in a way, she had. But only in a very small way.

In a moment I wish I could take back, I said, after a pause, "I can't believe you're giving up."

She sighed. "Well," she said, "believe it."

"You picked out your children's names in sixth grade," I said.

"All girls do that."

"I never did," I said.

"No," she said, "you did it for your pets."

Which was true. I'd forgotten. Funny, now, that I didn't even have a pet.

"Look," she said. "It's not going to happen. It's time to move on."

I don't know what I thought I was going to accomplish. It couldn't have ended well. But I just wanted her to have what she wanted. I felt like I couldn't be happy if she couldn't be happy. And, dammit, I wanted to be happy.

"There has to be a way," I said.

"Well," she said, "if you can fucking find it, be sure to let me know."

Her voice trembled like she might cry. And my sister never cried. She did not cry at *Terms of Endearment*. She did not cry when her prom date splattered ketchup all over her dress and corsage at dinner. And she did not cry on the summer night long ago when our mother died. At least, not at first. I, in contrast, cried at everything. I once cried at a tampon commercial. But Mackie was a pick-yourself-up, dust-yourself-off kind of girl, and when I heard her voice falter, I scrambled to backpedal.

"I take it back!" I said. There were plenty of terrible things about raising children. Maybe we just needed to shift our focus. "You know what children do?" I said. "They devour your life. My friends with kids are only hollow shells of the people they used to be."

"That's right," she said, nodding. "That's right."

"Maybe we've had this baby thing romanticized," I said. "Maybe we got it wrong. Maybe you've actually dodged a baby bullet."

"Maybe so," she said, and we were quiet while we tried that on for size.

After a bit, I went for a topic change. "I sat next to Everett Thompson on the plane today."

I was expecting an "Everett who?" I was expecting her to barely remember him—to have to remind her about who he was and the whole long story between us, even though there was nothing about the way I'd treated him that I cared to revisit. Later, we'd go over it. We'd have to. That's one of the things girls just do—circle around and around back through the past: analyzing, processing, searching for meaning. Though I wasn't sure there was too much meaning to search for in what I'd done to Everett: the way I'd agreed to go to the junior girls' Valentine's dance with him, but then, later, when the starting forward on the soccer team had also asked me, I'd said yes to him, too. And then I just kind of never told Everett. I just let him show up at my house in a rented tux with a handful of roses to find out that I'd already left.

That night, I'd wound up arguing with the soccer player about whether or not he could stick his hand down my dress (he won)—

and Everett wound up getting a lecture on the War of 1812 from my dad while they watched a nature program on mute and ate snicker-doodles. When my dad went up to bed, Everett said good night, but then waited on the front stoop for me to get home. I got home at twelve thirty—a half hour past curfew—found Everett waiting, and dumped him on the spot. I'm pretty sure I said something ridiculous and high-schoolish, like "Get a life." I know I didn't talk to him at school anymore after that. Or take his calls. Or read his letters. Or come to the window when he threw pinecones at it.

In the car with Mackie, I expected to need to walk her back through the whole story. But that's not the response I got. I got: "Oh, God! I forgot to tell you!"

"Forgot to tell me what?"

"Clive just hired him."

She was moving too fast. "Clive just hired my high school boyfriend? To work for him?"

Mackie was nodding. "Yes! On retainer! As a legal consultant!"

"And you forgot to tell me?"

"Well," she said. "I was going to tell you when I got to the airport." She took a deep, determined breath as she thought of the big decision she'd just made. "But then I forgot."

"Sure," I said. Of course. Then I said, "I thought he was in L.A."

"Was," Mackie said. "He moved to New York last year. Some big promotion."

That didn't add up. "Then why is he moving back to Texas?"

"Nobody knows. It's a big mystery. But we snagged him." Then Mackie squinted her eyes to remember way back. "What was it you did to him, again?"

"I don't want to talk about it."

"Does he still hate you?"

"Yes," I said. "He definitely still hates me."

"That's too bad," she said. "Because he's coming to the Thanksgiving party."

This was why I was home a day early. The Thanksgiving party. Clive's company had a party every month, and I had never been to one. It was all about morale and employee bonding—part of the management strategy that had made Clive the whiz kid of the online, all-natural, wooden-toy-selling world. The management strategy that had landed Clacker Toys on the cover of *Business Week.*

"It won't be like an office party," Mackie had sworn when she called. "It'll be a *party* party."

"People don't have Thanksgiving parties," I'd said. "It's not that kind of holiday."

"Well, it should be," Mackie had said. And then, "Clive's dressing up as a turkey."

"You're kidding, right?"

But she just said, "You never know with Clive."

Company parties were always at Clive and Mackie's house because it had great "flow." And it was a gorgeous house. I had contributed many things to the finished product, including the suggestion of concrete backsplashes in the kitchen and the breakfast nook, and I could go on and on about the design of it—sleek and contemporary but warm at the same time. Lots of windows and light, rough-hewn wood floors, an adobe fireplace. At the office parties, Mackie told me, she floated tea-light candles in glass bowls in the swimming pool that clinked against each other and made everything glow.

"Everett Thompson is coming to your Thanksgiving party?" I asked.

"I didn't invite him," Mackie said. "Clive invited him. And I didn't even know who Clive had hired until this morning. And Clive didn't know who Everett was until that same moment. And I still don't think Everett knows that Clive is your brother-in-law."

So that's why Everett had been on my plane in a bad seat. We were both flying home early for Thanksgiving to go to the same party. A party that, now, I would be skipping.

"You have to go!" Mackie said, reading my face. "You promised."

"That was before Everett called me old on the plane."

"He called you old?"

"He did."

"Did he call you old in a flirty way?"

"Does anyone ever call someone old in a flirty way?"

"He could have said it in a you're-not-really-old, I'm-just-sparring-with-you, you-foxy-lady, way."

"Well," I said. "He said it more in a you're-going-downhill-and-I'm-drop-dead-gorgeous-and-that's-how-it-should-be-because-the-universe-is-punishing-you kind of way."

"Is he really drop-dead gorgeous?"

"He's close."

"How did that happen?"

"I don't know," I said. "Last time I saw him, he was a skeleton with acne."

"There was something about him even then, though."

"Yes," I agreed. "There was."

"I wonder whatever happened to that soccer player you ran off with," Mackie said.

She knew, of course. Everybody did.

"I think he was abducted by aliens," I said.

"Didn't he get hooked on cocaine in college and crash his BMW?"

What an idiot. He was fine now, and working in finance. I shook my head at Mackie. "I'm sticking with aliens."

We had reached Mackie and Clive's driveway, and Mackie turned in and hit the brakes. At least she wasn't thinking about babies anymore. "I'm not coming to the party," I said. "I'll go to the movies instead."

"Of course you're coming to the party."

"No," I said. "I'm really not."

Clive was out of town until the next morning, so we had the house to ourselves. Mackie went to start supper while I went to the guest room to drop off my suitcase. And that's when I discovered something I really wasn't prepared for. The guest room where I always stayed when I came home had been painted yellow since my last visit. And there was a crib set up by the window, a changing table, and a zoo-animal mobile hanging from the fan. A stroller waited in a box in the corner. A watercolor of a hippo that had been in our bedroom when we were kids hung on the wall.

Mackie must have done it all during her most recent pregnancy—which had lasted three weeks longer than any of the others, but had ended just recently, in the second trimester. She hadn't told me about putting the nursery together, which wasn't that surprising. I could see how Mackie might not have wanted to open that topic up for discussion. I could see how decorating a room for a baby you stood a good chance of losing could be a private thing, an act of hope between mother and child.

I set my bag down. This, right here, was the room that she'd hoped to rock the baby in. This was the room she'd hoped to fold onesies in and play peekaboo in. This was what she imagined motherhood would feel like. This was the care she wished to lavish on her baby. It was one thing to know in theory that Mackie wanted a baby. It was quite another thing to stand on the inside of that longing. I stood by the crib and picked up a little rattle and wondered what it must be like to want something so desperately and not be able to get anywhere near it.

Mackie showed up in the doorway just then. "I forgot to tell you about the room," she said. She looked around and shrugged. "I got a little carried away."

"It's beautiful," I said.

"Thanks," she said. "I'm selling it all on eBay."

"Seriously?"

"Seriously." She turned and headed back toward the kitchen.

Here are the things my sister had that I wanted: a man who loved her wildly, a house with teak garden furniture, a storage closet larger than my entire apartment, and our mother's collection of Beatles albums. Here are the things I had that she wanted: a glamorous life in New York, a kick-ass (former) job, plenty of reasons to travel, and a sense of endless possibilities. She had stability and a Sub-Zero fridge. I had a subway card and H&H Bagels. She had never lived outside Texas, and I had gone away to college and never come back.

But I missed her. I really missed her. I called her on the phone at least once a day. Mostly because every time I had a free minute, she was the first person I wanted to talk to. The most important thing about this whole crazy year of our lives is how much I loved my sister. Because there in Mackie's empty baby room, as I cradled a sock monkey and eased myself into the glider rocker, I had an idea. An idea that would change all of our lives in ways I couldn't have imagined then. An idea that maybe we never should have tried. But what can I tell you? At the moment, it seemed brilliant. It seemed like the best idea I'd ever had. It seemed like, maybe for the first time ever, I'd found a way to take care of Mackie instead of the other way around.

Chapter Two

Here's what Mackie said when I made my suggestion: *No*.

She had made a corn-avocado salad with lime and bell pepper for dinner. We sat at the big farm table in her kitchen with wineglasses of San Pellegrino. The room felt airy and elegant. Every time I came home on vacation, I just couldn't get over all the space everywhere. I thought about my shower-stall-sized kitchenette in New York and how everything truly *was* bigger in Texas.

"You're not letting me finish," I said.

"That's right," she said. "Because you're not going to finish. Here's what I'm saying: No."

"Well," I said, shrugging, "I'm saying yes."

"It's not up to you."

I reached over and put my hand on top of Mackie's. "This is a good idea."

"This is a crazy, dangerous, very bad idea."

"Mackie," I said. "I can help you."

It took a fair bit of cajoling, but I finally wrangled a deal that I would accept her no if she would just let me finish. "All you have to do is really listen to me," I said.

"And then I can say no?"

"Then you can say no."

"And then we'll drop it?"

"Then we'll drop it."

I sat back in my chair. Maybe I'd pitched it wrong the first time. Maybe "Why don't I just have that baby for you?" had sounded a little abrupt to Mackie's ears.

I started over. This time, I put it this way: So what if her uterus wasn't working? She still had her eggs! If all she needed was a uterus, she could borrow mine. I had one going to waste up in New York. "This is my offer," I said. "Your egg, his sperm. I'll chip in the uterus."

Mackie just looked at me.

And then, mostly to be a pain in the ass, I said, "You make it, I'll bake it."

But now I had her thinking. "You make it sound so easy," she said.

"That's because it is," I said.

This was early on. This was back before I'd ever heard terms like "intrafamilial gestational carrier" and "intracytoplasmic sperm injection." Even the word *pregnancy* didn't mean too much to me then. Nine months didn't seem like such a long time.

Mackie remained against the idea in principle, but less so after I clarified that it would be her egg and not mine. Even so, she said, it seemed like a recipe for disaster. Days later, we would Google *surrogacy* and read about lawsuit after lawsuit, amicable beginnings that had gone bitterly awry. But even that didn't slow us down. By then, we were hooked on the idea. It had too much potential to not, at least, try it.

"I don't see what's in it for you," Mackie said that first night.

"Seeing you with a baby," I said, adding, "duh."

"But aren't you afraid it would feel like your baby?"

"No," I said. "That's not the way I see it at all." I saw it very clearly as Mackie's baby coming to visit its auntie for a while until it was ready to go home and live with its parents.

"I just don't think it's a good idea for the first baby you ever have to be for somebody else."

But that didn't seem like an issue for me. Mackie needed a baby now. I could make more later when the time was right for me. It just didn't seem like a big deal to me—in that way that things can seem so simple when you don't understand them at all. Like a television: *You just press the button and watch the pictures! Easy!*

"Why not?" I wanted to know.

"Because you don't know what you're getting yourself into," she said.

I threw my arms up. "Nobody who ever gets pregnant knows what they're getting into!" Then I put my hands on my hips in what I hoped was a wise and knowing posture. "All of life is a gamble."

Mackie studied my face. "It's not a good idea," she said again, but her conviction was gone. Whether she meant it or not—and whether it was, in fact, a good idea or not—by the end of the night, she was ready to try it.

I was ready, too. It was so simple. I couldn't stop applauding myself for coming up with it. There were so few problems in life that actually had solutions.

I proposed this plan: I'd move home for a while. Have this baby. Stay rent-free with Mackie and Clive. Figure out my life. Become a better person.

"What about your job?" Mackie asked.

"Oh," I said, waving my hand. "I got fired." It seemed so unimportant now. Looking back, I have to wonder if my baby-making enthusiasm was related to losing my job. If I was trying to replace the loss of one thing with the gain of another. At the time, I never would have admitted that, though. At the time, it was all about Mackie.

"You got what?"

"Um, fired."

"Please tell me you're kidding," Mackie said.

I shook my head. Supercasual.

"That job is your whole life!"

"Hello?" I gestured between us and then around the room. "Not my whole life."

I might have been willing to concede that my old job had been *most* of my life. Maybe even the *vast majority* of my life. But not all. In fact, taking a broad view, getting myself fired might have been a great stroke of luck. The universe freeing me up for something better. That was one way to look at it, right?

I told Mackie the Boob-a-palooza story, even hinting that the whole debacle was a little bit her fault.

"Not exactly," Mackie said, stopping me.

"You sent me the link," I said.

"But I didn't forward it to the CEO. That was all you, Einstein."

I was loving the idea of coming home. I made the arguments that I needed to regroup, I needed time away from New York, and I'd been feeling the itch to come home anyway—which were all true enough. My roommate's French boyfriend had been looking for a place. He could sublet for a while.

"You'd move away from New York?" Mackie said. "You'd move back home?"

"Not move home," I corrected. "Just visit." Then, to make it all extra clear, and with a little grimace that emphasized how preposterous the idea was: "I wouldn't *stay* here."

"Gotcha," Mackie said.

The pieces fell into place so nicely. Everything seemed so just plain perfect. Of course, in the long run, it was a dangerous idea. Just like my living with Mackie and Clive while I gestated their child was a dangerous idea. But in the short run it solved my rent problem. And they had such a great house. I couldn't wait to settle into all that space and sunshine. And maybe—though I didn't say this to Mackie—maybe it was just time for me to do something truly good with myself for a change.

Mackie was usually the one who put the brakes on things. She had stopped me from getting a yin-and-yang tattoo, from shaving off all my hair for an art project, from dropping out of graduate school when a professor admitted to giving every single student he had a B–. But here at her kitchen table, just the two of us and a rising sense of possibility, Mackie didn't have any brakes. How could she? When somebody offers you the thing you want most in the world, you take it.

All we had to do next was get Clive onboard.

Mackie and I did the dishes and locked up. Then we climbed on top of her king-size bed to watch TV. "Do you think he'll go for it?" I asked.

"He'll have to," she said.

"He seems very agreeable," I said.

I really didn't know Clive very well. He'd moved to Texas long after I'd moved away, and he and Mackie had met and courted and gotten engaged all on their own. I saw him only at holidays, though I knew a lot about him. His great-grandparents were from India, but he'd grown up in London, and after two generations in England, he was super-British. His hair was so black, it was almost blue. He'd gone to Oxford and then to Wharton Business School in the States. He drank Darjeeling tea every single afternoon with cream—not milk—and sugar, and if by some chance the cream had run out, he'd make a trip to the store to get some. He was a kind person, and a good listener. He was allergic to green peppers, but not to yellow or red. He used to do free diving and could hold his breath under water for more than two minutes. He wore cologne. He'd been bitten by a Yorkshire terrier as a small boy and was still afraid of them to this day. He was polite and sometimes a touch overzealous—and I suddenly wished I didn't know this—in bed.

But almost everything I knew about him I knew through Mackie. I hadn't ever thought much about knowing him better than that. Of course, if I was going to, you know, *have his baby,* I'd wind up knowing him far better than I'd ever planned on. But that seemed like a minor detail at the time.

Mackie felt certain that before he agreed to anything, Clive would make us think through every downside. He was a planner. He liked to be ready for disasters. It was part of the reason he'd been so successful with his company. He thought things through, and moved slowly, and avoided catastrophe.

So we made a list on a legal pad of every downside we could come up with. In addition to the myriad risks of heartbreak that accompanied a regular pregnancy, we came up with some extra doozies for the surrogate situation—two pages' worth, including: The pregnancy could fail to take, leaving us horribly disappointed, or I could have a bad experience with it and decide never to have kids of my own. Or—the most terrifying, and most likely, we thought, of all the possibilities: I might decide, in the end, that I couldn't part with the baby.

Funny, now, that the actual downsides of that year when we all made a baby together were nowhere on the list. They seem so obvious—so inevitable—now. But, at the time, we never saw them coming.

• • •

The next morning, Mackie woke me at six because her mind was racing. We'd finally fallen asleep in her bed only about four hours earlier, but now she was wide awake.

She poked me and whispered, "Do you still think it's a good idea?"

My face was smushed into Clive's pillow, which smelled, if I wasn't mistaken, exactly like Drakkar Noir. I peeked one eye open. It was still so dark, I couldn't even see her. "What?"

"The baby," she said. "Now that you've had a chance to sleep on it."

"I still think it's a good idea," I said, letting that eye close again.

"Good," she whispered. "Me, too."

A minute later, she was poking me again.

"Are you asleep?" she asked.

"Kind of."

"Okay," she said. But then she started fidgeting. She scratched her knee. She coughed. She rolled around and readjusted the blankets. Looking back, it was here, maybe, if I'd been paying attention, that I might have felt the first glimmer that I'd just made a decision that would take my life far out of my own hands. But really, at the time, I was just trying to stay asleep.

Finally, I said, "I guess we're awake."

She sat right up. "Great!" Then she was out of bed, pulling back the curtains, running the water, flushing the toilet. "What do you think of this baby name?" she called from the bathroom. "Indiana."

I still hadn't moved. "For a boy or a girl?"

She was already brushing her teeth. "For a girl. Of course. With an *a* on the end like that."

"Right," I said.

She paused from her brushing. "Except Indiana Jones was a guy, I guess."

I kept very still, playing possum.

There was a moment of quiet while Mackie flossed. Then she came into the room and patted a drumroll on my ass. "Let's go!" she said. "Let's take a walk."

Once I was awake, I felt chipper, too. I kept thinking about how satisfying it was to wake up with a project to look forward to. We hit the neighborhood in our exercise togs and passed my dad's house, the place where we'd grown up, now looking pretty ramshackle with the shutters missing slats and the azaleas overgrown. Though it was still much the same—a pretty brick two-story. Nothing fancy. We didn't stop, since it was so early, but we slowed as we passed, feeling the kind of electricity that layers of memories can give to ordinary things. The magnolia tree we used to climb. The place where Mackie once found a garter snake. And, next door, the house where I'd gone to sell Girl Scout cookies the day after we'd learned about rabies in school—and ran away screaming when our neighbor answered the door with toothpaste foaming at his mouth.

The same summer our mother died, Mackie had insisted she take me to the mall. I was in sixth grade. I had braces that always had something caught in them, and rubber bands that connected my top and bottom teeth. I kept my hair in a frizzy pom-pom on top of my head, wore a camouflage visor I'd found at an army surplus store in Galveston, and was—Mackie had recently pronounced to my mother—a true embarrassment to the entire family.

Mackie, in contrast, was fairly popular. She just had that gene for how to get along in middle school that I lacked. We hung out together at home, but at school, I wasn't supposed to talk to her. "I could help you get popular," she'd explained to me one night while we were clearing the dishes, "but then I'd have to be seen with you." In truth, she had tried to help. She had given me all sorts of makeup and fashion tips. She wanted me to benefit from her expertise. But, for whatever reason, at age twelve, I just couldn't absorb the information. "Take a toothbrush to school," she'd say. "Brush the spinach out of your teeth after lunch."

"Right," I'd say. But then I'd forget.

"Do not act out ghost stories with your friends at snack time," she'd say. "It makes you look like a crazy person."

I'd agree. But then, at snack time, my dorky friends would ask for ghost stories—and it was too fun to resist.

Mackie told me I needed bell-bottom jeans and clogs, but instead, when our mom dropped us at the mall, I'd forget to buy them and spend the whole time eating ice cream and watching the ice skaters.

Mackie was all of thirteen then, and her braces were already off. She curled her hair in hot rollers every morning and then tied it back with a pink ribbon. She wasn't the queen of the seventh graders or anything, but she was doing fine. She pulled my mom aside after dinner one night and said, "You need to take her to the mall and force her to buy some cute clothes." This was right after school had ended for the summer, and Mackie's idea was to make those months productive by transforming me. Grubby caterpillar to seventh-grade butterfly in three months or less.

My mom was up for it. She hadn't been feeling well, and she was scheduled to have her gallbladder out the next week. But she drove both of us to the mall that Saturday and, while my sister met her friends at McDonald's, steered me to the spots Mackie had written down. We bought three pairs of jeans and two Gap sweaters. We bought new sandals and my first bra. Later, at a stand next to the Italian ices, we got my ears pierced.

That night, I pranced around in my new stuff, doing fashion shows for my mom and dad, who kindly set down their books and clapped each time I came into the room. In two and a half months, I'd go to a back-to-school party, and I was dizzy at the prospect of arriving there transformed. I imagined all heads turning as I walked in, and kids whispering: *"Who is that?" "Sarah Harper!" "What happened to her?" "She got gorgeous!"* The boys would crowd around me, and I'd give a little wave to my old friends—far off, acting out ghost stories in the corner as if life could never be any different.

My mom's gallbladder surgery didn't turn out quite the way anyone expected. When the surgeons opened her up that Wednesday, they found cancer. Ovarian cancer that had filled up her abdomen. I remember my dad describing it to someone on the phone. He quoted the doctor, and said her insides were "weeping" with cancer. They drained some fluid, removed what they could, and closed her back up. But they perforated something in her body during the surgery—that was how I learned the word *perforated*—and then she got an infection that nobody was able to cure.

She went into intensive care two days after that and did not leave the hospital again. We visited her every afternoon. I made her a lanyard in art camp. I brought her a mix tape of the Supremes and an article on the healing power of music. One day, I lay in bed with her while she stroked my hair. She seemed fine to me in a lot of ways, and I remember talking on and on about the slumber party I wanted to have for my next birthday. She approved all my plans—even the idea of sleeping out in the backyard on the trampoline. But she died before the summer was over.

Many weeks later, when it was time for the back-to-school party, those clothes were still in their shopping bags under my bed. I got dressed and snapped off the tags, and my dad drove me in the Volvo. It's funny to remember now what I was thinking. You have to understand that death doesn't really make sense to a child. For ages after my mother died—and a little bit even now—part of me truly thought she'd gone on vacation. In my mind, she was on a cruise in Alaska, standing on the deck at night in the crisp wind, missing us but having too much fun to come home.

I knew she was dead. I'd been to the funeral, I'd seen the dishes piled up in our sink, I'd lain out on our driveway and tried to see her spirit whispering around through the night sky. But at the same time, I refused to know it. It seems so strange to confess it now, but as I walked into that seventh-grade party, I hoped her death might help my social standing. That I might not only be transformed in my new clothes, but also had become such a poised, tragic figure that the boys would all fall in love with me. As if a thirteen-year-old boy could possibly have done that. As if a boy with braces and a stack of comics under his bed and a perpetual boner could have been any kind of compensation for a mom.

But there was a hopefulness about me that night at the party. I still hoped to be a kind of hero, the bravest person in our whole class. Which, in truth, that year I was—even if nobody knew it. Including me.

I was fine now, of course. We were all fine. We were adults with adult problems and pleasures. Life had marched on, as it does, and that shadowy summer was something I didn't think about too often anymore. Not, at least, when I was in New York. Which may have had something to do with the fact that I was there in the first place.

When Mackie and I got back from our walk, we squeezed fresh orange juice, added a splash of lime, and did a few yoga stretches. We spent the rest of the morning rehashing our ideas from the night before. There was something delicious about the prospect of working together. It had been so long since our lives had been this integral to each other's. Mostly, we just talked on the phone about the things going on in our separate worlds. Now, suddenly, those worlds had merged, and we couldn't stop talking about our plans.

By the time Clive got home, around noon, we had printouts and spreadsheets and statistics for him. We had gathered facts online like squirrels hoarding nuts. He was a think-things-through guy, and we were ready for him. We were expecting some resistance. We thought he'd be tough to convince.

The plan was to wait to talk to him about it after he'd had a sandwich and put his feet up, but he hadn't even set down his suitcase before he squinted a little at Mackie and said, "What's going on with you?"

"Nothing," Mackie said, keeping a straight face.

Clive glanced over at me, then back to Mackie. "Something's going on," he said.

And then—despite all our planning about the best way to break it to him, despite our step-by-step outline for easing him into the baby waters, despite the number of times Mackie had said, "We just have to play it cool"—she told him. A grin took over her face, she said, "Sarah wants to have our baby for us!" and then she started jumping around.

Here is the amazing way that Clive loved my sister:

We did not even open our folder of charts. We gave him the basics about how it would work and assurances that the baby would be his and Mackie's, not his and mine. He left his suitcase on the kitchen floor and popped open a root beer as we chattered on about my epiphany and how I wanted, suddenly, to make the world a better place, and how I was ready to come home and regroup, anyway.

When we fell silent and waited for his response, he said, "Are you sure this is a good idea?"

And we both nodded and said in unison with total conviction, "Yes."

Then he studied Mackie carefully, like I wasn't even in the room.

"This is what you want?" he asked her.

And she nodded just the tiniest bit, as if she were doing it in secret.

Then he stepped closer and put his arms around her, and looked over to me. "We can put you on the company insurance."

"Hire me?" I asked.

"Well," he said, making quotation marks with his fingers. "Hire you." And then, as a clarification: "You'll be in charge of a Special Project."

Mackie hugged him. I hugged him. Then Mackie and I hugged each other. It was exactly that easy. Clive was onboard. Of course, none of us really knew what we were getting into, but Clive had seen Mackie jumping around—her body literally unable to tamp down her excitement—and that was it for him. She had him at the jumping. Though, of course, she had him long before that.

Chapter Three

Somehow, Mackie talked me into going to the Thanksgiving party. She made the argument that the only way to regain my equilibrium after Everett Thompson's insult on the plane was to surprise him at the party looking smokin' hot. She forbade Clive to tell Everett I'd be there, and she started working on what she called Operation Stealth Fox. "Like a stealth bomb," she said, "but sexier."

"I can't be a Stealth Fox," I said, in her master closet. "Don't you remember? I'm old."

Mackie was rooting in her drawer for something.

I went on: "You can't make me younger."

"But I can make you fabulous!" She whipped out a Boob 'em bra.

"I sent you that bra!" I said. "It was a free sample!"

"I know."

"It's evil," I said. "And also painful. That one is the worst of the bunch."

"Maybe so," Mackie said, "but it really works."

She held it out to me.

"I'm not wearing your bra."

"Why not?" she said. "It's been through the wash."

When I didn't take it, she threw it at me and it landed across my shoulder. Then she said, "Just because boobs are soft and feminine doesn't mean they don't make great weapons."

I knew that Mackie was going to pep-talk me into doing what she wanted, and I knew just as certainly that I was going to feel ridiculous. That was just our dynamic. She was the instigator and I was the reluctant participant in countless schemes that had expanded my horizons only slightly more often than they had landed me in trouble. But as much as Mackie was bad for me, she was good for me, too—only more so.

"The point is," I said, "Boob 'em bra or no, I'll still be old."

Now Mackie turned to face me. "You believed him!"

I thought about it. "I guess so."

"Crazy girl," she said. "You are not old. He was just being mean. And now we're going to be mean back." She lifted a gauzy white dress from the rack and held it up against me. "And here is the meanest dress I own."

Three hours later, I had on more makeup than a circus performer and was lurking behind the sashimi bar while Mackie's backyard filled up with strangers. Mackie had promised to stick right by my side and introduce me to every cute man at the party, but then the refrigerator had exploded or something and she'd disappeared. I watched Clive laugh and schmooze with everybody. There was jazz on the speaker system, a mojito bar near the Althea tree, and a gentle glow rising from Mackie's floating candles in the pool. It was a great party. And I was miserable.

I was skulking toward the back gate, about to slip out and take a walk, when Mackie found me and grabbed my elbow. "He's here," she said.

"Who's here?"

"E.T.," she said and winked. "He just walked in the front door. With a woman. And guess what?"

"What?"

"He's kind of cute."

"Kind of cute? He's gorgeous!"

"Sometimes," she said, "your gorgeous and my gorgeous aren't the same gorgeous."

"You don't think he's gorgeous?"

"Not really."

"We can't be talking about the same person," I said.

"If you say he's gorgeous, then he's gorgeous," she said. "We'll run with that." Then she started steering me across the patio. "Now I'm thinking maybe you two should get married."

"No," I said.

"You'd make the cutest little curly-headed babies!"

"No," I said again.

Mackie looked right into my eyes. "You need to think outside the negativity box."

"Mackie," I said. "He hates me. In a psycho, leftover-from-high-school, time-for-therapy way."

She raised her eyebrows. "Hate is kind of the same thing as love."

"Not really."

"They're two sides of the same coin."

"Sure," I said. "Except one side is love and the other side is hate."

But Mackie gave a brisk sigh. "If he didn't notice you, that would be bad. If he didn't remember you, or if he talked to you like a stranger, that would be bad. But insulting you in a hateful way? That's good. Hate is a strong emotion."

"Listen to yourself talking," I said. "Hate is not good. It's the opposite of love."

"No," Mackie said. "The opposite of love is indifference."

Later, after the party was long over and we were sprawled on the sofa, I'd remind her of the whole story between Everett and me. I would tell her that I absolutely did not want her to matchmake. And she would agree in principle to leave it alone and then say something like, "But if Clive winds up needing Everett to deliver certain things to our home from time to time and you happen to be here, I can't be held responsible." Mackie was bossy that way. She wanted everyone in the world to be as happy as she was. Especially me.

For now, we proceeded with our original plan. Mackie led me toward Mark, a graphic novelist who worked for Clacker Toys doing product copy. Almost every man there was dorky, dull, or emotionally unavailable, Mackie told me, and so even though Mark was "possibly all three," he seemed like a good enough place to start. Mackie advised me to laugh loudly at random intervals so it would seem like we were hitting it off.

Clive intercepted us on our way over.

"What are you guys up to?" he asked, looking my outfit up and down.

"We are punishing Everett Thompson with Sarah's fabulousness," Mackie said.

"Because?" he asked.

"Because he kicked her when she was down," she said.

"Remind me not to piss you off," Clive said, kissing Mackie on her lipstick.

"Do you need reminding?" Mackie said, touching him on the nose.

I wasn't so sure that I wanted to punish Everett Thompson. It didn't really matter what he'd said on the plane. There wasn't an insult he could hurl at me that could match the way I'd treated him in high school.

But a project with Mackie was hard to resist. She always made things fun. Everett Thompson did have it coming a little bit. Also, it didn't seem possible that I could get under his skin at this point. He had moved on—Mary-Louise Parker could vouch for that. The stakes for Everett seemed pretty low. I figured, if I had to be at the party anyway—and Mackie had made it clear that I did—I might as well muster up some sass.

Mackie sent every man on the patio my way over the next fifteen minutes, and by the time Everett and his very tall date made it out to the pool area, I was surrounded by guys.

Soon, Mackie came over and pulled me away. Everett hadn't noticed me yet, and she was getting impatient, and she wanted me to do a "walk-by." After that, she promised, we could relax. This whole elaborate revenge was not something I ever would have had the gumption to orchestrate, but I had to admit it was going well. Except that the party was getting pretty full. And in November in Houston, the weather is balmy enough that everybody wanted to be poolside. Mackie rushed the walk-by a little because we were running out of room. I was supposed to saunter past, look fabulous, surprise Everett by being there, and then rejoin my trove of men, leaving all his questions about why I was there at all unanswered.

Mackie was a big fan of women's inherent mystery.

The walk-by started out fine. But halfway to the target zone, we had to navigate a narrow gap between an impassable group of Web programmers and the edge of the pool. I've been over it a thousand times in my head, and I'm still not sure what I tripped on, but before I knew it, I was in the water.

I'm sure there are women in the world—Mackie comes to mind—who could have pulled off falling into the pool with a self-deprecating grace. But I just came up sputtering and dog-paddled toward the steps while a yard full of strangers held their drinks in silence. I want to say the jazz on the speaker system even fell silent for a minute, but that might not be true. Mackie showed up moments later with a towel as I climbed the pool steps like a submarine surfacing.

"What happened?" Mackie asked.

"I fell into the pool," I said.

She wrapped the towel around me. "No kidding."

"Do you think anybody noticed?"

Everyone was still staring, including Everett Thompson. "Nah," Mackie said, looking around. "You're good."

She furrowed me through the crowd again, but this time I wasn't strutting my stuff. I'd lost a shoe in the water. My flowy white dress was now clumping—and possibly even disintegrating—like Kleenex. I ducked down to hide behind the strands of my wet hair.

Mackie dropped me off at the back door with instructions to take a shower, "shake it off," and then come back to the party.

"I'm not doing that," I said.

She was irritated at the differences between us. "I knew you'd lose your gumption."

"I haven't lost my gumption," I said, though, in fact, I had. "I've just come to my senses." Which was also true. "The last thing I need to be doing is flirting with Everett Thompson."

"You weren't flirting. You were torturing."

"Same thing."

"What's your problem?" she said. "He's cute."

"The problem is, I don't like him." And here, I made myself sound overly certain. Because I'd always kind of liked him—even after he'd taken up with that theater girl who wore purple pumps with her school uniform, I still kind of liked him. I used to watch him on the sly in the cafeteria sometimes, but if he ever caught me looking, he'd drop his smile right away and take his tray to the conveyor belt.

These were feelings I wished to avoid these days: Feeling like a jerk. Feeling like a bad person. There was no way I was going to like him again if only to honor the remote but distinct possibility that if I actually caught him, I might not want him. After all, it had happened before.

"But you *do* like him," Mackie said. "I can always tell."

Mackie was kind of a black-and-white girl when it came to love. Emotions were pretty simple for her. You loved someone, or you didn't. You were happy, or you weren't. Life was good, or it wasn't. She liked to put things in broad categories, and she always tried to round up to happy. Sadness was a last resort.

I suddenly had this feeling that if I didn't put it to rest for Mackie, she'd never stop hounding me. I didn't want her analyzing my feelings, or passing judgment on my hesitations, or contriving scenarios for Everett and me to bump into each other. And this is a fine point—because Mackie was normally a person I was completely honest with. Too honest. "You've got a booger in your nose" honest.

So I shocked even myself with what I said to her next about Everett Thompson. Maybe I was blaming her for the Stealth Fox debacle. Maybe I was just cold and wet and wanted to be left alone. But there on the patio, for the first time in my entire life, I lied to Mackie about something important.

"I don't like him at all," I said then. "I really don't."

She tried to read me. "Even though you think he's gorgeous?"

"He's too gorgeous," I said. "He's Stepford gorgeous."

"In a Ken doll way," Mackie added, helping.

"That's right!" I said. "He's a Ken doll!" I matched them up. "The blue eyes. The blond hair."

"The plastic crotch."

"Let's not talk about the crotch."

"You sure? 'Cause that could be a fun conversation."

"The point is, I'm not attracted to him." I looked right into her eyes and waited until she believed me.

And then, finally, she did. Why wouldn't she? "Okay," she said. "Everett Thompson is out."

I sighed and said, "Thank you." I left her at the door and was almost to the stairs when she said, "Sarah?"

"What?"

"Can I set him up with other people, then?"

She was testing me, like a detective who throws one final question from the doorway on the way out.

She wanted to see if I'd hesitate, so I didn't. "Absolutely," I said. Then I added, gesturing toward the backyard with my eyes, "Though he does seem to have a girlfriend."

Mackie glanced over and then gave me a smile. She'd been on the job for an hour, and she already had the dirt. "Her? That's just a sex thing."

"Got it," I said, walking away on purpose.

I've thought about that little lie a lot since. It was such a tiny thing. People tell tiny lies to each other all the time—for self-protection, or to create some cover for themselves or give themselves some space. It wasn't an unforgivable or horrible thing to do. But it marked a change for us, and I always remind myself about it when I make the mistake of thinking that all our troubles started later.

Ten minutes out of the shower, I snuck back down to the kitchen for some ice cream. My plan was to consume an entire pint of cookies 'n' cream while I sat on Mackie and Clive's bed and watched *Biography* on their flat screen. Which was all I'd wanted to do in the first place.

I was not completely sure Mackie had bought my lack of interest in Everett. It was a tough sell, after all. You can't announce a man is gorgeous and then feign indifference. But I'd made a good start, and I'd played it cool. All I had to do now, I knew from my former career, was repeat it over and over until it seemed indisputable.

When it came to love, Mackie was a little like a meddling neighbor from a 1960s sitcom with curlers in her hair and fuzzy slippers. Always showing up at the wrong time, always listening over the back fence, always getting the wrong impression and trying to help, while making things so very much worse. Ruining things with her over-enthusiasm.

Deep down, she really wanted me to find a man. Deep down, although her women's studies minor would never let her admit it, she thought I could never be happy on my own. She wanted me to find someone so badly that she just couldn't be cool about it. Anyone I showed the slightest interest in, she was trying his last name on me within a day. Beating the marriage drums. Smoking the monogamy pipe. Wishing on the love star. It made her, in this one very particular area, difficult to talk to.

And so, instead, a trip to the refrigerator and then *Biography*: back-to-back Lauren Bacall, Betty Grable, and Marilyn Monroe. I had my pj's on, my hair wrapped up in a towel, and all the makeup scrubbed off. I was ready to put Operation Stealth Fox behind me. Revenge, I suddenly remembered, was always a mistake, anyway.

The cookies 'n' cream was out on the counter, lid off, and I had just shoveled a big spoonful into my mouth as an appetizer when the kitchen door swung open and Everett walked in. He stopped short when he saw me. I held up my hand in a wave.

"What are you doing here?" he asked.

"Getting some ice cream," I said, mouth full.

"But what are you doing *here*?" He gestured around at the house in general.

I swallowed. "You know Clive?" I asked.

"Yes," he said. "I know Clive."

I shrugged. "He's my brother-in-law."

Everett's shoulders fell a little, the way people's do when they get bad news. "Oh," he said.

"Yeah."

Then he brought his hand forward and held out the shoe I'd lost in the pool.

"Found this," he said, setting it on the counter.

"Great," I said, with a deliberate lack of enthusiasm.

There was a little awkward moment, and then Everett sized up my postshower ensemble and said, "You're not going back to the party?"

"No," I said, shaking my head. "I'm just"—and here, I made sure to look him in the eye—"so old." I stabbed my spoon into my ice cream tub and picked it up to go—despite a very strong urge I felt at that moment to stay. He seemed almost friendly. Like a person I would love to linger with in a kitchen chatting. But I was still smarting from his meanness on the plane, and more acutely from my pool debacle, and I wanted the last word. After a Bridget Jones moment like I'd just had, getting the last word seemed utterly essential.

I grabbed my shoe off the counter and headed for the stairs, yawning and talking to the room as if he weren't there. "I need to go upstairs to change my Depends. And soak my dentures. And rub Mentholatum on my bunions."

"Right," Everett said, remembering we were enemies.

I took the stairs two at a time with this weird feeling that he might just follow me up. But he didn't.

• • •

I don't want to say I'd never been in love. That makes it sound like I had no feelings at all, like I was some kind of robot. I'd loved people. Admired them. Set my sights on them. Flirted. Snuggled. Enjoyed their company. Missed them after they were gone. I'd lived a pretty normal relationship life of hits and misses—with, okay, a lot more misses than hits. From the outside, I looked pretty normal. If you weren't watching too closely. But I knew the truth about myself, even if I tried not to think about it. I had never been consumed by love. I'd never been overwhelmed or brought to my knees or set on fire by it. There was always a hitch for me. There was always some compartment of my heart that didn't give way.

Let me make one thing clear before you distrust me: I cared about love. And wished for it, and wondered about it, and longed for it in all those ways girls do. I just didn't know how to make it happen. And I was morally opposed to feeling desperate.

If I'd had a therapist, I'm sure she'd have said it was all about losing my mother. She'd have crossed her ankles and made a note on her pad that such a devastating loss—at age twelve, no less, just on the cusp of puberty, just at the moment when the body and the heart start to collide—was bound to have an impact on a girl. I'd certainly had enough conversations with Mackie about What Was Wrong with Me to have a coherent theory. I had, we all agreed, textbook intimacy issues. But it was one thing to know what was wrong. It was a much more impossible thing to know how to fix it.

The thing is, I believed in love. I believed in love the way little kids believe in Santa. It was real. It was out there. It was making toys for me at that very moment. And, on some very special night not too far away, it was going to load up its sleigh and squeeze its obese self down my chimney with a feast of unimaginable delights for me the next morning. That's what love was for me. Red, fur-trimmed, and three steaks away from a quadruple bypass. Oh, and something that I'd never actually seen.

One night, on the phone a few years earlier, after I'd walked out on a Norwegian named Oskar after he'd made a semiserious joke about getting married, Mackie'd had an insight about our respective love lives that was so true I'd hung up on her. And when she called back, I hadn't answered. And then, for a week, I'd screened my calls. Here's what she said: That we both approached love like my dad did. Except she was my dad before my mother died, and I was my dad after.

She'd apologized for saying that maybe a hundred times since it happened. But that didn't make it any less true. And it was something that the two of us had just come to accept about ourselves. Mackie was lucky in love, and I was my father, home alone on a Saturday night, cooking ramen noodles in my mother's ruffled yellow apron.

An apron that was about to wind up at Goodwill. Because the very next day my father brought a woman with him to Thanksgiving dinner and announced that she was his fiancée.

Our dad had told us he had some news. But he hadn't told us his news would be a fiancée. And he hadn't told us his news would show up in a sweatshirt BeDazzled with rhinestones. Or that his news would have on a pair of dangly turkey earrings that gobbled when you pressed a button on the back. Or that his news would be, as Mackie put it later, "such a hillbilly."

"This is your news?" Mackie said, when the two of them walked in.

"This is my news," my dad said.

"It's sparklier than I expected," Mackie said into her napkin.

"This is Dixie," my dad said to us at the table, before sitting down. "And we're getting married."

We all looked around for a reality check, and my dad, I decided, looked just as surprised as anyone. Then Clive and I said in unison, "Hi, Dixie."

And Mackie said, "You have got to be joking."

We had news for him, too, of course. But ours would have to wait.

It was a tradition in our family to eat Thanksgiving dinner at a Chinese restaurant. It was what we'd done the first year my mother died, and now we refused to admit that any other way of doing things might have more appeal. It was fine. We were all fine. We did not miss the turkey or the stuffing at all.

Without my mom, my dad had done his best for us. He started driving the carpool and rearranged his schedule so that he was home when we were. The university where he taught history was right near our house, and he rode his bike to work—but on carpool days, he'd ride home to get my mother's car.

He didn't know what to do with us, of course. Before, he had mostly related to us through our mom, especially once we were too old for the zoo. He was not that much of a people person, and without her he was utterly lost. Without her, the piles of books in his office and in their bedroom got waist-high. He drifted away from their friends and spent more and more time reading and scribbling in notepads. He was always, from then on, "working on a book," though he never actually wrote one. Looking back, it was a stroke of great luck that he got tenure before she died. He never would have gotten it afterward.

But he was there for us, in his way. He hung around every afternoon, working at the dining table, listening to the muffled sound of the stereos from our rooms. He fixed little plates of carrots and dip to supplement the fish sticks we ate most nights for dinner. He'd knock on our doors from time to time, and we'd open, irritated: "Dad! What? I'm on the phone!"

My dad didn't date anyone at all for years. At first, he was just grieving for my mom, and for everything he had expected his life to be. And then, later, I think he made a decision to close off that part of himself. Teaching and raising two girls was enough. We really didn't give him enough credit. We assumed he had just forgotten how to meet women—or possibly even how to talk to them. We assumed that he was alone because he had no other choice.

So many of my friends' parents wound up cheating on each other and tricking each other in marriages that crashed and burned. It was not lost on any of us that my parents' marriage had been working. They had been well suited. They had brought out the best in each other. They would have made it. For many of the early years, lady divorcées with clunky jewelry would sniff around my dad and leave messages on our answering machine. When we—either of us—heard those messages, we just went ahead and erased them. We couldn't imagine who those women thought they were. Or what on earth they saw in our dad.

Once we were off at college, my dad had some girlfriends. I knew there were women whom he "went to the movies" with. But we never met them. He never talked about them. And we didn't think too much about it. He was our dad, he was a good man, he'd been dealt a bad hand—and there wasn't much else to say. I guess I figured if he had someone worth telling us about, he'd tell us.

This is why it didn't feel strange to me when he showed up on Thanksgiving with the BeDazzler. I liked him, and I wished him all the best, but we had never been able to close the gap between us. To me, he was more like an eccentric old uncle than a parent, though Mackie disagreed.

"He's all we've got," she said over and over, as she brought him soup and invited him for Scrabble.

What shocked me about the engagement wasn't that he'd gotten to this point without telling us, but that he'd gotten to this point at all. I thought he'd given up not just on love but on people in general. That was the surprise: There was a heart buried under all those books. And it was still beating.

At the restaurant, my dad pulled out Dixie's chair, and she sat down while the rest of us tried to decide if the yellow confection on her head was a wig or just a crazy dye-job and a full bottle of hair spray.

Mackie went on. "You've never even mentioned this person."

My dad was pretty mild-mannered. "We've been dating for a little while," he said, as if that were a good explanation. Then he made introductions all around.

Clive and I were ready to run with it, if for no other reason than so we could go ahead and order. But Mackie was going to put up a fight. I could feel it. My dad could feel it. He picked up his menu and then, as if to close the topic, said, "Who wants moo shu?"

"I didn't even know you were dating anyone at all," Mackie went on. She looked at me. "Did you know he was dating someone?"

I shook my head, but only barely, as if my holding still would keep fuel from her fire.

My dad was hell-bent on a pleasant meal. When the waitress appeared, he ordered for the table, even specifying drinks. Then he turned back to the subject at hand—putting his hand on Dixie's as he started back up. "We just tried the relationship on for size," he said, "and it fit."

There was a little silence before I came up with, "So, are you from Houston?"

"No." Dixie shook her head. "I'm from up north." Then she got specific: "Cleveland."

This threw us sideways a little. Cleveland didn't make sense. From the accent to the acrylic fingernails, she was definitely a Texan.

So I had to clarify. "Cleveland, Ohio?"

And she let out a laugh. "Oh, no, sweetheart!" She put her hand on top of mine and frowned at me like she didn't even know there was a Cleveland, Ohio. "Cleveland, Texas."

"Gotcha," I said, and we were all relieved when the waitress brought the drinks.

Next, Clive gave things a shot. He turned to Dixie with "How did you two meet?"

She smiled. "I took over for JoBeth in the history department after her heart attack."

"She can type ninety-six words a minute," my dad offered.

Clive let out an impressed whistle.

My dad went on, "And she teaches self-defense classes at the Y."

We took that in.

My dad leaned in closer. "Don't let that sweet smile fool you," he said. "She could take down every person in this room."

Dixie looked down and smiled. But she didn't argue.

For a minute, it looked like the conversation might drift peacefully over to a discussion of self-defense tactics. But then I glanced over and saw that Mackie had set her jaw into a tiny pout that only someone who'd known her since infancy would recognize.

At that moment, I knew: Mackie was going to protest, and things were going to get ugly, and there was nothing anyone could do. I waited for it the way you wait for the pain after you stub your toe. Mackie was going to say something so mean about Dixie's fingernails, or cleavage, or little slight double chin, Dixie would have no choice but to stand right up and leave the table.

And here, I want to defend Mackie a little. Dixie was clearly the vulnerable one, with her high-heeled boots and rhinestone bracelet. It seems obvious that the only kind way to react to her joining us was to welcome her so convincingly that we convinced even ourselves. But I knew what Mackie was thinking; she didn't stand for injustice. And as the sister who had always tried so hard to keep us all together enough to call ourselves a family, it must have seemed unreasonably wrong to her that my dad would finally decide to get together with someone who had nothing to do with any of us.

Maybe she thought our dad was lost enough to us already. Maybe she thought, in that moment, that Dixie was only going to pull him further away. But what I can promise you about Mackie is that even in her meanest moments, some part of her heart is always in the right place. I know she saw herself as protecting our tenuous little family unit—protecting all of us from a threat she hadn't even defined yet, but that had something to do with change, and how change always leads, in its way, to loss.

So even if she'd actually done what I knew she was about to, I'd have defended her.

But Clive decided to save the day. I thought I was the only one who knew what was coming, but clearly he sensed it, too, because he turned to Mackie before she could say a word and kissed her— a long, meandering kiss that required not just lips and likely even tongue, but both his arms and part of his torso. Dixie and my dad and I looked down. Mackie batted at Clive in protest, but she kissed him back anyway. And by the time they came up for air, she was laughing, and he turned to us and lifted his glass before saying, "How great is love?"

Then, just as our dumplings arrived, we all picked up our glasses and clinked a toast to love.

Dixie nudged me then and leaned over to whisper, "That one's a keeper."

And right as she said it, I realized something important about Clive: He definitely was a keeper. And looked like a good kisser, to boot.

It was amazing how little it took to turn Mackie completely around—although maybe an unexpected kiss in a Chinese restaurant would have that effect on anyone. She reapplied her lipstick, while we all waited in a fragile silence to see if we were in the clear. It looked like we might be.

More dishes arrived: beef with broccoli, moo shu chicken, pan-fried noodles. All my dad's favorites. Then Mackie said, "Dad, we have some news, too."

As my dad gave a polite "Oh?" Mackie looked at me for the go-ahead.

But I gave her a frown and a shake, like, *No, no, no.*

So she lifted her brows and nodded, like, *Yes, yes, yes.*

I tilted my head to say, *Mackie, are you insane?*

And she rolled her eyes to say, *Don't be such a pain in the ass.*

Then my dad, always much sharper than we gave him credit for, said, "What is this, girls? Charades?"

That's when Mackie turned to him and said, "Guess what? We're having a baby!"

"Who?" my dad asked.

"Me and Sarah," Mackie said.

"And me!" Clive waved at Mackie. "Hello?"

"Wait!" my dad said, shaking his head. "Who is having a baby?" Then, with timing any sitcom would envy, Clive and Mackie pointed at me and said, "She is," just as I gestured at them and said, "They are."

Then Mackie launched into the whole story. And I'll give her this: She went for it. The whole shebang. Her description of how the doctors would gather her eggs by scraping them off her ovaries and implant Clive's sperm "smack-dab in the middle" before transferring the whole operation over to me would've done *Scientific American* proud.

My dad took it in.

"The eggs look just like caviar," Mackie went on. "Only not black or stuck together."

"I always picture them like those little orange sushi eggs," Clive said.

"That's so cute," Mackie said, pausing to gaze at him a second before turning back to conclude, "And *presto*! A grandbaby."

"Not exactly *presto*," I piped up.

I glanced over at Dixie, who was the only one eating, and who had already abandoned her chopsticks for a knife and fork.

My dad scanned our faces back and forth.

He often made the mistake of thinking that personal topics were the same as academic ones. Time and again, when he heard about issues in our lives, he'd respond as if he were with colleagues discussing something from the distant past. The French and Indian War, say. Or the signing of the Constitution. And he always looked so befuddled when one of us burst into tears over something he'd said. Like the time Mackie had asked him how she looked on her way out the door to a party, and he'd lifted his eyes from his book and said, "Well, sweetheart, you've definitely put on a few pounds. But that's a beautiful dress."

With the baby, Mackie should have known better than to think he'd gloss over all the moral, ethical, historical, educational, and conversational nooks and crannies the topic provided. It was impossible to ask my dad to think about anything without him doing just that—at length. He was a college professor, after all. And so here in the restaurant, he compared and contrasted the historic roles of adoptive parents, offered varying cultural views of motherhood, and summed up an article he'd just read on the emotional and intellectual status of the first set of test-tube babies before Mackie had had enough.

"But Dad," she said, when he finished. "Isn't it exciting?"

He looked up, confused. Then he touched his thumb and fingers to his beard and dropped his gaze as he thought about it. We all found ourselves waiting for his response as if he were a judge deciding a verdict.

Then, at long last, he shook his head. "Nope," he said. "Nope. It's a bad idea."

Finally, Mackie said, "What?"

My dad shrugged. "I don't think it's a good idea." Then he pointed back and forth between the two of us with his chopsticks. "I don't think you two should jeopardize the most important relationship of your lives." Then he glanced at Clive. "No offense."

Clive lifted his hands. "None taken."

Mackie looked shocked, and I confess I was, too. We had worried so much about Clive, and he'd been easy. It didn't seem fair for my dad to make trouble.

But my dad didn't know he was making trouble—not, at least, until Mackie made it clear.

She stood up. "You can bring the Grand Ole Opry to Thanksgiving dinner and announce you're getting married and we're all just supposed to dive into our fried rice, but I give you the fantastic news that we have finally found a way to have a baby and you talk about child labor laws in Malaysia and then try to tell me no?"

My dad looked puzzled. "Sweetheart, I'm not telling—"

"Well, guess what?" Mackie went on. "You don't have any more authority over my bad decisions than I have"—and here she shifted her eyes to Dixie—"over yours." We all watched as she looked back at my dad and then turned to march out of the room, Clive scrambling after her. Even though they'd been my ride home, I stayed right there at the table.

Then, in the silence that followed, I set down my chopsticks and picked up my fork.

That night, I lay awake in my single bed in the nursery for a long time.

It turned out that I could hear Clive and Mackie through the wall. Or possibly the air-conditioning vent. I never did figure out, after many nights of puzzling over it, just what, exactly, was conducting the sound from their room into mine. But their voices might as well have been amplified on speakers. I could hear them not just as well as but slightly better than the sounds in my own room.

I should have marched next door as soon as I realized this problem, but instead I got caught up listening to their conversation. They were discussing my father, and my mother, and the BeDazzler. They were coming up with intricate theories about what we all meant to each other. Mostly Mackie was, actually. Clive seemed to be a pretty good listener, though. I found myself nodding along with her insights, even, for a little while at least, after the conversation drifted over to the subject of me, and how I refused to open up to anyone, and then led to a whole set of musings on my chances at happiness. By the time I heard Mackie say, "She wants to be alone. She won't let anyone love her"—and Clive respond, "No one wants to be alone"—it was truly too late to knock on their door. As I rooted in my suitcase for my iPod, I made a mental note to keep the thing charged. I'd be falling asleep with it every night for a very long time.

Lying in bed, I found myself thinking back on the girl I'd been that summer my mother died, and how incredibly goofy I was. I was a kid who'd taught myself to draw Garfield and had made sketches for all my teachers as end-of-year presents. I used to practice magic tricks in front of a full-length mirror in my room in the earnest hope that I might one day have an impromptu chance to amaze a group of onlookers. I dug a hole out behind our garage in my spare time with the idea of building an underground clubhouse. Even at twelve, I was truly still such a child—so able to rely on the imaginary and the whimsical.

I had no idea that it was my mother who made it possible for me to trip along so unself-aware. That's what I lost when I lost her, in addition to the universe of things a girl loses when she loses her mother: I lost the one person who knew me exactly for who I was and adored me anyway.

Once she was gone, all my goofiness went, too. I got myself in order and held myself in check. I was still me—just less of myself, somehow. A tighter, simpler, more presentable version of myself. I watched what the other girls did, and I did the same. I wore what they wore and said what they said. I stayed as normal as possible at all times. I applied myself to the task of becoming cool. I social-climbed. I traded in my old friends. I bought a curling iron. I became anonymous, acceptable, quiet, and pleasant. Part of that was just middle school—everybody panics in middle school—but the stakes shifted for me the instant my mother was gone. Because the one thing I knew without her was this: If someone hated my hair or my outfit—or anything about me at all—there was no one left in the world to tell me they were wrong.

I guess I was still angry at my dad—even now, as irrational as I knew I was—for not being my mother.

But I did know he had tried. He hadn't left us, and even now, even getting remarried, he wasn't leaving us. He wasn't even leaving his house: Dixie—they'd told me over fortune cookies—was going to move in with him.

I gave her an apologetic wince. "Have you seen the house, Dixie?"

My dad lived in that house like a creepy old guy, forgetting to re-cycle his newspapers and wearing a path in the carpet. The dining table was piled high with student papers and scholarly journals and junk mail. The sofa sagged in the middle. I couldn't imagine any nor-mal person wanting to live there. Even I had refused to stay there in recent years when I was home on vacation. My childhood bedroom was still waiting for me, with its R.E.M. posters, but I hadn't slept in it once since Clive and Mackie built their house.

Though it turned out that Dixie did not intend to live in that house as it was. She had "divorced well" and loved to decorate, and she had sketched out a total redo of every room except our old bedrooms and my father's office. She'd drawn her plans for me on a napkin and talked about paint colors like Key Lime Pie and Hibiscus and Daiquiri.

At the table, I had felt antsy at the idea of her "resculpting" the inside of my childhood home. But in bed with my mellow playlist on, I tried to talk myself down. It was hardly the home I'd grown up in anymore. My dad had already transformed it himself, through neglect. Maybe it needed a woman's touch. Maybe it needed—as Dixie had described at lunch—a Jacuzzi pavilion in the backyard and a "Napoleonesque" kitchen. I certainly couldn't argue with fresh paint—even Sorbet or Purple-icious had to be better than the dinge that was there now. If the BeDazzler wanted to use her first husband's money to "rejuvenate" my dad's house, I couldn't complain. Or, at the very least, I wouldn't.

I wouldn't complain, but I might lie awake thinking about it. All these years, we'd been living with my mother's absence. Those piles of newspapers would have been bundled with twine and put out by the curb if she'd still been alive. The laundry would have been folded and the curtains would have been pulled back. Once my mother was gone, my dad stopped shaving. With my mom, he'd been a clean-shaven guy. Without her, he'd become a grizzled old mountain man who forgot to get his hair cut or his eyebrows trimmed. I hadn't seen my dad's face without a beard since I was thirteen. It was as if he had become a different person. It was as if he were hoping that if he refused to take care of himself for long enough, my mom would be forced to come back to life and do it for him.

Lying there, I knew this much: My father deserved to remarry. He deserved a person to eat dinner and take evening strolls and go to the movies with. He deserved someone to take care of him when he was sick and cook him fried chicken. I wanted him to have those things.

I wanted him to have a person in his life who knew about every little thing he did all day long. I didn't want him to be alone.

So what if two more different-looking people did not exist on the earth—Dixie in her sequins and my dad in yesterday's rumpled brown slacks? So what if they wouldn't have anything to talk about? So what if Dixie had wild horses flame-stitched onto her purse? If my idea of love was Santa Claus, why couldn't my dad's be Dolly Parton? Who was I to criticize? I didn't know the first thing about it.

Chapter Four

And then, suddenly, I was pregnant. In the way that two months later can be sudden. The getting pregnant was remarkably easy, though the being pregnant would turn out to be quite a bit trickier.

The week after Thanksgiving, I'd flown back to New York to ship my things home, taking a few days to say good-bye to the city. And everywhere I went—the airport, the subway, the flea market on Columbus and Seventy-ninth for one last hurrah—I walked around with a great sense of importance. I was doing something truly self-less. I was helping another human being in a profound way. I was a good person, a giving person—and, best of all, I was about to be an auntie!

While I was there, I went back to the office to pick up a few of my things. They had a file box waiting for me behind the security desk in the lobby, but even a trip back to that building couldn't bring me down. I bumped into Kid Dy-no-mite in the lobby right near the revolving door, and I was as aglow as if Mackie's bun were already in my oven.

We chatted a minute, and he acted overly sympathetic about my new unemployment, squinting his eyes as if we were friends and saying, "What will you do now?"

"I'm going home to Texas to have a baby," I said, walking backward toward the revolving door. It was all I could do not to squeak with pleasure at the way his mouth fell open in surprise. This from the workaholic ex-girlfriend. This from the girl he'd dumped and then fired. This beautiful news. This glorious adventure.

"You're pregnant?" he asked, as I stepped in.

"Almost," I said, and gave him a big wink as the door spun closed. And why not? I had happiness to spare.

My trip to New York might have been a great time to pause and really think about what I was about to do. There were certainly moments, like when I was packing or when I was saying good-bye to Bekka, when the enormity of the shift could have hit me. But it never did. Mostly because I saw all the upcoming changes as temporary: a temporary pregnancy, a temporary—if lengthy—stay back in Texas, a temporary break from my advertising career. If any of these changes had seemed permanent, I never would have made them. But I framed them all as essential components of an intermission. I was going to take a little break from my life and return back to it refreshed in a year or so. Better than refreshed, even—whatever that was.

Back home, I moved in with Mackie and Clive—at their insistence.

I should have had my pick of rooms in their palatial house, but I didn't. Mackie and Clive had built the place with four bedrooms, assuming they'd have at least three kids. But as the fertility struggle had gone on and on, the rooms had found other uses for themselves. Clive had claimed one of the bedrooms for his home office, Mackie had claimed another for herself. All that was left was the baby room.

There was a garage apartment, which they'd designed with me in mind, but I couldn't stay there, either, because they had rented it to a tenant. Actually, the tenant was the little sister of Mackie's roommate from college, which was how the whole thing happened. She was a med-student-slash-marathoner-slash-professional-sunbather named Barni ("with an *i*"—she had stated to Mackie when they met) who was finishing up a surgical rotation. I'd heard about her but never met her: Even though I came home most holidays, she was off visiting her own family in Dallas. We bumped into each other for the first time ever on a warm December day just after I'd come back from New York. She was sunbathing by the pool, bottom up, in a thong bikini. And I knew at that moment that she was one of those women whom guys always love and women always hate.

"You must be the sister!" she said.

"You must be the tenant!" I countered.

She was rubbing actual baby oil on her body as she flipped a magazine in the sun. And sunbathing in December! In New York, it had been 7 degrees. In Houston, it was 83.

"She's giving herself cancer!" I said to Mackie later. "Who does that with baby oil anymore? Don't they cover skin cancer in medical school?"

"She's young," Mackie said, with a beats-me shrug. "She skipped like two grades."

"I don't like her," I said. "I can tell already."

Mackie never hated anybody. She said, "Maybe she'll grow on you."

"Like a melanoma," I added, but Mackie didn't think that was funny.

The longer I knew Barni, the more I would come to resent the fact that she had my apartment. She turned out to be one of those supercompetitive women who want every man in the world to obsess over her, who are willing to go to all kinds of trouble to outrank every other woman in the world. She jogged six miles every day, ate plenty of leafy greens, flossed morning and night, and made straight As in school—but also bought the naughtiest possible underthings at Victoria's Secret, hit the bars every weekend, cursed at the TV when sports were on, and smoked the occasional cigar. Lean, sexy, high-achieving, raunchy, and half-naked much of the time, she was a patched-together version of all the things women think—or fear—men want, and even the thought of her exhausted me.

Plus, she was kind of a bitch. And I would never use that word lightly. Like the time her washer was broken and she borrowed our laundry room. She found a pair of my perfectly normal white cotton underpants, and she lifted them up with a wire hanger, walked into the kitchen where we were all eating breakfast, and said, "Whose grandma left these in the dryer?"

But she had squatter's rights on the garage apartment, since Mackie had finally given up on my ever coming back. So I took the baby's room and its attached bath, carefully boxing up the duckie-themed towels, soap, and toothbrush holder Mackie had already set by the sink. I replaced the single bed's gender-neutral green gingham sheets with a set of plain white, and then unplugged the dish-and-spoon night-light. Mackie sealed all the baby gear in Tupperware boxes and packed them away alphabetically in her enormous storage closet. Using a label maker. And color-coded labels.

"This pregnancy's going to be fun," I said to Mackie.

"You bet your ass it is," Mackie said.

Houston was not the town I remembered. Visiting your hometown on vacation is not nearly the same thing as coming back to stay. Everything looked different, and, in part, it was. Grocery stores, shopping centers, and movie theaters I had gone to growing up had disappeared or changed beyond recognition. Houses I'd grown up playing in were gone. Entire neighborhoods had lost their original houses one by one and become entirely new places. I had noticed these changes from time to time over the years. But with the total immersion of coming back to stay, I got the whole picture. It was exactly the same town, but totally different, which left me in a constant state of looking for things that were long gone.

"That's just Houston," Mackie and Clive said about it one night. "That's just how we roll."

They didn't want Houston to bother me. They envisioned my pregnancy as a long stay at a family-owned spa. They were going to cook for me and pamper me and spritz me with gratitude every day. Mackie had read every book in existence about optimizing those nine months, and she fully believed that a happy mother made for a happy fetus. And I was willing to run with that. They were going to play Brahms on their house-wide speaker system to nurture the baby's intelligence—as well as Billie Holiday for wisdom, Al Green for passion, and James Brown for total badass-ocity. Mackie was going to cook feasts every night and keep the house stocked with organic, high-fiber food that was free of trans fats, artificial colors, synthetic hormones, and phthalates. They were going to buy me a gym membership (no pressure!), a feng shui pebble fountain, and a birthing ball that converted into an ergonomic desk chair.

They said I didn't have to worry about finding a new job until after the baby. That way I'd have my options open when we were done. I could follow my plan to go back to New York and resume my fabulous ex-life, or "Please, please, please stay in Texas." Either way, everybody won. They were getting a baby, and I was getting a forty-week, all-expenses-paid, health-and-wellness-oriented, baby-rific vacation. Easy.

Mackie's old fertility specialist referred us to a new in vitro specialist whose office was on the top floor of the tallest building in the Medical Center, and we took to calling her Dr. Penthouse. She had hunched shoulders and a Dorothy Hamill hairdo.

"I love her," I said after our introductory visit. "She's so retro."

"You know there's an Ice Capades tutu under that lab coat," Mackie said.

Then Mackie and I went out for chile con queso and margaritas as a last hurrah. That night also signaled my last coffee, last deli meat, last sushi, and last shampoo with either sodium laurel sulfate or sodium lauryl sulfate, since neither of us could remember which one was worse. A few other lasts that snuck up on me: chocolate, hair spray, sugarless gum, fluoride toothpaste, and antiperspirant (though I hid a travel-sized one in my underwear drawer). Mackie offered to go without all the same things as an act of solidarity, which I found very touching. And I wasn't missing any of them yet.

At our first official visit, Dr. Penthouse gave us a stern talking-to about what we were undertaking. She let us know that it was her responsibility to safeguard not just our physical but also our emotional health. She gave us lengthy questionnaires with inquiries like "Do you ever think about death and dying?" and "Have you ever struggled to stay happy?" and "Do you find it hard to let go?" She also gave us cards to keep in our purses with the signs of depression on them. "Feelings of anger," "feelings of resentment," "overeating or loss of appetite," "sleeping too much or too little," "feelings of dread or worthlessness," "lethargy," "excessive worrying," "temper fits," and "questioning the meaning of it all" made up the list, and Mackie looked it over and said, "Sounds like a typical day to me," as she dropped the card in her purse.

Dr. Penthouse had cautioned that the process could take months and months, try after try, and also declared that she was "not comfortable" with my first pregnancy being a surrogate one. "Women typically do this after they've had their kids," she said.

"Women typically do this for hire," I pointed out. "And we're in a different situation."

"Sarah's doing it for love," Mackie added, giving me a little hug.

"Love and adoration," I corrected.

"Fair enough," Dr. P. said, shrugging.

With all the new technologies, there was a pretty good success rate, but we had to pace ourselves and be prepared for an emotional toll. Dr. P. used words like "tension," and "resentment," and "angst." She was definitely a worrier, and we decided to let her head up the Worst Case Scenario Department.

We, in contrast, just felt grateful. We took hormones to get in sync for the embryo transfer and downed prenatal vitamins like they were M&M's. We had something to do, which was far better than the nothing we'd had before. In truth, we got consumed by the project. It became as sisterly an activity as planning a wedding or throwing a shower. We became a Girls' Pregnancy Club of two, and looking back—though he might have liked to be in on at least some of it—we left Clive out entirely. His contribution, to put it plainly, was about the size of a petri dish.

We were so consumed by the project, we found ourselves wishing we had nothing else in the world to do. But the world had a thing or two in mind. Because on the same crisp January morning that Dr. Penthouse implanted several of Mackie and Clive's hand-fertilized zygotes into my plump and waiting uterus—possibly even the very same hour—Dixie, who was apparently knee-deep in her home improvement project at my dad's, discovered my mother's chest of drawers. Discovered, I mean, that it was still full of her stuff.

And when I say "stuff," I mean T-shirts, jeans, panties, lingerie, socks, bras, hairbrushes, jewelry, letters, magazines, grocery receipts, ballpoint pens, hand lotion. Everything. Seventeen years after her death, it was all still right there. All still folded just exactly as my mother herself had folded it—that last load of laundry before she went into the hospital. Everything stacked in drawers and completely untouched. Every drawer exactly as she had left it. Only the top drawer was a total mess. And it was the one Dixie opened first.

Somewhere during that long year after my mother died, there had been a night when my mild-mannered dad—who wore his grief zipped up around him like a Mister Rogers sweater—freaked out.

Mackie and I were making cereal and hot dogs for dinner in the kitchen and heard a crash in his bedroom, then his feet clomping down the stairs, then the jangle of keys, and then a door slam. After an appropriate pause, we tiptoed up the stairs together to find that he had swept every item off the top of my mother's dresser. The floor was covered with makeup, and jewelry, and perfume bottles, and broken pieces of the Deco vase that had been our grandma's. Even the things that hadn't broken looked broken down there on the rug: hand lotion, powder, a jewelry box, a papier-mâché tiara I'd made in second grade.

Mackie insisted she wasn't crying as we picked every tiny piece up off the floor. Even the glass shards went into Ziploc bags. Anything larger than a pebble we saved. It was stupid, we knew. But these pieces of glass were our mom's. They had been carried by her hands. They had her fingerprints on them.

Mackie and I moved quickly, neither of us ready to deal with our mother's things yet. And I remember having the crazy thought that when our mother came back, we would probably all spend several nights at the kitchen table, gluing the pieces back together, sorting them patiently like we were working a jigsaw puzzle. She'd understand. She'd be pissed about the vase, but she'd understand.

After that, the top drawer of her dresser became the repository for anything of my mother's we found around the house. The scarf on the coat rack, the compact in the bathroom. "Put it in the drawer," my dad would say, without even looking.

As we got older, we raided the drawer now and again for fancy barrettes and earrings—most of which, despite our best intentions, we eventually lost. Mackie insisted our dad had thrown our mom's wedding ring in there at one point, but I'd been in the hospital room when he'd lifted her finger to take it off. I'd seen the way he'd stopped halfway at the knuckle and pressed his face against the back of her hand, and I knew he'd have found a better place for it than that.

Though Mackie had asked to have it when she got married, and my father told her he couldn't find it. "Don't worry, sweetheart," he'd said. "It's in the house somewhere." Then, as if this were a good thing: "I never throw anything away."

I can't imagine what it must have been like for Dixie to find that drawer full of my mother's things. She'd seen the house before, of course, and she knew it was not livable. "We mostly go to her condo," my dad had told me. Though it was really too small for the both of them.

"Why don't you guys just get a new place together?" I had asked him.

He shrugged. "I don't know." And then, after a minute: "She likes to fix things up."

Dixie had started her renovations to my dad's place right after Thanksgiving without either of them mentioning it to us. She wanted to get the place ready before she moved in, and she wanted to move in right after the honeymoon. Maybe she was just efficient and moving fast, or maybe she just didn't think to tell us. Or, more likely, maybe Mackie hadn't picked up when she'd called to talk to us about it. Either way, we didn't know a thing about the work crews she'd had swarming the place until January—the very same day Dr. Penthouse implanted the very first fertilized egg in my body.

As we walked in from the appointment, the phone was ringing.

Mackie checked the caller ID and didn't pick up, explaining, "It's Tammy Wynette." But then the phone rang again. And again. By the time Mackie had me set up on the sofa in my sweatpants with a cup of herbal tea and a copy of *People,* Dixie had called four times.

"Give me the phone," I said when it went off again.

"No," Mackie said. "She is bad for our chi."

But when I stood up to get it myself, Mackie gave in right away. She pointed at me and said, "Down!" She didn't want me to be vertical, afraid I might shake the zygote loose. She grabbed the cordless and tossed it to me.

Suffice it to say, Dixie was pretty freaked out by the drawer.

"He just kind of forgot about it," I found myself saying—though I'm not sure that was entirely true. I hadn't looked in that top drawer in years, but I hadn't forgotten it was there. It wasn't something I mentioned at cocktail parties or anything, and I guess I tried not to think about it too directly. But in the back of my mind, I knew. And, more than that: I liked that it was there. And my dad probably did, too.

I learned a lot of things about my dad during that five-minute conversation with Dixie. And I learned a lot about Dixie's ability to yell. So much that when it was over, I stood up and told Mackie, who was making sandwiches at the counter, that we had to leave.

"She found Mom's stuff," I said.

"So?"

"And it sounds like Dad never cleaned out Mom's closet, either."

"Yes, he did. When we were at camp. The year I broke my nose."

"Sounds like, actually, he didn't."

"He didn't?"

I shook my head. Then I added, "And it's possible he never threw away any of her prescription vials from the medicine cabinet."

"Okay. That's weird."

"Dixie sounds kind of upset."

"And?"

"And we need to go over there and talk to her."

"No," Mackie said.

"Mackie," I said. "It's the right thing to do."

"You shouldn't be vertical. You should be horizontal."

"That's just a theory you have. That's not actually true."

Mackie was back to making lunch. She had a plan, and we were sticking to it. "You're saying theories can't also be true?"

"Macks," I said. "I'm saying we have to go. And here's why."

Mackie did not look up.

"At this very moment? Right now?" I said. "She is pouring herself a stiff drink. And as soon as she finishes it, she's going to start hauling every single thing that ever belonged to our mother out to the curb in Hefty bags."

Six minutes later, we were ringing our childhood doorbell, and Mackie was saying, "A hundred bucks says she's got the inside lit up like Vegas."

When Dixie opened the door, Mackie pointed at me and said, "She might be pregnant, okay? So no sudden movements."

Dixie tried to summon the appropriate response. She looked me over and composed herself. "Well, sweetheart, that's wonderful." I looked her over, too, in her pantsuit—in a way I hadn't at Fu's Garden. She had a delightful late-fifty-something body, with dancer's legs, a soft belly pooch, and a rack like a Swedish grandma.

Then Dixie's cell phone started going off—with an Elvis ringtone: "Hound Dog"—and her attention shifted. She gestured us both to follow her inside as she clacked down the hall in her high-heeled sandals to find it.

We stepped in. I had braced myself on the walk over for some changes. But I hadn't expected what I saw from the entryway: Except for two deluxe dog beds for Dixie's rescue shih tzus, ZaZa and Snippers, the entire downstairs was empty.

Not that long before, if you'd stepped into my dad's foyer, you'd have seen stacks of papers on the front hall table, clumps of mail on the floor from past avalanches, a top-heavy coatrack, books and manuscripts piled on the stairs in heaps, pictures askew, stacks of recycling, an old bicycle with no chain. I'd done some reading on the subject, and there was a term for the way my father lived: "pathologically messy." Mackie thought this was an exaggeration, but it was true. My dad was the type of messy person who might well at some point get crushed by avalanches of his own stuff.

"It's like he's trying to lose things in there," I'd said to Mackie once.

And she'd nodded and said, "Himself."

He kept the dishes done, though. It wasn't like there were rats crawling around a sink full of dirty dishes. It wasn't squalor. But at that moment, standing in the cleaned-out entryway, I suddenly got a whiff of what the house had looked like when it was normal—and I realized the long distance my dad had drifted from that place.

I thought about his medicine cabinet still full of my mom's things, about him opening and closing that mirror to get his toothbrush or aspirin or floss. How many times a day did a person open and close a medicine cabinet? And what did that add up to over seventeen years? And all the while his dead wife's old penicillin bottles were right there on the shelf, her name typed out on a label from a pharmacy that had long since been demolished. Did he not notice them? Could he not bear to part with them? Did it comfort him to see her name, all spelled out as official proof that she had, at least, once shared this bathroom and borrowed his razor and argued with him about who used up all the hot water?

Suddenly, Dixie seemed pretty good to me. Her energy. That

plunging neckline. Those glitter-pedicured toes as she clicked back over to us. So what if she had enormous hair shellacked into a crisp shell? She was alive. She was in motion. And around this place, that was a hell of a thing.

She also knew how to get things done. I had to admit, the downstairs looked a lot better. Especially after we'd made it up to the second floor and saw the section of the house that Dixie hadn't worked on yet—the contrast between "before" and "after" seemed more and more like a miracle. The floors were shiny and mopped, the dust was dusted, the curtains were gone, and sunlight was touching parts of the rooms that hadn't felt it for years. Everything down there felt brighter and breezier.

Dixie watched us look around. "Girls," she said. "It was time to bring this place back to life."

"Where's all the stuff?" Mackie asked, and I knew she was worried about the same thing I was: that Dixie had sent it all off to the dump without any regard for what it might have meant to us—as if there had been no treasures among the trash.

But Dixie knew exactly where all the stuff downstairs had gone. She ticked the categories off on her fingers as she led us back to my parents' bedroom. "The trash is in the trash. The almost-trash is at Goodwill. The keepsakes are in storage tubs. And the good stuff is waiting for you in the garage." Never mind that Dixie lacked the authority and experience to know which of those things should have gone into which category. Her decisiveness appealed to me. Even as I felt, at the same time, exactly like we'd been robbed.

Dixie agreed to let us—actually, just Mackie, because she didn't want me lifting anything—store most if not all of our mother's things down the hall in our bedrooms until we had time to sort through them properly. Dixie swore up and down over and over that she was not going to touch our bedrooms at all. "I won't even open the doors," she kept saying.

So the boxes of junk—hand lotion bottles, lipstick tubes, love letters, books—wound up in my old room, and the clothes wound up on Mackie's old bed, along with photo albums and yearbooks. The only thing we brought back to Mackie's house that day was a collection of six fancy dresses of my mom's that we used to play dress-up in. They'd been zipped in plastic bags in my parents' closet, and Mackie carried all of them on the walk back home. Dixie had offered to drive them in her Escalade, but Mackie gave a polite no.

As children, we'd tried those dresses on often, stuffing Kleenex into the bodices and walking on tiptoe so the hems didn't drag. We'd smear on bright red lipstick and too much rouge. We'd stab at our eyes with mascara and give ourselves beauty marks—sometimes doing so many, our mom would come after us with a wet paper towel.

"One is a beauty mark," I remember her saying. "Twenty is chicken pox."

On the walk back, Mackie fretted about all the standing I'd done and all the dust I'd inhaled and the emotional toll of watching our mother's things get evicted from their rightful home by "that redneck lady."

"This is the last thing you need today," she said, stomping along. "Sorting through your dead mother's things."

"Mackie," I said. "I'm fine."

"You don't know that," she said, glancing at my tummy. "You have no idea what's going on in there." And her voice sounded sad enough that I just let her be right.

Mackie was so discouraged by the time we got home that she didn't even make me lie down. I was already a lost cause. Instead, I wound up comforting her while I boiled water for a pot of Clive's Darjeeling.

"So it won't happen this month," I said. "Big deal."

"It was a big deal to me," she said.

I wanted her to feel better. I gave her a kiss on the head and then looked her in the eyes. "Don't you know?" I said as convincingly as I could. "Nothing good ever happens on the first try."

Chapter Five

But it did happen. On the first try. Despite all our pessimism, within a few weeks, I'd taken seven positive pregnancy tests, visited the doctor to confirm, and was vomiting up a storm. The vomiting lost its luster pretty quickly—though the first time was a kind of thrill. Mackie and I had even high-fived before she scurried off to find her stockpile of pressure-point motion-sickness wristbands and cans of ginger ale.

And then, on the morning of the official eight-week mark, on a Friday in mid-March, I woke up with a tumor.

"I have a tumor," I announced to Mackie at breakfast.

"Again?" she said.

"Feel it," I demanded, while she squeezed my orange juice.

"No," she said.

"I need a second opinion," I said.

"And that's why I'm not going to feel it." She was not going to spend the morning discussing the dimensions of any lump anywhere on my body. "I'm good with the tumor conversations," she said. "I really feel satiated on that front."

"Come on," I said.

"We're not talking about this. You already know what I think."

"What do you think?"

"I think you're fine."

"Why?"

"Because you're always fine."

She had a point. "But," I said. "Someday I won't be. Someday I'll have a tumor that will actually be a tumor. And when that day comes, won't we want to catch it early?"

"Yes," Mackie said. "When that day comes, we should definitely catch it early."

I tried to work in a Big Worry at least twice a year. I remember a time in college, worrying that I had skin cancer:

"Where?" Mackie kept asking.

"Here," I'd say, pointing at a little place on the back of my hand.

"That's a freckle."

"No. Next to the freckle."

"All I see is the freckle."

"You're not trying hard enough," I kept saying. "Here. Right here."

Mackie hated these conversations. She was not a person who got bogged down in irrational fears. She did her best to keep level-headed and steady and preferred to keep her anxieties tied to sensible things, like pesticides and global warming. Life had not left the same marks on her that it had on me, and her only response to my moments of panic was teasing. And then, after a few days, exasperation. "Dammit, Sarah," she'd say. "Pull yourself together."

Given everything—the way we lost our mother so quickly and the way I had never quite been able to get every single piece of my life back in place, fear of illness didn't seem so unreasonable. Fear of a cancer that arrived out of nowhere, wept from every corner of my body, and then obliterated everything.

All these years later, I didn't feel sad about my mother's death anymore, exactly. I could remember her with fondness and look through photo albums just fine. But there was still something aching inside me that I could feel only in refracted ways: vacation cruise commercials that brought me to tears; news stories about abandoned newborns; starving horses on *Animal Cops;* and, of course, as always, phantom illnesses that grabbed hold of me like nightmares in the yellow light of day.

Because cancer did sneak up on people, appearing on the night of the big promotion, say, or during a honeymoon in Paris. There were countless stories of people who had saved their own lives because they'd "caught it early." Vigilance, attentiveness, and even obsession could pay off. By worrying about every little thing. By looking for death around every corner. By making your sister feel your tumors.

I'd found this one in the shower. An armpit lump. Exactly the kind that took down Debra Winger in *Terms of Endearment*—a movie I never should have been allowed to see, and which, in retrospect, my dad admitted he should have screened first. He'd thought it was about astronauts, and he'd always been a big Jack Nicholson fan.

That morning, I thought, *Of course*. Things were going so well these days. Really too well. Except for the vomiting, which was frequent, and the nausea, which took up maybe half the day, I felt great. I felt so amazed and grateful that this pregnancy had worked—and been so easy. Everything had gone beautifully and perfectly right. Which seemed like just begging for trouble.

On the way downstairs after my shower, I'd tried to imagine what to do about the baby. In my mind, I refused chemo to protect it, telling Mackie and Clive that the next generation was "all that mattered now." In my mind, I was noble and selfless and brave—and Mackie was desperate to talk some sense into me. "You have to fight this," my imaginary Mackie said.

But down in the kitchen, my real Mackie just said, "I'm not sticking my fingers in your armpit." She was slicing banana coins. "What are you saying?" she went on. "You have armpit cancer?"

"No," I said. "It's a swollen lymph node."

"It's not a lymph node," she said. "It's a sweat gland." She plopped a glass on the counter in front of me in a way that said we would not be talking about this again today. "Drink your juice."

I'd freaked out over too many illnesses for her to take me seriously. I'd cried too many wolves. I understood that. I didn't even take myself seriously. But still, I wanted to check.

"I'm just going to Google my symptoms," I said.

"No!" she said, grabbing my arm. "No Googling. Breakfast."

No wonder Mackie rolled her eyes. I would have, too. I knew I was being crazy. *This is crazy,* I'd say to myself. *You're fine.* But no matter how firmly I said it, some tiny, rebellious voice somewhere in my head always squeaked, *But what if I'm not?*

Breakfast that morning was whole wheat toast from the bread machine, organic cream cheese, and toxin-free lox. Plus a fruit salad, all organic, and my prenatal vitamin in a little Japanese wasabi dish.

"You're so full-service," I said as I knocked the vitamin back.

"Everything but the armpits," Mackie said.

That same afternoon, we went for our first ultrasound, and by the time we left the office, the tumor was completely forgotten, never to return again—entirely replaced by something new.

The technician laid me back and squirted the gel on my tummy. Then she ran the sensor all around as Mackie and I searched the monitor screen for something, anything, that was identifiable as human. Mostly, it was just fuzz—and some blobby shapes. I guess I'd expected to see a tiny little person waving at us. It was oddly disappointing.

Until the technician made an almost imperceptible gasp and said, "Oh."

"Was that a good 'Oh' or a bad 'Oh'?" I asked.

"Hold on," the technician said.

"What is it?" Mackie asked.

The technician, of course, had no sense at all of my capacity for panic. Or she would not, next, have said, "Just a second," and then left us to wait while she studied the screen. I watched her face, and came up with a billion troubles she could have been studying. My first worry was that she didn't see anything at all—that none of the blobs added up to a baby. My second thought, of course, was cancer, the grande dame of bodily fears. Ovarian, uterine, bowel, pancreatic. Something bad. Something very bad.

We waited. Mackie and I watched the technician's face now instead of the monitor, but it was equally inscrutable.

The technician froze the screen in a picture and said, "There." She touched her finger to the image, showing us something that didn't look like anything.

"What is that?" Mackie asked.

"A tumor?" I suggested, but Mackie swatted me on the arm.

"Guess again!" the technician said.

But Mackie said, "You don't want her to do that."

"It's another baby!" the technician finally said, breaking into a smile. "You've got twins!"

Right as she said it, I felt a little flutter of excitement. And not the kind of excitement you feel when something good happens to someone else, but the kind you feel when something good happens to you. It was a tiny moment, but it scared the hell out of me. Because I suddenly understood that no matter what my brain had decided I was supposed to feel about these babies, my body could decide something different all on its own. And right there, for the first time, I thought words that would become a mantra for me over the coming months: *This is not your pregnancy. It's Mackie's.*

We'd been hoping for twins, of course—to get, as Mackie put it, a "twofer," which is very common with IVF. But we'd only ever heard one heartbeat on the Doppler, and the twins were a real surprise. Mackie hugged me. Then she hugged the technician.

Then we all studied the screen. "Are they sisters?" Mackie wanted to know. "Can you tell if they're sisters?"

"No, no." The technician waved her hand. "It's way too early for that."

"I'm kind of hoping for sisters," Mackie admitted. Then she gave me a shoulder-squeeze. "I can't imagine my life without my sister."

"Best not to hope too hard for any one thing," the technician told her.

"In pregnancy and in life," I added, but only Mackie gave me a smile.

Later, Mackie and Clive would decide that they didn't want to know the sex of the babies. They'd decide to be surprised. Even though, with twins, there is so much monitoring and so many ultrasounds, it really takes a lot of work not to find out. "Don't tell me!" became Mackie's catchphrase for every doctor visit. She'd shield her eyes and say, "We want to be surprised." The drama got pretty over-the-top near the end, and I remember one day meeting eyes with the ultrasound technician as we had the same thought at the same time: *Ai, ai, ai.*

I, of course, knew. I knew as soon as it was possible to know, and I liked knowing. It helped me feel like the babies were a wonderful gift I was making for Mackie and Clive—something I was in charge of. Every now and then, Mackie would stop what she was doing and turn and say, "Okay, tell me." But I never did.

On this first visit, though, all that still lay ahead. On this first visit, Mackie and I were in sync, equally in the dark. Mackie stared at the white shapes on the monitor. "It's sisters," she said. "I can tell. They totally look like girls."

"Mackie," I said. "They're blobs."

"Sister blobs," she said, and then we slapped high fives.

We were halfway to the elevator when Mackie realized she'd left her purse in the exam room. I waited by the front desk while she ran back to get it, and after a little pause, the receptionist and I felt like we had to make eye contact. As we did, I patted my belly and smiled.

"Good visit?" she asked.

I nodded. "Twins," I said.

"Wonderful!" she said with a delighted lilt. And then her voice dropped about an octave. "Kiss your body good-bye, though. I gained eighty pounds with mine. And don't believe what they tell you about vitamin E preventing stretch marks. I had a hundred and seven."

"You counted them?"

She nodded. "A hundred and seven."

I gave a polite laugh and then came to the final moment of a realization that had started somewhere back in the ultrasound room and been building ever since. It was not the moment when I reached the point of no return, but, instead, the moment when I realized that I was already well past it—and had been for quite a while. My smile faded until I realized the receptionist was still waiting for a reply. So I patted my belly again and said something like "Okeydokey."

I was so relieved to see Mackie come around the corner that I almost shouted her name. The receptionist gave a little wave as Mackie took my arm and we turned away.

"Seriously," the receptionist called after us. "You will really miss that body when it's gone."

. . .

The good news was that Dr. Penthouse had recommended scheduling a C-section. Of course, nowadays, for twins, a C-section was a given, but it was nice to get it on the calendar. And it shaved three weeks off my waiting time. Due date: October 15. C-section: September 20.

"We're happy to wait until the due date," Mackie had told Dr. P.

But Dr. P. shook her head. "She'll never make it that long." And before I had time to decide what, exactly, Dr. P. was trying to say about me, she clarified: "Twins always come early."

Clive was out of town that day, not due back until the next afternoon, and Mackie called him from the car on the way home. I counted the number of times she said the word *twins* into the phone. Twenty-three. It might as well have been a hundred and seven.

Back at home, we swam for a while and then decided to watch movies, but somehow found ourselves in Mackie's gargantuan storage closet instead, playing dress-up with our mother's dresses for the first time since we'd brought them to Mackie's—aware on some level that it was not nearly as much fun as adults as it had been when we were kids, but determined to do it anyway on principle.

The dresses still fit, sort of, though we couldn't zip them all—especially around my belly, which, at eight weeks, was already starting to pooch. And my boobs were bigger, too, I suddenly noticed, and I spilled over in a new and alarming way. Wriggling in and out of the dresses, it was pretty undeniable. I was definitely pregnant.

I tilted my head at my cleavage in the mirror.

"It's a little hookerish," I said.

We found another one for me, slightly looser.

"That's better," Mackie said, looking at my reflection. And then, "Great boobs."

"Thanks," I said, pushing the bodice up a little to see a new angle.

Mackie paused a minute and then said, "You could nurse the babies if you wanted to." And then, "I wouldn't mind."

"I'm not nursing the babies," I said.

"Okay," she said. "But it's actually kind of better for them to get breast milk."

"I'm not nursing any babies," I said again. "And you'd better bring champagne to the hospital," I went on, "because as soon as it's over, I'm done."

"You sound like you're not having fun," she said, with a hurt-feelings pout. This was, I realized then, what I'd gotten myself into. It wasn't enough to do this. I was supposed to love every minute of it, too.

At the beginning, when I'd framed the pregnancy as "two sisters having fun," I was able to turn everything into a funny story. But now it wasn't just two sisters anymore. It was two sisters and two little creatures swimming around in my abdomen, and suddenly I could feel them gliding around in there like koi in a pond. And we weren't going through it together anymore, either, because one of us was on the precipice of gaining eighty pounds and getting 107 stretch marks and losing her body forever. Why hadn't I known this would happen? I guess Angelina Jolie just made it look so easy.

After that first ultrasound, the tone of the project shifted for me. It was like we'd been dancing around the living room to the Go-Go's, and then somebody had unplugged the music. You can keep dancing like that for only so long. But Mackie's music was still going. She was bouncing and shimmying with no idea that I'd already collapsed on the couch. And that would pretty much be the rest of the pregnancy: her trying to get me back up and dancing, and me saying, "Mackie, give it a rest."

And something about the fact that I couldn't change my mind had me thinking a lot—a whole lot—about changing my mind.

"I am having fun," I told Mackie, feeling a twinge of nausea. "For exactly forty weeks."

"Okay," Mackie said, and let it drop. Then she looked down at her feet and announced, "Shoes." With that, we were in her dressing room, negotiating who got the sling-backs with the bows.

In the end we took turns prancing around in front of the full-length mirror, mesmerized by the silhouettes of our fancy, retro selves. We looked so different, so transformed in our white gloves and pillbox hats, that we decided to do our makeup. We gave ourselves thick cat eyeliner and ruby lips. We put on powder and perfume. We rolled pretend cigarettes with paper and tape and called each other "Darling."

Then Mackie asked if she could straighten my hair, and at first I said no.

"I'm trying to accept myself as is," I said.

"Oh," Mackie said. "Okay." And then, "But if you had straight hair, we'd look like twins."

"Or if you let yours go curly," I countered.

"Or got electrocuted," she added.

In the end, I suggested we switch hair—that I'd let her straighten mine if she'd let me unstraighten hers. I should have guessed, when I agreed to go first, that we might not get around to Mackie.

When she finished with me, we both just stood staring because, really, she was right. When we had the same makeup and the same sixties outfits and the exact same straight red hair, we really did look remarkably alike—and we really did look a lot like our mother, who had been exactly my age when she was pregnant with Mackie. At that moment, I found myself thinking about my dad and how much he must still miss her, and feeling so glad for his sake that he wasn't there to see us.

We had just decided to hit the town to show ourselves off when a wave of nausea came over me so fast I threw up in Mackie's lingerie drawer, though I had barely apologized before she had all the contents in the delicates cycle. And then I hardly had time to get the dress off before I did it again, this time—and I tried to count my blessings here—in the toilet.

Mackie helped me change into a pair of her pajamas and put me in her bed while she went down for a glass of ginger ale. Then, when I was better, she climbed onto the bed beside me, still in her prom dress.

"Maybe we should just watch a movie," Mackie said. She had one she'd been wanting to show me, a Jane Austen knockoff. She'd Netflixed it on impulse and wound up loving it enough that when she saw it on sale at Target for $9.99, she bought it.

"It's cheesy," she warned me, "but you just have to look past the cheese."

I took a sip of my ginger ale. "That doesn't sound good."

"It's a great story," she insisted, "tangled up in some very bad writing."

I agreed to watch it with her. I was always up for anything Jane Austen, even a knockoff.

Maybe I was just feeling bad, though the nausea passed again pretty quickly. Or maybe I was tired. Or maybe the movie was just way worse than Mackie wanted to admit. But for some reason, I hated it.

"These people are too weird," I said. "She looks like Homer Simpson."

"You get used to them," Mackie said.

But I didn't. They had facial tics and bad dialogue and the production values were awful. At one point, I swear I saw the boom in the frame.

"This is the worst movie ever made," I said. I could not believe that my smart, sophisticated sister had actually bought it.

But Mackie was getting up off the bed, and walking across to the TV. "Fine," she said. She was mad. She was the kind of mad you get only when people who ought to know better are really disappointing you. She put the DVD in the box and glared at me. "I'm going to go rent us something else."

"I'm sorry," I said, but it was way too late.

I offered to come along, but she didn't want me throwing up in her car. She had a whole library of DVDs in her TV cabinet, but it was clear that she could use a minute to breathe.

But at the door, she stopped to say this: "Just because you have morning sickness doesn't give you the right to complain about every single thing."

"You want this morning sickness?" I shot back, all fire and fight. "You can have it!"

She took a deep breath then and let it out. "Actually," she pointed out, "I can't."

Before I could react, she closed the door, and clicked her heels away down the hall. I felt relieved that I hadn't had time to say anything, because, even if she'd wanted a response, I wasn't sure what I would have said.

I climbed into her bed to wait. The TV was off, and I could hear the palm tree outside brushing against the window. A stupid fight, for sure. But sometimes stupid fights have a smartness to them.

I waited so long for Mackie to come back that I fell asleep in her bed—and that's when a crazy thing happened. Because the next person to come home wasn't Mackie. The next person to come home was Clive. Maybe he didn't notice that Mackie's car was gone. Or maybe he was just on autopilot. There was really no reason at all he should have expected that I would be in his bed. In his bed, in a dimly lit room, on Mackie's side, asleep, with my red hair straightened like hers, and wearing her pajamas.

Of course he assumed I was Mackie. He didn't even hesitate. He just dropped his bag and climbed up on the bed in his suit, stretched his body out against his wife, buried his face in the crook of her neck, took in a deep breath of her, whispered something like "I missed you," and then started kissing her neck. Kissing her with the kind of kiss that just about anybody would kill to wake up to—mouth against neck, hand on the rib cage—not rough or overpowering, just the right amount of firmness and pressure. Just exactly right.

Except not exactly right, since I wasn't his wife.

We can say that I wasn't fully awake, that I didn't know what I was doing. We can argue that I was dreaming about somebody else. We can point out the truth: that hormones and dehydration made me feel a little dizzy and disoriented most of the time. I can promise you that up until that moment I had never even thought of Clive's kissing abilities in a first-person way. Even watching his great smooch with Mackie at Fu's Garden had not sparked the tiniest thought about what it would be like to kiss him. He was just a person. Not a guy, not a man. Up until that point, he was just my sister's husband.

And now I have to confess something else. It was the best kiss I'd been anywhere near in a long, long time.

I pushed him away, of course—as soon as it hit me. I sat up and turned away and shouted, "I'm not Mackie!" all at once. Clive scrambled off the bed and rushed back across the room, tripping on the gown I'd left on the floor and falling backward onto his butt, a butt I had never noticed before—but one I'd realize, in the days and weeks to come, was first-rate.

On the floor, Clive was staring at me in disbelief as I said over and over, "I'm not Mackie, I'm Sarah!"

"But that's Mackie's hair!"

"She straightened it for me!"

"But you're in our bed!"

"I was resting!"

"But you're in her pajamas!"

"I'm borrowing them!"

"Well, where the hell is Mackie?"

"She went out to rent a movie."

"Bloody hell."

Clive breathed in and out while he took it all in. He stayed on the floor, and I stayed hunched over on the edge of the bed, not looking at him. We were quiet there for a minute.

"You're supposed to be out of town," I said after a bit, eyes on the carpet.

"I'm home early," he said.

"Obviously."

Then another pause. Neither of us moved, and neither of us was going to move until Mackie got home to make things okay again. We just sat. And waited.

"So," Clive said, to fill up time. "Twins, huh?"

"Yep," I said.

"That's fantastic," Clive said.

And then, reading my silence, or my body language, or maybe even my thoughts, he said something that Mackie herself had still not said. "Thank you for doing this," he said, "by the way."

"My pleasure," I said, almost in a whisper, hoping I didn't sound sarcastic.

Then we heard Mackie's heels clicking in the hallway. When she walked into the room, still in her fabulous sixties dress, she looked like a movie star. She'd seen Clive's car, and the empty glass of milk on the counter.

"Hey!" she said to Clive. "Why are you on the floor?"

I wasn't sure what Clive was going to say, or how much he was going to confess. He hesitated a bit before he said, "Sarah scared me. I thought she was you." Not a good liar—which struck me as sweet. Then he realized he needed something more. He pointed out the dress beside him. "And then I tripped on this."

True. All true.

Mackie wasn't listening too hard. "Did you see Sarah's hair? Doesn't she look great?"

"She looks exactly like you," he said.

"It's crazy, isn't it?"

"I mean, exactly."

Mackie dropped the movie on the bed and went over to help Clive up. "You're back early."

"Yep," Clive said.

"Were you missing me?"

"Yep."

She leaned in for a quick kiss, and I made a break for it. "Good night!" I called at the door.

"Wait!" Mackie said, and grabbed the movie she'd rented. *It Happened One Night.* My favorite. A peace offering. "I'm sorry," she said.

"No, I'm sorry," I said. And then, "I'm just not feeling great today."

"Climb back in bed," she said. "We can all watch."

I did not look at Clive. "I just need to sleep," I told her.

"Okay." She gave up easily—like a person who had a better option, home early from his business trip, just across the room.

Then she leaned in to kiss me good night on the cheek. In that moment, I was sure she was going to figure it out. She'd sniff his scent on me, or she'd find one of his hairs—some forensic moment would bust us. But she didn't notice anything. Just pecked me on the cheek and said, "Feel better."

Of course, there wasn't anything to figure out. Which is why I decided Clive was right not to tell Mackie. Telling her would just give her something to worry about when there was, in fact, nothing to worry about. Telling her would just complicate every aspect of our living and childbearing arrangements. Best to just forget about it as quickly as possible. Nobody had done anything wrong. Except me, maybe. I didn't fault myself for the moment, since I was practically asleep, after all—but I did kind of fault myself for liking it.

Clive would forget it very quickly. By the next morning, he'd be joking around with me like he did with everyone. No lingering looks, no special significance to anything he said or did. The kiss would be gone from his mind—replaced, no doubt, by countless subsequent and legitimate kisses from the love of his life.

Me, I didn't have any kisses to replace it with—and I wouldn't forget it quite so fast. That moment with Clive would linger in my head for a long time. Maybe we had all been too cocky, thinking we could outsmart the love-and-baby-making tides of human evolution. I was, after all, carrying the man's child in my body. Even though it hadn't gotten there in any way that remotely resembled nature, my body couldn't have been expected to know that. Maybe it felt some connection. Maybe it made assumptions about the two of us. Maybe this whole having-a-baby-with-my-sister's-husband project was going to have complications and ramifications down to the cellular level that I'd never bothered to anticipate. It was possible that that moment with Clive hit me the way it did because I had stumbled onto some invisible Gulf Stream of passion and humanity and life that I had never been privy to before—something infinitely larger and more powerful than myself.

Maybe that was it. Or maybe, more likely, it was just because my most recent previous kiss had come from a vegan blind date named Maurice who had tasted like baba ghanoush and cigarettes and had used this line to try to get upstairs to my apartment: "Red in the head, fire in the bed." Or maybe it was just because I could count on one hand the number of tender human touches I'd felt in the past six months. None of which were exceptional. Except, I had to admit, for Everett Thompson's elbow.

That night when I got back to my room, I took out a piece of paper and wrote the C-section date in inch-tall block letters: September 20. Then I centered it on my pillow and stared at it. March to October didn't seem so impossible. I'd traveled that distance countless times before without even noticing. Through the vent, I could hear Mackie and Clive making little happy murmurs, so I cranked up some Chaka Khan on my headphones. Then I pulled out the calendar in my day planner and counted the weeks, and when I was finished counting the weeks, I counted the days. Next time I was out, I'd get a big calendar to put Xs on, and a fat red pen. One thing was clear: It was time to add some forward momentum to this pregnancy. It was time to get things moving.

I knew of course that you can't speed time up, any more than you can slow it down. It plods along at its own stubborn and infuriating pace. But that didn't mean I couldn't try. It seemed important to try.

Even after the whole house, including Chaka, had fallen silent, I lay awake for hours. Whenever I tried to curl up and doze off, I would feel the echo of Clive's palm on my rib cage, and I would literally have to thrash my body around to shake off the memory. By morning, the covers were piled up like a little shrine to insomnia.

When I went downstairs for breakfast, Mackie took one look at me and said, "What the hell happened to you?"

"I couldn't sleep," I said.

She assumed it was the pregnancy. She brought me a fruit plate and started a pot of decaf. "Vomiting?" she wanted to know.

"No," I said. "Just restless."

"I was restless, too," she said. And then, "Clive and I had a big talk about what happened."

I froze with a strawberry in my mouth. He'd told her. I felt a flash of anger at him. It just didn't seem like Mackie's business. The last thing I needed was her getting angry at me over something so accidental. Something I never saw coming. Something I already felt angry at myself about anyway. I didn't need both of us to be mad.

"I think you and I should talk a little, too," she said.

"Sure," I answered, forcing myself to swallow.

I stabbed another piece of fruit, and that's when I noticed that

Mackie had arranged the pieces into a smiley face. Kiwi eyes, banana nose, strawberry smile, blackberry hair. I felt my eyes fill with tears.

I wasn't even sure what to say. If she'd been anybody else, I could have talked about that nuzzle with Clive all morning—not so much the moment itself, but its lingering effects on my psyche. Something about it had started a warmth inside my body, a burble of molten feelings that I would have given just about anything to discuss. But I couldn't ever have that conversation with Mackie. Or Clive. Or even myself. I'd have to hold all those words in so tight and for so long they'd simply disappear into my body.

I held my breath.

Then Mackie said, "Clive could not believe I got mad at you because you didn't like my dumb movie."

This was it? This was the conversation? I met her eyes. "He couldn't?"

"Nope. He said, 'You yourself said it was a bad movie.' "

Which was true.

Mackie went on, "And I said, 'But with a spark of something meaningful.' "

"I just wasn't feeling well," I said.

"That's just what Clive said! 'Maybe she wasn't feeling well'!"

"He said that?"

"He did! And then he said I should apologize to you."

Clive taking my side! At that moment the continents in my heart drifted one more time and settled into a full-blown fixation. "You don't have to apologize to me," I said. "I should be apologizing to you."

Let's not call it a crush. Let's call it an "awareness" or a "longing" or a "spark." I'm fully aware that "crush" and "brother-in-law" are not terms that should be anywhere near each other. It's creepy. And wrong. And violates all kinds of social contracts. You just don't go there.

But, with this nutty pregnancy, we were going all kinds of places people just don't go. We were in uncharted territory. So I won't use the word *crush,* but believe me that however we wrangle the semantics, it was the real deal.

For three unbelievable months after that crazy night, I found myself in an agony that I'd never known existed. I guess I'd felt like this before, but not for a long while. And never so intensely. Never with stakes like these. Never while I was pregnant, for example. Never regarding the person whose baby I was gestating. Before, I'd always liked guys who had, at the very least, a remote chance of liking me back. With Clive, that wasn't possible. Even if it had been—even if that nuzzle had knocked him sideways like it had me—getting what I wanted would have actually made things worse.

When I say "made things worse," I mean "ruined my life." And everybody else's, too.

I couldn't even be in the same room with Clive after that. The pleasant breakfast-and-dinner routine the three of us had fallen into since I'd been home withered on the vine. I ate with Mackie if Clive was out of town, but otherwise, I took my food to my room. I told them I was nauseated, I was sleepy, I was hormonal. But I did not tell them that I spent every meal we ate together scrutinizing Mackie's face and voice and body language to see if, by some infinitesimally small chance, she happened to be losing interest in her husband. Which, by the way, she wasn't.

In fact, that was the only fantasy I could permit: Mackie leaving Clive. I spent quite a bit of time working that one out in all its variations. Mackie would meet a French or Scottish or Hawaiian traveler in line at Starbucks or the dry cleaner. They would start chatting, and she would spill her coffee or drop her pile of blouses. He would bend down to help her and their eyes would lock. Within days, she'd be packing her things, off to start a new life in a faraway land, sorry to leave Clive and me behind but desperate to follow her heart. Clive would grieve for a while and then perk up to realize I was the better sister anyway. Then we could make out against the fridge worry-free. Then we could have it all. Except, of course, for Mackie.

There was an upside to this fixation, though. It brought the world into delicate focus. There is a deliciousness to feelings like that, to a life so ripe and ready and brimming with emotion. There's something inherently hopeful and alive about it. What's more: After that accidental kiss from Clive, for the first time in a very long time, I felt lonely. In my single bed at night in the nursery, watching the horizon of my pooching belly rise and fall with each breath, I was fifteen feet away from what I wanted most, with no possibility of getting it, ever. And something about that kind of suffering just has to be good for you.

In New York, at least, I'd had my work. And no shortage of dates, either. A woman with intimacy issues has a special appeal for men. They could sense that I was unavailable, so it was easy to want more from me. More dates, more interest, more passion. In the case of Kid Dy-no-mite, more time in the supply closet with the door locked. If it had been a ploy, it would have been working brilliantly. But it wasn't a ploy. I wasn't pretending to be disinterested to trick them; I truly was disinterested. So none of those men really did me any good.

Mackie and I often talked about the way life had two big categories in it—work and family—and that most people seemed to have only one or the other figured out. People who had great jobs longed for better relationships, and people who had great relationships usually longed for better jobs. Clive, with both, was an exception. But Mackie and I, up until I moved back home, were perfect examples of each extreme. Mackie loved her husband passionately, despite his flaws, and I felt the same way about my job.

But now I was home. I didn't have a job or a relationship. Or a house, for that matter. Or a car. Or a group of friends. Or any prospects for any of these things. All I had was a growing belly, significant bouts of morning sickness well beyond the first trimester, and a sharpening awareness that nine months was a longer span of time than I'd ever thought possible.

I hate to admit all this. I'm embarrassed just remembering what I was thinking then. But what I've decided in retrospect is that what I really wanted was not Clive himself but what Clive represented. Living there, I was getting to witness a real, functioning marriage up close. And even though Clive never took his plate to the sink or put his newspaper in the recycling bin, he also went out on Sunday mornings for croissants and stroked his wife's hair whenever they watched TV. The two of them made married life look pretty good. For the first time in my life, I wanted it. And as for the convergence of that awareness with my pregnant state and Clive's accidental kiss, I dare anyone to walk in my identical shoes and not feel the exact same horrible way.

Chapter Six

Three miserable months went by, and I can't even tell you what I did.

I remember a few things. I ate well and exercised and tried to be a good incubator for the babies. I kept a journal where I examined issues of Truth, and Longing, and the Meaning of It All. I developed a fixation with the mesquite chicken burger at a nearby taqueria and ate one nearly every day. I watched cooking shows. I shopped for maternity wear online. I marked my C-section date—September 20!—on the calendar I'd bought and dutifully added an X for each day I'd survived. I lurked in the self-help section of our neighborhood bookstore and sneaked peeks at books with titles like *Big Bad Love, Don't*

Even Think About It, and *Don't Screw the Pooch! How to Stop Making Yourself Miserable and Get Your Life Back on Track.*

It was a strange time, no question. For six straight years, I'd been working my tail off—forgoing things like weekends and New Year's parties—for the not unsatisfying reward of always having the most dedication, the best ideas, and the most kick-ass presentations in the entire agency. I wasn't as recognized for it as I should have been, which is a whole other topic of conversation, but I knew, even if the guys at the helm didn't, that there were five, maybe six, people in our office who really ran the place. And Kid Dy-no-mite was not one of them, despite his corner office. I was. Take a look at my portfolio sometime if you don't believe me. I was a star. A star just twinkling away in my little, shared, windowless office by the elevators.

But I didn't regret sending that boob email. If anything, I felt guilty for the contributions I'd made to our collective unhappiness. The image of a hot branding iron sizzling on a woman's cleavage, now that I stopped to think about it, was clearly a little hostile.

Now, unemployed in Texas, I told myself I was cocooning. I had not stopped to reflect on anything at all in six years, and now it was time for me to learn something—anything—about how to live a better life. When was I ever going to live rent-free in a house this beautiful again? When could I ever press the Pause button on my life in this way? It was a once-in-a-lifetime opportunity, and I knew I ought to be making the most of it. So I tried to cocoon—even though I suspected that somewhere on the other side of it all, when I finally emerged, I might easily still be the same caterpillar I'd always been, and even though cocooning sounds better in theory than it turns out to be in practice. Especially when your brother-in-law keeps swimming around outside your window in his boxer shorts.

"He can't afford a bathing suit?" I asked Mackie one day.

"It's our backyard," Mackie said. "Who's looking?"

In truth, I missed my job, and the passion I'd brought to it, and the drive I'd felt every morning. I missed my morning walk with my coffee and my banana and my bagel. I missed feeling in charge of my life, feeling like I was heading somewhere, and feeling like a grown-up. I missed being good at something. I could tell myself I was on a journey of personal growth, and I could tell old acquaintances at the grocery store that I was on "sabbatical," and I could read every self-help book out there. But whatever I was doing felt a lot like nothing.

I should have made some changes. Looking back, I want to heckle myself and shout, "Get a job! Take a class! Get your own apartment!"

But I didn't do any of these things. It didn't make sense to get a job or an apartment if I'd be moving back to New York after I'd finished up the baby project. Which I most certainly would be—though when I had declared to Mackie on a particularly grumpy day that I was "not under any circumstances *staying* in this backwater little town," she had reminded me that it was the fourth largest city in the country. Then she crossed her arms and said: "New York, L.A., Chicago, *Houston.*"

There were things I couldn't do—but there were many things I could. I just didn't. I thought about the little depression cards Dr. Penthouse had given us all those months ago. I'd lost mine already, of course. What had the list said to watch out for? Feelings of jealousy? Fits of pointlessness? General inertia? Fear of ghosts? I couldn't remember.

Mackie didn't understand why I was acting so distant. "Clive kind of bugs you, doesn't he?" she asked one night.

"Not at all," I said, making a puzzled frown. "I think Clive is terrific."

"You always make a horrible scowl when he comes into the room."

"I don't."

"I'm telling you, you do."

"And I'm telling you I don't have a problem with Clive."

Mackie thought about it, deciding whether or not she believed me.

"Is it because he said women are bad drivers?"

"No."

"Is it because of the time he made those pretend fart noises?"

"No!"

"Is it because he calls Dad's beard a 'beaver'? Because that's just a British thing."

"No!"

"Then, what?"

"Nothing! Jesus!"

"Clive agrees with me."

"He does?"

"He thinks you don't like him."

I took this in. I wondered if it bothered Clive to think that I didn't like him. Then I reminded myself that it didn't matter.

"I do like Clive," I said. "It's just—"

"It's just that this whole pregnancy thing isn't as much fun as you thought it would be?"

I nodded.

"Me, neither."

If I'd been in a better frame of mind, I might have paused to think a little bit about what this whole pregnancy must have been like for Mackie. Here I was, doing the thing she'd tried hardest to do in her whole life. As far as I could remember, it was the only thing she'd ever failed at. And I was taking it all for granted—grouching and complaining, rolling my eyes at good fortune. It's really a wonder she was as nice to me as she was.

But Mackie was not a person who gave up on things. As for me and Clive, she decided that we all needed more togetherness. She was sure I would come to like Clive if I only got to know him a little better, and so she created a regimen of forced bonding. In restaurant booths, she'd seat us next to each other. In the car, she'd snag the backseat and leave the two of us up front. She'd duck out anytime she could to leave us alone to make conversation.

It didn't work, of course.

Finally, one night, after weeks and weeks of watching me mope and push my organic dinner around my plate, after the first trimester had come and gone, after my belly had already begun to look like it had a watermelon stuffed inside, and after a major shopping spree for ultrastylish maternity wear didn't even dent my funk, on the night Mackie had baked cupcakes to celebrate my fifth month being pregnant, she slammed her palm down onto the dining table.

"Snap out of it!" she yelled.

I blinked at her. "Snap out of what?"

She framed her hands in front of my face. "This!" she said.

I pretended there was nothing to snap out of, but she didn't buy it. She had a theory—and a plan: "You're a workaholic," she said. "And a workaholic can't just quit cold turkey to sit around the house in maternity sweats! We need to get you back into the workforce."

It turned out that Mackie, who had her own organizing business called A Fine Mess, had a client looking for a temp. "I've talked you up already," she said. "You're a shoo-in." Then she wrinkled her nose. "He's a little prickly, though," she added.

"What do you mean, 'prickly'?"

"Um," Mackie said. "He's only nice if he likes you. And he doesn't like anybody."

"Peachy," I said.

It was a research job at the Preservation Society in midtown. And she'd already set up an interview.

"I don't know anything about preservation," I said.

"You like old buildings," Mackie said. "You have an eye for design.

You'll be perfect." She reached over and patted me on the head. "Plus, I have to get you out of the house. You are making me crazy."

"Don't forget: I was fired from my last job."

"Only because you had a breakdown and screwed your boss."

"It wasn't a breakdown. It was an epiphany," I said. "And he wasn't my boss when I screwed him."

"Well," she went on, patting my round, five-month belly, "now you're in no condition to screw anybody."

I did need to get out of that house. Mackie was right, even if she didn't know why she was right. Clive divided his time between the warehouse and his home office (and playing rugby on Saturdays), but even though he traveled a lot, he was still home too much, shuffling down the halls in his Tevas, making cucumber sandwiches and getting Snapples from the fridge. When he needed a break, he'd take a swim in the pool, and now that winter was suddenly gone—how had it become May?—he was swimming every day, sometimes twice. I'd hear the splash from my room and stand at the window, watching him zip along the bottom like a deep-sea fish.

Mackie was out most of the day, spending mornings and afternoons organizing her clients—a job that had completely lost its luster after five years, even though it had seemed like such a great concept for a be-your-own-boss business. Organization had always come so effortlessly for Mackie. It had been an appealing idea, almost an altruistic one: She was helping people take better care of themselves and their workplaces. She was making the world better, one filing system at a time.

"How come you never organized Dad?" I asked one day.

"I have my limits," she said. "Plus, he wouldn't let me."

"But he let Dixie do it," I pointed out.

Mackie shrugged. "The things we do for love."

Over the years, Mackie had seen it all: the banana that had been forgotten in the wastebasket for so long it calcified into a black boomerang; the closet that collapsed in on itself when the rod got too heavy, and was never opened again; the porn garage stacked to the ceiling.

"Don't tell me about the porn garage," I'd said once when it came up. "I do not want to know."

"Babe," she'd said, "I'm not making it up. Half the men you meet have a porn garage."

Mackie was good at her job. She'd float in like Mary Poppins and put everything in proper order. The clients were always ashamed of their messes, and part of her job was to reassure them that these things happened, they were normal, everybody had times when all the stuff of modern life got away from them. Officially, she had "a dream job." But after all this time, she was feeling less sure. She was tired of getting down on her hands and knees in strangers' houses, sorting through their detritus and breathing in their dust. And, also, the recidivism rate was atrocious.

Mackie couldn't believe I was pooh-poohing the job she found me.

"I should take that job," she said. "I'd love to have that job." Then she sighed. "But you need it worse than I do." She put her hands on her hips and studied me from head to toe. "You really, really need it bad."

The morning of the interview, Mackie lent me her car with one important stipulation. "Don't lock the door," she said. "Just always leave it unlocked."

"You leave your Mercedes unlocked?" I asked.

"Yep," Mackie said. "All the time."

She'd bought it used, and it had been a bargain—in perfect shape, with hardly any miles—except for this one little problem. The alarm couldn't be fixed. Anytime you put a key in the lock, the alarm would sound, and Mackie had never found a way to turn it off without disconnecting the wires.

"You know how to do that?" I asked.

"I do now," she said.

"Maybe you should teach me," I said. "Just in case."

"As long as you don't lock it," she said, "you're good." She'd taken the car to three mechanics, and they all agreed: There was some kind of short somewhere.

"It seems like that ought to be fixable," I'd said.

"They can fix it," Mackie said. "But for more than I paid for the car."

On the way, I drove carefully, wearing a little maternity interview suit Mackie had mail-ordered, and it's so funny to think back on that morning now, my five-months-pregnant, grumpy self in my pointy shoes and stockings with my hair tamped down in a little bun, trying so hard to make a change in my life. Taking yourself that seriously is sometimes just begging for a pie in the face.

Halfway there, I realized I'd forgotten the little map I'd printed out so carefully the night before, along with the purse that I'd placed on top of it—in a genius attempt not to forget the map—and the cell phone that was inside the purse. I could have turned around, but I was already right on the edge of late, and I'd looked at the map the night before, and I thought I could remember the way. I had a general sense of the area. So I just forged ahead through the little historic neighborhood, hoping with each corner I turned that I was going to see the building from the website. Instead, before I knew it, I found myself on a one-way on-ramp for the freeway, and minutes later I was caught in a construction zone that had traffic down to one lane. Not to mention the air-conditioning was broken in Mackie's car, and though it wasn't technically hot on that May morning, it was certainly humid. I could feel my mascara smudging. I could feel my armpits getting damp with sweat. I could feel my curls frizzing up and doubling in size. And with my maternity suit jacket on, and all the internal padding I'd accumulated, I couldn't seem to shed my own heat. I could feel my five-month belly expanding block by block.

When I finally found the office and made it inside, it was almost an hour past my appointment time. The receptionist told me that the director of personnel was on a call, but I was welcome to wait.

So I waited. I found a place on the putty-colored sofa. I let the air-conditioning cool me off and I took what I hoped were deep and relaxing breaths. And I waited. For a very long time. It must have been thirty minutes, at least, though I didn't have a watch.

It was a long wait, but I wasn't bored. Because the calmer my body got, and the more I settled into the sofa, the more I had a chance to look around. And I realized that I was in a beautiful place. The house was a grand old mansion with crown moldings and floor-to-ceiling windows. The staircase had a carved oak railing as thick as my arm. The alcove had an archway with curved molding. And there were historic photographs everywhere—in frames on every table and every wall. Black-and-white images of buildings and people and moments gone by: a trolley car, a pair of twins in front of the Sam Houston statue, a horse 'n' buggy parked in front of the original courthouse, one of the city's first fire crews.

After a while, I stood up so I could get a closer look. I loved the photos. I loved the feel of the building—how solid it was, and how grand. I loved the idea that people came to work every day in this beautiful place, and as I tried to imagine myself doing that very thing, I felt a tug of longing. I wanted to be here. I had come to the interview grudgingly, mostly to appease Mackie. But now that I was here, it seemed like the perfect place for me, and I felt so grateful that I'd managed to find it, and so hopeful that I might somehow, despite this terrible beginning, find a way to convince Mackie's client that I belonged here. I couldn't recall the last time I'd felt this certain about anything. It was love at first sight.

And then Howard showed up. Mackie's client: Howard Hodgeman, director of personnel. "You're late," he said from the top of the stairs.

"I'm sorry," I called up. "I got lost."

Howard Hodgeman did not break his stride. "And I've got three other candidates I like better. One whose father ran track with me in high school."

"I wound up on a freeway?" I said. "With construction?"

He still had not come down the stairs. He was just standing at the top, looking down. Finally, he said, "All right." And he turned and walked out of view.

I looked over at the receptionist. "Should I go up?" I whispered.

She nodded and waved me toward the stairs, whispering herself. "Go! Go!"

Howard Hodgeman's office looked like a library—shelves of books covered every wall all the way to the ceiling, a whole collection of books on architecture and design stacked every which way: vertical, horizontal, diagonal. Walking into the room felt like walking into another place in time—leather chairs, an enormous walnut desk, a dark red Oriental rug, potted palms by the window. If Howard Hodgeman hadn't been checking his email on his laptop, I'd have expected him to pull out a monocle and a pipe.

"Have a seat," he said, to no one in particular.

But the chairs were stacked high with books.

"Would you like me to move the books?" I asked. "Or sit on them?"

He looked up and saw what I meant. "Good God, girl, I don't want you to sit on my books!" He moved them for me, in one big stack, and then balanced them all so precariously on the radiator that I couldn't resist making a bet with myself: If they fell during the interview, I'd get the job.

Once I'd sat down, I was about a foot lower than Howard. He actually had to peer over the edge of his desk to see me. He was a walrus of a man, with a stiff oxford shirt and brown corduroy slacks. It was clear that he took care with his appearance and had a flair for colors. He dressed like a much handsomer man.

I waited while he sent a few more emails, and then he seemed to remember I was there.

"Okay," he said, shoving a stack of papers out of the way. "Let's get started." And then, as he reviewed my résumé, he said, "I've never interviewed a person so underqualified and so overqualified at the same time."

He didn't seem to be inviting me to speak, so I just sat still.

Then he looked up over his glasses. "The salary for this position is so low, it's practically volunteer." Then he pulled his glasses off. "You knew that, right?"

I hadn't, but I nodded anyway.

Then we moved on to some questions—like "How would you describe the look of our city?" and "What's your favorite period of architecture?"—but he didn't seem interested in my answers. Then he turned pretty quickly to hard-core architectural terms, like "What's a barrel-vaulted pediment?" and multiple-choice brainteasers, like "Which type of limestone is native to Texas?"

Toward the end, I got question after question wrong, and he seemed to enjoy watching me squirm. I felt inexplicably guilty, as if I were taking a test I hadn't studied for. "I hope you're grading on a curve," I joked, but he shook his head solemnly. No.

"I'm a fast learner," I offered up. And then, as if this information were relevant: "Those Boob 'em ads all over town? Those are mine."

Howard looked skeptical.

"You can Google it," I promised.

Howard looked at me. "What are you doing *here?*"

I'd known this question was coming, and I decided to give it my best shot. "I had an epiphany one day that the ads I was spending my life making were a bit evil. I just want to make the world a better place," I went on, "or, at least, not make it worse."

He was listening a little. My personal confession seemed to have snagged his attention. And he was waiting for me to say more, so I kept on the same track. "If I'm not going to have anything else in my life—if that's my destiny: to be a person who works all the time—then I want it to be worth something. You know?"

But he didn't know. Somehow I'd lost him. Maybe I'd confessed too much, or hit too close to home, or missed the mark of "refreshingly honest" and hit "a little bit sad" instead. When I looked up to meet his eyes, he had looked away.

We were done. Then he started wrapping things up, arranging the papers in his file, putting his pencil back in its holder. I wasn't getting the job. I could feel it. And he was so smug that it made me mad. Something shifted in me at that moment. I felt an urge for self-defense. I would have been great at that job! He hadn't even given me a chance! Without thinking at all, I stood up for myself—in a way that, as always, looked just as clearly like self-sabotage. "You didn't ask me if I had any special skills," I said.

He gave a short sigh like I was really pushing his buttons. Then he said, in a flat voice, eyes on his email, "Do you have any special skills?"

I spoke loudly. "Break dancing."

He looked over.

"The moonwalk, mostly," I went on. "But also the caterpillar and the inchworm. I can do all the insects."

Howard Hodgeman stood up. We were done.

"I can walk like a chicken, too," I added. "Though that's not dancing so much as it is strutting."

He looked at me with new eyes. "You're kind of a pain in the ass, aren't you?"

"You haven't asked me one real question," I said, still sitting.

He thought about it. Then he lowered himself back into the chair.

I'd gotten his attention. By complete accident, I'd managed to crack the conversation back open—a tiny bit, at least.

"Okay," he said, squinting a little. "Tell me about the house you grew up in."

It was my moment to dazzle him. To show him that even though I had no experience with preservation, I somehow belonged in this job—even if I myself didn't exactly know how yet. I could tell, even in the moment, that I had a tiny chance to charm him. And I also knew, suddenly with total certainty, that this was exactly where I wanted to be.

The house I grew up in. That seemed easy enough. I had a million things to say about that house, at least. Howard had lobbed me an easy pitch, and I took a deep breath to hit it out of the park.

And then, instead, I started to cry. The tears sprang up and over, my nose started to run, my belly bobbed with each tremor of my diaphragm. Howard Hodgeman looked away, hoping I'd pull myself together, and then, when I didn't, started rummaging in his desk drawer and found me a package of Kleenex. After an interval, he started checking his email again.

"Just ignore me," I said, as I cried on and on.

"I'm doing my best," he said.

When I blew a big honk into his last Kleenex, he stood up. "I think we're done," he said, and I didn't argue—even right then when the stack of books fell off the radiator. I knew it was too late.

I gathered my things and followed Howard down the stairs to the foyer of the building, my heels knocking the steps and my pregnant thighs rubbing their panty hose against each other like giant cricket wings. And though I wouldn't realize it until I checked my reflection in the mirror on the drive home, I'd cried my mascara into raccoon smudges all down around my eyes.

We paused at the door and he stuck out his hand. I took it and said, "I'm never going to get this job, am I?"

"Not a chance," he said, almost tenderly. He touched my shoulder, apparently with no awareness that I was pregnant, and said, "Go home and have yourself a stiff drink."

"You bet," I said, patting my belly.

But then, just as I touched the doorknob to go, the door pushed open from the other side and a woman with a salt-and-pepper bob stepped in. I recognized her. But more important, she recognized me. When we met eyes, she tilted her head a little, and then, when Howard Hodgeman introduced her as Barbara Tierney, I knew exactly who she was.

"You're Everett Thompson's mother!" I said.

"And you are the girl who broke his heart in high school," she said.

She wasn't wrong. "Great memory," I said.

In the pause that followed, we all noticed my puffy, red face.

Barbara Tierney turned to Howard Hodgeman and said, "What did you do to her, Howard?"

"Sweetheart," he said, touching her arm. "What did *she* do to *me*?"

"We just had an interview," I explained.

But Howard Hodgeman stage-whispered, "We just had a psychotic break."

It turned out Barbara Tierney was the executive director. She had been there for seven years, and she had saved fourteen buildings, though she had failed to save many more. Still, saving fourteen was quite a thing for Houston, and she was a little bit famous. I'd heard of her many times without realizing who she was. Without realizing

I'd once helped her make a birthday lasagna many years before for her soon-to-be-heartbroken son. But she'd been "Thompson" then. She must have gotten divorced in the interim. And then remarried.

Barbara Tierney looked over at Howard Hodgeman, still thinking about the job. "Well? Is she going to get it?"

Howard Hodgeman shook his head and rolled his eyes a little, as if to say not just *no,* but *hell, no.* Then he turned to me. "But it was great to meet you!" And he made an escape up the stairs, calling out, "Good luck with your post-traumatic stress disorder!" and leaving me alone with Everett Thompson's mother.

Everett's mother had a kind face. "He's just mean," she told me. "It's part of his charm."

I shrugged an *Oh, well.*

And then—right then—through the door stepped Everett Thompson himself.

His mouth fell open a little to see me there—mine probably did, too—and he just stared at me until the door closed behind him. In that little pause I realized something: Mackie had set this all up. She knew Barbara Tierney was the former Barbara Thompson, she knew Everett was good to his mother and met her on occasion for lunch, and she knew that if I worked here, we'd be bound to run into each other. It was a matchmaking scheme that no one had been in on but Mackie, but as soon as I put it together, I suddenly felt complicit. Which made me blush all the way to my earlobes. A fact that did not escape Everett Thompson, who was still staring at me and seemed to be holding his breath.

Barbara Tierney stepped in to fill the pause. "Everett, I believe you know—"

"Sarah," he said, sounding just like he had on the plane.

"She just interviewed with Howard," Barbara Tierney explained. "I think he made her cry."

Everett nodded. "Howard makes everybody cry," he said.

It was much easier for me to look at Barbara Tierney than at her son. She was attractive on a normal scale: that no-nonsense bob, those straight teeth, the long beaded necklace that almost touched her belt. She was pleasing to the eye without going overboard. But her son, no matter what Mackie said, was really too good-looking. Most people in the world depend on their clothes, or their makeup, or their personalities, to compensate for their ordinary, regular humanness. But for me, looking at Everett Thompson was like looking at the sun. It hurt my eyes. It hurt my whole body. I had no choice but to stare down at his shoes.

"I had no idea your mother worked here," I said, almost as an apology, eyes down.

"Yeah, well," Everett said. "It's a small town for such a big city."

"Fourth largest city in the nation," I said.

"Is it?" Barbara Tierney asked. "That's surprising."

Finally, I knew something. I turned to her with an informative nod. "New York, L.A., Chicago, and Houston."

"That's wonderful," she said, like we'd won a prize.

Then, we stalled. I wanted to escape, almost as badly as I wanted to stay, but it seemed impolite to leave too quickly. An appropriate amount of time had not passed, and even though I had already lost this job—and, for that matter, these people as well—instinct took hold in that second and I found myself trying to jump-start the conversation, grabbing the first topic that popped into my mind.

"My sister wants to set you up with the tenant in her garage apartment," I offered, glancing up.

"Great," Everett said. "I love tenants."

He was teasing me, but I pushed on. "She's very young and sexy," I said, feeling more like an idiot with each word. "She sunbathes in a string bikini with baby oil."

"Bull's-eye," he said.

"And smart, too. Apparently, on her SATs, she got a perfect score."

He was just playing with me now. "Is there any other kind?"

I pushed on. "She's actually one of those girls that men love but women hate," I went on. "Though that might work fine for you—being a man."

Everett didn't know what to say to that one, and even I could tell I sounded like a nut job. He tilted his head. "Do *you* hate her?"

It was time to shut things down. I said, "My sister thinks she will mellow with age."

"Don't we all?" Barbara Tierney said then, and I noticed I'd forgotten she was even there.

At that, I glanced up, ready to excuse myself, and realized that even though I hadn't been looking at either of them, they'd been looking at me. Staring right at my belly, in fact. A belly Everett Thompson had not seen since long before it looked pregnant. And I knew exactly what they were thinking and why they were staring. They could not imagine what on earth had happened to me.

And so without wasting a second on a transition, I just patted my stomach and said, "I'm pregnant!" And then, "With twins!"

Without wasting any seconds himself, Everett said, "Who's the father?"

I felt a quick urge to tease him with "You are!" But then it didn't seem like he'd think that was funny. And my second option was almost as alarming. "Clive," I said. "Clive is the father."

"Your brother-in-law?" Everett asked.

Everett was translating the conversation for his mother, who didn't know who Clive was. I met her eyes to explain. "I'm acting as a gestational carrier for my sister and her husband." Then I turned back to drive the point home to Everett. "So Clive is the father, but Mackie is the mother."

Everett looked relieved. His mother looked delighted. "You must be a very good person," she said then.

"I am really trying my best, Mrs. Tierney."

It was a good exit line, and as I said it, I knew it was time to go. The conversation was about to die again. Keeping it up was like trying to fly a kite with no wind.

And then, in short order, I had made it out into the parking lot and was walking toward Mackie's car—Mackie's broken car—and was noticing with each step that I was feeling dizzy. As I reached the door, it struck me that I might possibly faint. And that's when I saw my reflection in the window: curls popped out of their pins and pointing in every direction like snakes, collar all wonky with one flap tucked under my jacket and one flap on top, mascara smeared all down my face from crying.

I didn't want to faint. I didn't want to pass out in Everett Thompson's mother's parking lot, belly-up like a beached whale. I leaned against the door and put my key in the lock. Forgetting, of course, as I tried to stay conscious, that I was never, ever supposed to do that.

The car alarm went off: a siren so loud and frantic it was the sound of panic itself. My fate had actually been sealed when I parked the car, because in my flustered state, I had locked it.

"Shit!" I said, my brain racing to think of a way to make it stop.

But there was no way to make it stop. I knew that. Mackie had warned me of that. So what was I going to do? Drive home with the siren going? I climbed in and started locking and unlocking the doors, flipping every switch, starting the ignition. I think I even popped the hood and the gas tank.

It wasn't until Everett showed up and knocked on the driver's window that I realized taking off with the siren going would have been my best option. At least then I would have escaped from the parking lot. But now there he was, offering assistance—mostly to be helpful, but maybe, possibly, also to delight a little bit in my humiliation. I didn't want to look at him—or even acknowledge he was there—but the siren was so loud that I was forced to read his lips. He was shouting something I couldn't hear.

I cracked the door open.

"Do you need help?" he was saying.

"I can't turn this off!" I yelled.

"Press the Off button!" he said, reaching in for the keys.

I gave him a *duh* look. "It's broken!"

"Let me try!" he shouted, but I had already turned away from him and lunged for the glove compartment.

Then I felt his hands on my hips as he pulled me back toward him across the driver's seat and gently—careful of the belly—hooked his arms under mine to lift me out of the car. When I was standing, he took the keys, slid past, and turned the ignition three times fast. The alarm stopped.

For a minute, the silence was too shocking to believe. In that brief pause, I thought about my crooked collar and my crazy hair and my smeary mascara. And, knowing it was hopeless even as I did it, I started wiping my fingers under my eyes. At the very least, it gave me something to do.

When Everett stood up and saw me, he pulled a bandanna out of his pocket and handed it over. It must have been washed a thousand times; it was as soft as suede.

"Don't worry," he said. "It's clean."

So then I tried the bandanna—even though every woman who's ever taken off mascara knows a dry cloth doesn't work any better than dry fingers. But it kept me from having to look up at Everett, which I really didn't want to do.

It also, of course, meant he was waiting to get his bandanna back. And while he was waiting, he just watched me.

"I'm not totally pulled together today," I said—of course, a ridiculous understatement. I had never had days like this in New York. In New York, I had myself in line. I had dignity. I wore great clothes and stood up tall and strutted around the city like I had it all figured out.

In New York, I was completely untouchable. What was it about coming home that had pulled everything out from under me?

But Everett wanted to tell me a story: "One time, when I was a kid, my mom took me to see *The Nutcracker*." He leaned back against the hood of the car, and went on. "It was the holidays and the place was swarming with kids, and somehow I got separated from her. I wandered around for a long time and I don't know how, but I wound up backstage in the dancers' dressing room. That's where they found me, just resting on a stool and watching everybody getting dressed. Once my mom got me to my seat, the ballet itself was a big disappointment."

"Sure," I said, still not looking up.

"I think that's true about me," he went on. "That I'm much more interested in people when they don't have their costumes on."

Then I couldn't help but lift my eyes. "Or maybe you just like naked women."

His face crinkled up into a smile. "That, too."

I handed back the bandanna. It was time to go.

Before I drove away, I thanked Everett one last time, called him a car-alarm genius, and possibly even shook his hand. And then I drove home exactly at the speed limit—the doors unlocked, my suit coat unbuttoned, my mind shuffling through the events of the day, and the memory of his hands rising off my body like steam.

Chapter Seven

At home that night, I was mad at Mackie for many things: for being so happily married, for not having fixed her broken car alarm long before now, for matchmaking when I'd expressly asked her not to, for telling me I was a shoo-in with the meanest job interviewer I had ever met, and also, if I'm really honest, in some remote and extremely unfair way, for getting me pregnant and stealing my youth and beauty. Although those last ones were a stretch.

I was still eating in my room a lot, especially when Clive was home, but on this night I was too exhausted and strung out to take myself away. Plus, I really wanted to be with people. So what if the best I could do was Mackie and Clive? I was a beggar these days, not a chooser.

Mackie's offenses were swirling in my head as we ate together. She and Clive sat on one side of the table and fed each other from their plates, mixing their salad ingredients in infinite delightful combinations that the other just *had* to try. Caressing each other's forks, wiping each other's mouths with their thumbs.

"What is this, *Tom Jones*?" I said. "You guys are obscene." They giggled in that way that happy people do, but I said, "Could we talk about something, please? Or do something, anything, other than lick each other's fingers?"

"Sorry," Clive said. Then he offered up a conversation topic by telling me that Clacker Toys was being sued.

"It is?" I asked. "Why?"

"It appears," Clive said, "there's a little toy store in rural Montana called Clicker Toys that's decided we're stealing its business."

"That's crazy," I said.

"Yep," Clive said. Their old lawyer had seen it as just a little nuisance, and he ignored it. But now it was a big nuisance. So Clive would be spending the whole day on Saturday with Everett Thompson figuring out a strategy for response, and Mackie would be bringing them lunch.

She wondered out loud what to bring, and I said, "Just bring some love. You can eat that, can't you?" But they'd gone all kissy-kissy again—Mackie feeding Clive a roasted new potato with her fingers—and didn't notice me mocking them.

"Hello!" I said, waving. "I'm still here! I'm just right here at the table with you."

"Sorry," Mackie said, forcing herself away.

"You guys are an affront to common courtesy." I stood up to take my plate to the sink.

"Sorry," Mackie said. "It's just our anniversary tonight."

I almost dropped my plate. "It is?"

"Yep," Clive said. "Eight years."

"Eight fabulous years," Mackie corrected, pointing at him.

"That's not possible," I said. They were newlyweds, practically. Weren't they?

Mackie said, "I know, right?"

What had I been doing for the past eight years? Working my tush off in a career I'd eventually not just leave but totally renounce? Rejecting suitors I'd eventually forget? Shopping for home furnishings I'd eventually put in storage? Reading books I'd eventually forget the plots of? Gestating babies I'd eventually give to other people? I flipped through the time in my mind, looking for even one thing that had lasted, but I came up short. Now I felt even crankier. And I added "being married for eight years" to my list of things Mackie had done to make me mad.

But Mackie didn't know I was mad. She was just licking butter sauce off Clive's fork and chattering away like always. She careened from topic to topic—the guy who'd slipped on the wet floor at the grocery earlier, an earring she was missing in case anybody'd seen it, a song she'd forgotten the words to—and then she settled on one. A topic I didn't want to talk about. One she could so easily have left alone.

"Let's talk about Everett Thompson," she said.

"Let's not," I said.

But she had spent several days that week doing some organizing at the Clacker warehouse while Everett was there. In his "on retainer" capacity for Clacker Toys since the fall, Everett had spent quite a bit of time with Clive, and they'd become buddies—shooting hoops in the parking lot and going to Rockets games. And after Mackie's week of organizing, she was acting like she was a third musketeer. I'd assumed that Mackie had avoided Everett on principle, out of loyalty to me—which she had, until this week. But now she was more determined than ever to marry us off. Now we were going to talk about how wonderful he was, whether I wanted to or not. For my own good.

"I know you're not interested," Mackie said. "But he really is the sweetest." And then she turned to Clive. "Isn't he the sweetest?"

"He's the sweetest," Clive said.

"We're not talking about him," I said again.

But then we talked about him anyway. After the long, absolutely insane day I'd had, I was drained of the strength to protest. And maybe I needed a distraction. Or a lively conversation. Or both. I dropped my protest and arranged the grilled vegetables left on my plate into a little circle as I let Mackie go on and on.

She had learned all kinds of things about Everett this week, including his favorite color (moss green), his favorite cuisine (Vietnamese), and his favorite book (*Lonesome Dove*). She also had the skinny on why he'd left a thriving New York legal career to move home. She'd weaseled it all out of him over chicken salad sandwiches in the lunch room.

"Don't you want to know why he gave up everything to come back?"

"No," I said. "I don't." And apparently Clive didn't, either, because he excused himself to take his plate to the sink and then snuck on up to bed.

"It's his stepdad," she whispered. The stepdad who had adopted him when he was a baby.

That fast, she got me. Now it came back. I remembered his stepdad a little. He used to take Everett waterskiing back in high school. "What's wrong with his stepdad?" I asked.

A short question with a very long answer. And Mackie had every detail: It all began when Everett's stepdad had left his mother after cheating on her with more women than Everett would disclose. Everett was twenty-three.

"He divorced her," Mackie explained, "to marry a twenty-three-year-old grocery checker who left him when he wouldn't buy her a Jet Ski." She looked up to see if I was paying attention, and, I confess, I was. "And then, after that divorce, he married again a year later, this time a massage therapist with a collection of porcelain cat figurines. And she left him, too."

But I'd regrouped. I was not going to ask why.

"Don't you want to know why?"

"Nope."

"Because," Mackie announced, "he got Alzheimer's."

I didn't know what to say to that.

Mackie went on. For a long time, Everett's mother had refused to take care of him on principle. But then it got so bad, she had to. There was nobody else to do it and no money for a nurse. Everett's mom didn't tell Everett, because she wanted him to live his life unfettered. His stepdad was sick for five years before anybody told him anything.

I thought about it for a while. Then I said, "Everett never noticed?"

"They were estranged," Mackie whispered.

So now Everett had given up everything and moved home. Even though he disliked the man, and even though his stepdad barely recognized him anymore, he'd found a top-notch facility for him and went out to visit him once a week. Everett did it because it was the right thing to do. "Mostly, though," Mackie explained, "to ease the burden on his mom."

That was Mackie's argument. Definitive proof that Everett was the greatest man in the history of the world.

I shrugged. "Maybe."

Mackie raised an eyebrow. Then she tossed this into the conversation: "Did you know that after you dumped him, he carved 'I love you, Sarah' into the bark of the magnolia tree in his backyard—and the tree died like six months later?"

"He told you that?"

"Uh-huh," Mackie said, crossing her arms at me, as if she were expecting some kind of answer to her question. But I couldn't believe we were having this conversation on a day like today. I couldn't believe we were having it, period.

"No," I said. "Okay? I didn't know that! What do you want me to say?" My voice was louder than I realized. "It was high school! It was high school! So I killed his magnolia tree! What do you want me to do?"

My voice got Mackie's attention. "What is your problem?" she wanted to know.

"You're not supposed to hang out with him!" I said. "He's the enemy!"

"A job's a job," Mackie said.

"Then, why didn't you tell me about it?"

Mackie shrugged. " 'Cause I knew you'd be mad."

I was mad. I was super-mad. Wildly, irrationally mad.

"And you tricked me into going to his mother's office!" I was shouting now.

"Hey!" Mackie shouted back, pointing at me. "That was an accident. I didn't know she was his mother."

I took a deep breath, and when I started again, my voice was quieter.

"Yes, you did." I was going on a hunch.

"No, I didn't."

"Mackie"—I put my hands on my hips—"you did!"

She put her hands on her hips, too. Then she threw them up in the air. "Fine!" she confessed. "I did."

"Dammit, Mackie!"

"What's the big deal? I can totally see you guys together!"

"The big deal is, I said no!" I threw my dirty napkin on the kitchen floor as a gesture of defiance. "I said no, Mackie!"

"You said no, but you meant maybe."

"No! I meant no!"

Now Mackie was mad. "Why are you fighting me on this? What exactly is the point of being so goddamn stubborn? Why do you insist on ending up a spinster?"

That word shocked me dead still. *Spinster.* The judgmental, anachronistic meanness of it. The sound of it on my sister's lips.

For a minute, I expected her to be shocked, too. To raise her hand to her mouth as if she could stuff the word back in. I expected her to be mortified. I felt a quick second of sympathy for her, even. Once her own voice hit her ears, she'd be hating herself for weeks.

I waited for her to cringe. Or crumple. Or burst into tears. But she didn't. Either she was so busy talking that she couldn't hear herself, or she was so self-satisfied that she didn't care. She pushed on, and now she was almost shouting: "I just want you to be happy!"

I regrouped. And then I stood up for myself, in my own sideways way.

"I don't want to be happy!" I shouted. "Isn't that painfully obvious? I'm living here with nothing to do and no friends and no car and I'm as big as a house and my back hurts and I'm frumpy and I have to watch you and your husband suck on each other's fingers and I don't want to eat organic wheat germ in my organic yogurt every single morning and I don't want to take fifty prenatal vitamins at every meal and I don't want to sleep in that crazy bedroom and listen to you guys all night long and I don't want you to set me up with anybody ever again—least of all Everett Thompson! I will never, ever in my sad, stupid, pathetic life want to date Everett Thompson! If you try to set me up with him one more time in even the tiniest way, I will set myself on fire. Can you hear me, Mackie? I will douse myself with gasoline and light a fucking match!"

There was a pause. We blinked at each other. Then Mackie said, "Okay." She rubbed the back of her neck with her hand. "No more Everett Thompson. I hear you."

My voice was quieter now, but not exactly softer. "Can you remember it, or do I need to write it on your arm with a Sharpie?"

"I can remember it."

"Good."

Mackie got the broom out of its closet and started to sweep a little. Then she stopped to look at me with a question that was almost a whisper. "Can I just ask one other thing?"

"What?"

"Can you really hear Clive and me in our bedroom?"

I was all yelled out. I let out a breath. "Every whisper," I said, "and every sigh."

Later, we both apologized for yelling so much that night. I was just "tired." I was just "freaked out." I was just "pregnant." And she was just "busy with work" and "stressed-out" and "worried" about me.

I apologized, and she accepted, but—as often happens—we never got into the specifics of what I'd said to her that night. We just let it all lie.

Mackie bounced back fast and was cheerful again. "Don't worry about it," she said. Though I did.

Me, I was still a long way from cheerful. I was tired of fighting with her, and of feeling so irritated and angry all the time. And on some level, I knew it was crazy to be angry about the matchmaking. After all, I had just been flirting with him a little bit not two hours earlier. Or, if not flirting, having a pleasant conversation, at least. But sometimes context is everything, and the context of our lives right now was this: Mackie was in charge of every square inch of my life, both inside and out. And when you're that tethered, all you can do is flap like hell to get free—long after your feathers are gone, or even maybe your wings.

I'm not sure why I went to the monthly Clacker party the next night. I certainly wasn't feeling festive. A party was probably the last place I needed to be. But I was busily insisting to Mackie that I was fine about our fight the day before, and still atoning some for my outburst. And I knew she wanted me to be there.

So I decided to go—but I didn't dress up. Even as the hour for guests to arrive got closer, I just sat in the maternity T and shorts I'd been wearing all day, leaning over my belly at the edge of the pool with my feet on the top step, while Mackie and Clive bustled around getting ready.

"You just rest," Mackie kept saying as she passed me in her heels with big trays of food. "I've got all this."

"Great," I said, sloshing my feet around in the water. "I'll just gestate these babies."

Any minute now, the yard was going to start filling up with guests. I noticed a yogurt stain on my T-shirt from a little spill at lunchtime, and even though I knew I really ought to go in and change, I found I couldn't summon the energy. I leaned back instead to lie flat against the patio and watch the clouds float past overhead in the darkening sky.

And that's when I noticed Everett Thompson standing beside me, looking down.

"What are you doing here?" I said, squinting up.

"Your sister set me up on a date."

"With the tenant?"

"Yep. She called me this morning and said, 'I've got the perfect girl for you.' "

I had a funny moment of disappointment in Mackie. I felt like she should have just let him alone. Even though I had worked hard to convince her that I didn't care one way or the other who Everett dated, or didn't. Plus, she did this kind of thing all the time. And I could imagine what she was thinking: No sense letting a good man like that go to waste.

"Sorry if I ruined the surprise," I said.

"Oh, no," Everett said. "Anticipation is always better than surprise."

"You're meeting her here?"

He nodded. "I am."

I sat up then and looked around the empty backyard. "Guess you're a little early."

He sat down cross-legged next to me. "Guess so."

We watched the pool for a little bit, him waiting for his date and me waiting to feel better enough to go inside.

"Heard you and Mackie spent the week together," I said.

"Well," he said. "A few hours."

"And she never told you I was pregnant?"

"Nope," he said.

"She says you're a 'total sweetheart.' Would you say that's accurate?"

"I guess that depends on how you define 'total.' " He thought about it. "And also 'sweetheart.' "

"Those definitions can be tricky," I said.

One of the floating candles in the pool had drifted over to the edge, and I gave it a little shove with my toes.

"You bouncing back from yesterday?" he asked, finally.

"That guy Howard really hated me," I said.

"Howard hates everybody," Everett said. "But I think he hated you in a good way."

"Can you hate somebody in a good way?"

"Absolutely." Everett reached over to dip his fingers in the water. Then he added, "And now we all know you can break-dance."

"Oh, yeah," I said. "I've got a bunch of trophies."

"My mother likes you, by the way," he added.

Then there was a long pause. A little breeze ruffled the pool water and the palmetto fronds by the stucco wall. Everett picked up a flat landscaping stone and skipped it across the pool, narrowly missing a floating candle.

It caught my attention. I'd never been able to get a stone to skip. And I'd tried plenty.

I grabbed a handful from a nearby planter and flicked one into the water. *Plink*. It sank.

"What was that?" Everett asked.

"I was skipping a stone," I said.

"It didn't skip," he said.

"I think I knew that."

"I could teach you, if you like."

"No, thanks," I said, and flicked some more. *Plink. Plink. Plink.*

He picked up one of my stones and skipped it. It skipped eight times.

"Fine," I said. "Teach me."

So he did. When I said, "Teach me," I was thinking of a demonstration and maybe a few pointers. But instead, I got a barrage of words like *torque, thrust, drag, lift, resistance,* and *pitch and yaw*. I got a thorough consideration of angles, aerodynamic coefficiencies, surface-to-weight ratios, and propulsion. And still, I couldn't make it work. "Don't overmuscle it," Everett kept saying. "And don't hit the candles."

"Okay," I'd say, and flick another stone to the bottom. Mackie would make me dive for them all later, but it was okay for now.

I didn't notice myself relaxing, but before I knew it, we were talking like normal people talk. I suddenly found I had a question for Everett. A real one. "How are you liking being home again?"

He thought about it a minute. Like he wanted to give a careful answer. Like he wanted to say something true. "It's not the town I remember," he said at last.

"Is it better or worse?"

"It's both."

I nodded. I knew about that. We were both home again after years and years away. We both walked through our days with the past lapping at our ankles.

"What about you?" he asked. Polite. Taking turns.

I meant to say something equally thoughtful and broadly true. But instead, I heard myself say, "It's torture."

Everett lifted his eyebrows. "Why?" he wanted to know.

The reason, of course, was Clive. Or at least that's what I thought. And I probably should have excused myself at that moment, or offered Everett a margarita, or burst into song. Or perhaps even started break dancing. The last thing one ever wants to do with a secret crush is talk about it. Because, of course, once you talk about a secret, it's not a secret anymore.

But I guess I'd had enough of secrets, because in response, without even hesitating, I just said it—even though there was no reason on earth I should have felt comfortable cranking open my heart for Everett Thompson, total sweetheart or not. We were not by any stretch of the imagination friends. We walked across a tender landscape of pleasantries, each careful word informed by the ones that had come before it—even the ones we couldn't remember. But a strange intimacy—hostile as it sometimes was—hovered in the background. We had a history. We'd known each other a long time. And, at the moment, he was being nice to me.

Besides, this secret was ready to come out. It was at a rolling boil inside my body, like water in a kettle. Who else was I going to tell?

"The thing is," my voice said then, really without my permission, "I have a crush on someone." The words rushed out like steam.

"You have a what?" Everett leaned closer.

"A crush on someone," I said, a little louder. "A horrible, pathetic, impossible crush on someone I can never be with." Then I added, "And it's making me feel a little limp."

Everett studied my face. Then he said, "Are you talking about me?"

I looked over. "No, I'm not talking about you. What is this, *The Brady Bunch*?"

"It sounds like you could be talking about me."

"Well, I'm not."

"Then, who are you talking about?"

"I can't tell you."

"Because it's me."

"Why would it be you? You're not even nice to me."

"That's exactly why. You want me because you can't have me."

"But I don't want you."

"So you say."

We watched the water, and the flat stones sprinkled across the bottom of the pool. The sun had gone down now, but there were no guests yet. Mackie's candles made everything glow. Then Everett said, "If I kissed you right now, you'd melt."

"No, I really wouldn't," I said.

"Yes, you would."

"Don't forget," I said, "I already know what it's like to kiss you."

"But you weren't in love with me then."

"Like I'm not in love with you now."

"Prove it," he said.

"Fine," I said. "You want me to prove it? I will."

I grabbed his shirt just under the collar and pulled him over to me. I meant it to be a quick "so there!" smack—feisty and defiant—but by the time our mouths actually met, Everett had brought his arm around behind me, and then he held us still, in that kiss, which softened into a tender, deeply suggestive thing. And here's the truth: I did melt. A little. Though I was never going to admit it.

I hadn't noticed, but Everett had leaned forward on his knees to reach me. After a minute, he started to lose his balance, but rather than stop kissing, he brought his foot around to steady himself and wound up plunking it into the pool, top step, shoe and all. And then the kiss came to an end because, yep, that was his shoe in the water, and his pants leg, too. And then we were laughing about it a little, and then Everett sat back and plunked the other foot in, too, like, *Oh, well.*

We watched his feet there for a minute, both of us kind of waiting to see what they might do next, and then I was amazed to see Everett stand up and take a few steps down deeper into the water. To his knees, then past his belt buckle. "This pool is great," he said. "Remember the time you fell in?"

"Like it was yesterday, buddy," I said.

"That dress was completely see-through once it got wet."

"Sounds like you remember, too," I said.

He lifted his eyebrow the tiniest bit. "Like it was yesterday," he said.

Everett was chest-deep in the pool now, and then he turned back and reached out for my hand, and I let him pull me in. The water felt cold, but I didn't want to splash or squeal about it. I just kept calm and let Everett lead me deeper into the water, in all our clothes, out toward the floating candles. Soon we were shoulder-deep and I was on tiptoe. Suddenly, I almost didn't feel pregnant anymore. The water held me up, and I could be my real self again. And it wasn't just the water, it was Everett. There we were, doing this crazy thing, and it felt like we were the only people who had ever done anything like it. Like this was exactly where we belonged, and nobody else belonged here, and nothing was more important than that one true thing.

The candles were all around us like stars.

Then Everett dunked under the surface, and when he came back up he shook out his hair like a dog. He'd picked up a stone from the bottom, and he sent it skidding along the surface of the water to the other side of the pool. "That was a great kiss," he said.

I wasn't going to give it to him. "It was okay."

"Say whatever you want," he said, "but you melted."

He took my hand and started pulling me closer. He was going to kiss me again, I could tell. And it was the strangest feeling right then: It was like I'd been holding my breath for months and months and finally, with that one moment of tenderness, I could let it out. And it wasn't until I could breathe again that I realized how tired I was—how very tired I'd been for so long—of not being able to breathe. It felt like the most important thing that would ever happen: Everett Thompson was going to kiss me, again, right there in the pool in all our clothes, and I was going to kiss him back. Probably a lot.

And then, just as our eyes locked, we heard Mackie's voice. "What are you guys doing in the pool?"

She was walking toward us fast, and Barni, all done up in a slinky minidress for her date with Everett, was right on her heels. They stopped at the edge to wait for an answer.

Barni bent over toward me with fake sympathy and lots of cleavage. "Did you fall in again?"

Everett turned to me with an expectant look. "What are we doing in the pool?"

"Just swimming," I said, supercool. "Just taking a little swim."

Barni stood up, irritated. She was late, but not that late. It wasn't like she had forfeited. She put a hand on her hip. "Are we still having our date?"

Everett looked at me, as if I were the person who was supposed to make that decision. He glanced from me to Barni and back to me. "Are we?"

I didn't see that I had any other choice but to let him go.

"Of course," I said, all politeness, as I swam to the edge and hoisted myself up. Everett followed, and then we were standing side by side as still as naughty children, dripping wet in our clothes as Mackie and Barni tried to decide what to make of us.

Before anybody had decided anything, Everett leaned over to whisper in my ear, "I like your other wet outfit better."

Everett wound up borrowing some dry things from Clive—the very same shirt, in fact, that Clive had been wearing when he had climbed into bed with me months earlier. Barni led Everett into the house, saying in a low voice like a purr, "Let's get you out of these wet clothes." I went and changed, too, into a red halter top—the sexiest maternity outfit I owned, which wasn't saying much.

"Do I look like a tomato?" I asked Mackie when I came back down.

"Good enough to eat," she said with a nod. I expected a question about what Everett and I had been up to, but it didn't come, and Mackie's silence on the topic had an air of defiance to it. I'd asked for it, and I got it. No more Everett. Instead, she led me over to meet Graham, a programmer who was taking a year off from Princeton to intern with Clive.

"He's in college," I protested as we walked.

"But it's Princeton," Mackie argued as she squeezed my arm, "so we can give him bonus years."

"I think, for Princeton, you subtract."

Talking with Graham turned out to be more fun than I'd anticipated because while he was explaining to me about the new code they were switching to, I noticed Everett watching me. He was standing in a group next to Barni, who was touching his arm over and over, and he was laughing at all the right moments and participating. But his eyes kept drifting over to meet mine.

He was right, of course. I had melted. He'd certainly worked on his kissing since eleventh grade. And something else, too: That kiss had been tender. Tender enough to convince me that he did not hate me after all. He hadn't been actively mean to me since that day on the plane, but a little meanness goes a long way.

I felt a connection to him—hell, an *attraction*—but it had seemed masochistic to pay much attention to it. Besides, I'd had my stupid fixation on Clive to keep me busy.

But something happened to my crush on Clive in the aftermath of that kiss. It disappeared in a puff of smoke like a magic trick. As impossible as it seemed, all those wrong feelings I'd been having for Clive just jumped right on over to Everett and became right. Maybe I was tired of pining. Maybe I'd wanted to fall for Everett all along and had just needed some encouragement. Maybe when a man that beautiful—no matter what Mackie says—kisses you, you're just a goner. I can't explain it, or understand it, and it makes me sound fickle, I know, but suddenly, as I stood with Graham, nodding my head about Flash and social media and Twitter, I felt my skin tingling with the pleasure of Everett's gaze.

Then, as an experiment, I glanced over to Clive to see what that would feel like. And it felt—for the first time in months—like looking at a brother-in-law. It felt like nothing. Or as close to nothing as gazing at the father of the koi in your belly can feel.

Later, I would struggle with what to make of it all: two heart-in-the-throat longings for two different guys in as many trimesters. Was I so starved for human contact that any touch at all could send me into spasms of love? Was I so easy that all you had to do was kiss me, anywhere at all, and I was yours, heart and soul? What had happened to my iron heart? I was the Chuck Norris of love, and now I'd gone all girlie. Twice. And this new time felt like a doozy.

And what did I even know about Everett Thompson that wasn't a distant memory, anyway? Here are the things I could tell you about him: He'd had a full drum set in his high school bedroom, a life-size poster of Bob Dylan, and every Rolling Stones album ever recorded. He'd won the English award two years in a row. He used to eat pickle sandwiches every day at lunch. He loved to read history books about doomed expeditions to the Arctic. He used to let me drive his car, even when I didn't have a license yet—and one night, racing home for curfew, I'd taken us the wrong way down a one-way street. We came about three inches from getting hit by a Cadillac, and after the honking was over and we'd pulled into a side street and I'd put us in park, his first order of business was to unbuckle and dive across the front seat to kiss me for the very first time. When we paused for breath, he said, "I can't believe I almost died without ever getting to do that."

But this was all trivia—and outdated trivia at that. I didn't know anything about the grown-up Everett. Was he a Republican or a Democrat? A cat person or a dog person? Did he believe in God? Did he balance his checkbook? Read the paper over breakfast? Listen to NPR? Follow sports teams? Drive too fast? Though maybe that was the whole point of having a crush—feeling curious enough about someone to want to find out these things. Maybe that was all there was to it, and I just didn't have enough experience to know.

There at the party, I played a game with myself. I forced myself not to look at Everett for a few minutes—to let Graham complete his entire story about the time he'd dropped his laptop in a puddle on the way to his programming final. I forced myself to keep an eye on his one canine snaggletooth while he talked, and wound up asking, "Is that the end of the story?" three times before we ever got there. When we made it at last, and I finally let my gaze skip across the night air to find Everett's face, the sight of him made me swoon. Or maybe it was just the babies kicking. Or maybe I hadn't eaten in a while. But, honestly, I lost my balance for one second at that exact moment and had to grab on to Graham's arm.

I thought nobody noticed but Graham and me, but in less than a second, Everett was right by my side. His hand was on my arm and I looked down at the electricity I felt at the touch, and then met his eyes and said, "I'm good. I'm just"—and here I was about to say, in that little private moment, the word "melting." Even though he was now on an official date with somebody else, it felt exactly like the right thing to do.

But before I could say it, Barni arrived—her face in mine and her voice as loud as a siren. "Clive was just telling us that story again about how you fell in the pool! Weren't you so embarrassed with everyone laughing at you? Didn't you just want to die?"

The moment was lost. I found myself wishing I had fainted outright. At least, if I'd done that, Everett could have rushed me to the hospital and had an excuse to leave. But an imperceptible swoon was not enough reason to ditch a date. I gave Everett a look that was meant to say, *Come find me again as soon as you can possibly get free.*

And he gave me a look that I could have sworn said, *I absolutely will.*

But the night turned out to be long. Because Barni lived right here, Everett couldn't exactly take her home. They stayed and stayed, Barni preening and posing and hooting with laughter at every single word from Everett's mouth—funny or not. I was hoping Everett might walk her home and come back to find me, but once when he suggested taking her home, she leaned her body against his and said, "It's not even midnight! What are you—a pumpkin?"

She was sexy. I had to give her that. Or maybe she was a caricature of sexy. But she sure knew exactly what to do with herself. Where does a person learn how to move like that—and how does a medical student find the time? She could have been in a music video, or on a runway, or doing a pole dance.

I couldn't wait them out. Mackie, earnestly wanting to give them a little privacy so their love connection could blossom, insisted I say good night and pulled me by the hand into the house.

The irony was not lost on me that just as Mackie had officially given up on matchmaking me with Everett, I had gotten interested in him. But I don't think I was trying to spite her. I think the timing was just bad. And the communication was even worse.

That's the trouble with matters of the heart. It's so hard to be honest, to just lay things all out plain. There's such an infinite number of ways to be hurt and humiliated when it comes to love that it's crucial to hold back a little. You can't roll in like a steam shovel and say, "Love me, love me!" You can't jump up and down and yell, "What the hell is wrong with everybody?" You just have to take it inch by inch, make the best guesses you can, and hope against hope for the best. Which is what I planned to do.

I went upstairs to my room to find my cell phone, feeling certain in a way I hardly ever felt certain about anything that Everett was going to call me as soon as he could shake Barni loose. She had wound up drinking too much—shouldn't an almost-doctor know better?—and he literally had to carry her up the stairs to her apartment. I watched her lights go on inside and then waited for him to come back out. But he didn't.

I was tired, so I lay back on my little single bed, watched the ceiling fan spin, held my cell phone on my chest, and waited.

Then I heard Clive and Mackie kissing in their room—now aware that I could hear them, and shushing each other—but, for the first time in ages, I didn't feel jealous or lonesome or tortured. It was fine. Awkward and gross, but fine. I put on my headphones and switched the phone to vibrate with a strange, solid kind of certainty that everything was going to work out. True, I was unemployed, single, and more and more pregnant every day, but these things were starting to seem temporary. As of tonight, I couldn't help but take a broader view. In a year, it seemed, everything would be resolved. I'd be far along whatever good new path I was surely about to discover. My buzz of well-being was so strong, in fact, that I dozed off that night without even noticing that Everett never called.

Chapter Eight

Falling asleep so hopeful like that was wildly optimistic for me. Uncharacteristically optimistic. So optimistic that the next morning, when there were no missed calls on my phone, I worried that I'd jinxed myself somehow, just by daring to look forward to something.

Then, over the course of the day, as Everett continued to not call, I felt my optimism roll over into pessimism. Noon passed. Then one o'clock. Then two. Soon supper was done, and I was in bed again, just as I had been the night before, but this time there was no buzz of well-being. No pleasant anticipation. This time, I felt a thudding kind of hollow certainty that no call was coming. Possibly ever.

It would have been a perfect problem to discuss with Mackie, if

Mackie were a person I discussed anything with anymore. I had just, for example, started getting a weird pain in my earlobe whenever I talked or chewed. But I didn't even mention it to Mackie, because I could just hear her say, "What? You've got earlobe cancer now?"

Instead, I kept out of her line of sight. Mackie was in a busy patch with back-to-back clients, and Clive had gone out of town until Saturday. I had the place to myself, and I did all the things I imagined people who felt bad did to feel better: I took a bubble bath. I made gazpacho. I played Earth, Wind & Fire at top volume on the stereo, read a novel about a French spy cover to cover in an afternoon, and took a stab at a Pilates pregnancy video. All to little effect. I did not feel better. I felt worse. I circled some want ads in the paper, but the end of the week came and went, and I was too depressed to even make the calls.

By Saturday, the day Clive was returning home, I refused to even look at my cell phone. And I wasn't sleeping. I'd stayed up all night for days—truly, until five in the morning—watching TV. I couldn't sleep. I didn't want to. I didn't even want to try. Instead, I watched reruns of *All in the Family* and *Eight Is Enough*. I watched extreme cooking shows where the hosts ate spiders and eyeballs and poisonous fish. I watched televised gospel churches and infomercials for the Monkees' greatest hits. My eyes would get puffy as the night wore on, and I'd press them with cold washrags. My legs would get crampy from sitting so long, and I'd do deep knee bends. When morning came, I'd go to sleep and stay that way until two in the afternoon, or three, or even, sometimes, four.

Mackie didn't like it. She'd try to serve me plates of fresh fruit and whole wheat toast. Sometimes I'd run the shower and hide in the bathroom with a book. "Come and eat something," she'd say through the door. "This isn't good for you!" She didn't add "or the babies," but she didn't have to. Then she'd set the tray down in the hallway and add, "People are not nocturnal."

By Saturday afternoon, I was officially a lost cause, and though Mackie and Clive invited me to join their farmers' market run to get some fresh things for supper, they knew in advance what I'd say. I waited until they were gone, then sat at the farm table in the kitchen, doodling these words in my journal: "What was I thinking? What was I thinking? What was I thinking?" The question seemed to sum it all up, and I wrote the words big and small, in print and in cursive, slanting forward and then backward. I wrote them again and again and I might have kept writing them all afternoon if the doorbell hadn't rung.

I set down my pen. I walked to the door. I looked through the peephole.

It was Dixie. In a tae kwon do outfit. A hot-pink tae kwon do outfit.

"Hey, Love Bug," she said, wiggling her fingers.

"I love that color," I said as I opened the door.

"I'm glad to hear it," she said. " 'Cause look what I have for you!" She held out another one just like it, all folded and pressed.

"Are we going somewhere?" I asked.

Dixie nodded. But we needed a few things first, and she counted them off on her fingers: a pair of sneakers, a water bottle, a sports bra, and an attitude.

"I think my attitude is still in the wash," I said, and Dixie smiled and gave my cheek a little pinch.

Then she said, "Just go grab it, darlin'. You can wear it wet."

She'd showed up too last minute for me to think of an excuse. And what could I say? Her pink sensei look won me over.

Within minutes we were buckled into her Escalade in our matching pink uniforms on our way to the Downtown Y, and I was feeling better already. It turned out Dixie needed some help with her self-defense class. Her co-leader, Danielle, who lived down in Galveston with an unneutered standard poodle named Bob, was having car trouble today. "It's the first class," Dixie said. "And the first class is always a doozy."

"Anything I can do to help," I said.

"Just follow my lead," Dixie said. "Though that won't be as easy as it sounds."

"Am I too pregnant?" I asked, and Dixie—who, I'd noticed, was never shy about touching people—reached over and gave my belly a little rub.

"No, no," she said. "Today, it's mostly shouting." Then she looked over and winked at me. "You know how to shout, right?"

"Like a champ," I said.

Next thing I knew, we were standing in front of a group of thirty older ladies who were ready to rumble. I felt a little self-conscious up there, especially since my pink jacket didn't quite reach around my belly. With the white strip of my T-shirt underneath, I truly looked like I had split a seam. But the truth was, nobody was looking at me. Everybody was looking at Dixie.

"Welcome, girls," she was saying, as she took a shoulder-width stance in her matching pink sneakers. "Today we're going to practice being strong and fierce and taking charge." She took a deep breath and lifted her arms above her head, and the ladies in the class did, too. She took a second deep breath, but then got distracted by somebody in the back. "Oh, no, sweetheart," she called to the woman. "You don't have to take off your rings. Jewelry makes a great weapon."

She started again. "Now, we all love our men. And none of us likes to fight. But I know nobody here will argue when I say that every now and again in life, we ladies will need—and I mean really need—to kick somebody's ass."

I had never heard Dixie curse before. I had heard her talk about the needlepoint pillow she was making for the shih tzu rescue auction. I had heard her describe the lemon drop cookies she always made at Christmas. I had heard her rhapsodize about her grandmother's pear preserves. But the cursing was new. And even after I'd heard it, it still just didn't seem possible.

Dixie went on. "And that brings me to one of the mottos of our class—a phrase I want you to say over and over. Whisper it to yourself in the grocery store. Sing it in the shower. Print it up on a bumper sticker. Are you ready? Here it is: 'Don't fuck with me.' "

Hearing Dixie say the word *fuck* almost put me over the edge. It was a terrible word. But filtered through her Texas twang, it took on a second syllable and became almost musical.

She nodded at us. "Say it with me now. Try it out."

And we said it. "Don't fuck with me." But we didn't sound as good.

"Good," she said. "That's the attitude I want you girls to practice." She leaned over and started doing some stretching, and we all copied. "How many of you girls have been menaced?" she asked, and every single person in the room raised her hand. "That's right," Dixie said. "You're just minding your own business, getting gas in your housecoat and thinking about that phone call from your mother, when some fella in a pickup decides to give you a little scare. These are the magic words that you will think, say, and—if need be—scream at him to call up your power. Let's try them again."

"Don't fuck with me," we all said in unison.

"Now, I'm not a big fan of bad words," Dixie said. "But words are strong, and words are powerful. And when you need them, they'd better be there."

Then she told us that the only things we were going to do today were: one, curse—and two, scream. The rest of the course would be all about how to beat men up: how to use their size and strength against them, identify their vulnerable areas, outsmart them, and— just as important—find the will inside our own selves to fight back and keep fighting until our attacker was either "crippled, unconscious, or dead."

But that was later. This class, today—which she claimed would be the toughest of them all—was just about words.

Then she got us cursing. She clapped her hands and said, "All right, ladies! Top of your lungs!" Then she yelled at us—just like that—from friendly grandma to psycho drill sergeant in two seconds flat. We started with "No," and worked our way up.

"What do we say if somebody tries to grab us?" she shouted.

And it was our job to shout, "No!"

"What do we say if somebody wants to hurt us?"

Again, we shouted, "No!"

"What do we say to anybody who thinks he can tell us what to do?"

"No!"

"Say it like you mean it!"

"No!"

"Say it for yourself! Say it for your friends! Say it for all the women in the world who don't know how!"

"No! No! No!"

And that was only the beginning. At first, I tried to lip-synch, like I used to do in school chapel when we sang hymns. I didn't want to be the only person singing, the lone off-key voice. But Dixie created such an energy in the class, such a feeling of shared outrage, such an I-am-woman-hear-me-roar fierceness, that it was impossible not to get caught up.

She wanted us yelling. She wanted our faces turning red and our jugulars popping out. She said women were taught to be polite, and quiet, and apologetic. She said we had to teach ourselves to use those voices—because our voices, believe it or not, were the very best weapons we had.

I found myself wishing I'd brought a notepad. I'd thought we were just going to practice some karate chops and then head home. But Dixie wanted us to understand the psychology of power. She said that men who attacked women felt afraid themselves and saw the world in only two groups: the attackers and the attacked. For them, everyone had to be one or the other. Then she said, "If you take nothing else away from this class, take this: If you scream obscenities at an attacker, eight times out of ten he'll turn tail and run."

The women in the class looked around at each other, pleased to hear that it was going to be that easy. But then Dixie warned us that it wasn't going to be easy. "In fact," she said, "it may be the hardest thing you ever try to do."

I didn't think it sounded that hard. I'd screamed before. And I could curse like a sailor: Mackie had already started shushing me so I wouldn't be a bad influence on the babies. Now, at six months along, I was not as nimble as I used to be, but if yelling and cursing were the central activities, I figured I could ace this class no problem.

Then Dixie gave us our next assignment. "Okay, ladies. This one's tough. Think of a person you find threatening, and, when I point at you, yell, 'Get the fuck away from me, you stupid-ass motherfucker!' "

I so wished Mackie were there so I could turn to her in amazement.

Dixie gave us a minute to think of our guy. Then she said, "Got him?"

We all nodded. This didn't seem so hard.

But the first woman she pointed at just started laughing, collapsing into giggles each time Dixie tried. The second woman had similar trouble, her voice shrinking into a breathy falsetto. The third burst into tears, and the fourth declared she was morally opposed to cursing and walked out of the room.

And then it was my turn. I was ready. But when Dixie actually pointed at me, I felt a tightness, almost like a hand grabbing hold of my throat and squeezing. Dixie gave me a few seconds to pull myself together, and then she took my hand with a surprising gentleness and walked me toward the door.

"Get a drink of water, sweetheart," she said, and so I did.

Dixie had known this would happen. It had happened, she told us later, in almost every self-defense class she'd ever led. Women who knew perfectly well how to use their voices to talk to employees or scold their children or remind their husbands about the dry cleaning had no idea how to access those same voices in a pinch.

"Are you afraid you sound silly?" she yelled at us. "Are you afraid you're being too loud? Are you afraid the other ladies are going to go home and laugh with their husbands about you making all this noise? Fuck those ladies! Fuck their husbands! Now give me a 'Goddamn stupid-ass motherfucker!' "

And finally I ceased to be shocked by the cursing. Dixie had turned out to be a superhero, and she could say any damn word she pleased.

"I can't hear you!" she was shouting. Her mouth was wide open, her fists were clenched. "Wake up the security guard! Shake the walls! Bring down the building! 'Goddamn stupid-ass motherfucker!' "

We were louder this time.

"Yell it at the guy who cut you off in traffic this morning!"

"Goddamn stupid-ass motherfucker!"

"Yell it at the office supply store that put you on hold for half an hour today!"

"Goddamn stupid-ass motherfucker!"

"Yell it at the boy in middle school who made fun of your bra!"

"Goddamn stupid-ass motherfucker!"

"And yell it at the goddamn stupid-ass motherfucker who scared you into taking this class!"

And then we finally hit the fierceness she was looking for. She got us there, and then she kept us there: "Again! Again! Again! Again! Don't tell me you think cursing is tacky! Don't tell me women should be seen and not heard! These words are your best friends! These words are your bravery and your passion and your self-respect! Now stand up and let me hear you fucking say them!"

Of course, we were standing up already. But we stood up taller, and we screamed our hearts out.

We yelled so loud that the security guard came in to check on the ruckus. And when we saw him appear in the doorway, his uniform pulling apart between the buttons on his doughnut belly, we all in unison gave one last great impromptu shout for the evening. "God-damn stupid-ass motherfucker!"

He shook his head and wandered off.

And then the hour was up, and Dixie started clapping. "Give yourselves a hand, girls! You really did yourselves proud!" We clapped for ourselves, and for Dixie. We took swigs from our water bottles and caught our breath. Then Dixie gave us homework to practice our curses. "They're best done out loud," Dixie said. "But you can do them in your head if you have children."

That class was the most fun I'd ever had, and I didn't walk to the car, I galloped. On the drive home, I asked Dixie all about how she'd learned to do that, but all she'd say was "My first husband was a real son of a bitch." Then she told me there were two things in this world that every woman needed to learn about. One was self-defense. And the other one wasn't covered in her class.

"What's the other one?" I asked.

Dixie took a long, slow breath before saying, "Comfort."

I thought about that. "How does that one work?"

"Well," Dixie said, "everybody's different. What comforts me won't be what comforts you."

"What if I don't know what comforts me?"

Dixie pulled up in front of Mackie's house. "Well, sweetheart," she said, kissing her fingertips and touching them to my cheek. "It's time you found out."

I cruised up the front walk, eager to tell Mackie all about the class and get her signed up pronto for next week. For the first time in months, I felt good. I felt ready to talk to Mackie and help her chop up something organic for dinner and maybe even take a late-evening walk.

I felt so good, in fact, that I decided at the front door to call Everett and confront him as soon as I could. This was the new millennium, after all. I did not have to sit around waiting on him and wondering what the heck had happened. I could use my newly discovered voice to ask him myself. I could draw upon my bravery and my passion and my self-respect. Or, at the very least, Dixie's.

But first, I had to tell Mackie about the class. "I just set the world's record for curse words!" I was calling out as I slammed the front door. "You are not going to believe it!"

But then as I rounded the corner I stopped midstep at a sight that I, myself, could not believe. Right there, at our dining table, was Everett Thompson. On some kind of a double date. With Mackie and Clive. And Barni.

The four of them were halfway through their beers and eating Clive's world-famous chicken masala. I could not speak. For a minute, I couldn't even breathe. I just froze and stared at them. Everett. On a date. With Barni.

They seemed to be having a great time. I looked at the table, everybody so young, so done up, so freshly washed and fragrant. In the face of it, I felt tragically plump and middle-aged and off balance and slow, my big belly weighing me down. Suddenly, all that cursing at the air with a roomful of ladies in pink sweats and power bras didn't seem so cool. Barni wore a strapless sundress and light silver bangles on both arms. Her baby-oil-basted skin looked as delectable as the meal itself. I felt completely deflated. All my sassiness just hissed right out of me.

"Sarah!" Mackie said. "We set a place for you!"

"Oh," I said. I couldn't meet Everett's eyes.

He must have been tricking me with that kiss. It was all I could figure. Some kind of sadistic, twelve-years-in-the-making, leftover revenge from high school. It seemed incomprehensible to me that he could have seemed so very smitten that night in the pool and then lost interest so quickly. The only answer I could come up with was that he must be a very good actor—and he'd faked the whole thing. Either that, or I hadn't given Barni enough credit, and—given a choice between Barni and me—the person he chose was Barni.

"Join us," Clive said, waving me in.

I could see an outline of Barni's pink lipstick on the mouth of Everett's beer bottle. "Oh," I said again, trying hard to make some—any—words. "I can't. I have somewhere to be," I said. I was backing up, and then I hit the wall.

"You just came in," Mackie protested, trying to wave me to the table.

"It's a busy day, chief," I said.

"We've got aloo gobi and home-baked naan," Mackie said in a singsongy voice, as if there were anything in the world that could tempt me to stay.

They'd had some drinks already. They were feeling good. They wanted to chat. They wanted us all to be friendly friends, and they waited with pleasant faces to see if I'd pop over to the table and join them—all except Everett, who was looking away. I wanted to turn and leave, but I couldn't move my legs.

Finally, Barni broke the silence and pointed at Everett. "You two really used to date in high school? That's so funny!"

"Isn't it?" I said then. "Isn't it hilarious?"

"So?" Barni went on, as if she and the entire table had been waiting for this question all day: "Was he a good kisser?"

In my peripheral vision, I saw Everett study his plate.

I surveyed the scene. I couldn't remember the last time I'd done something as carefree as have a beer with friends. Everything in my life now was prescribed by what was safe for the babies, or optimal for their development, or best for their intelligence. I lived in a lab-rat cage of maternal healthiness, reminded at every turn that I was a vessel. And the person I was doing it all for was halfway through a bottle of Shiner Bock with her perfect husband in her perfect house on a perfect double date. In that instant, I hated everyone in the room, including myself, and after a long evening of screaming curse words at both everyone and no one in the world, it was all I could do not to shout a handful of obscenities right then.

But I didn't. I just walked over to the table and picked up Everett's beer bottle. I wiped Barni's lipstick off the rim with my thumb. I held the bottle up high in a toast while I turned to her. "Everett was," I said, stretching out the moment, "a phenomenal kisser."

Then I put the bottle up to my lips and took a hearty swig.

Mackie gasped. Everybody else froze, staring at me while I made my grand protest against heartbreak and injustice and people who don't call you when they're supposed to. Even Everett was too shocked to move for one short, glorious second. I clanked the bottle back down on the table.

It was a good moment for me. I felt fierce and mean and bad to the bone. I was proud to be able to summon up some moxie. Next step was to take Mackie's crappy car and hit the open road. I didn't have anywhere to go, but that had never stopped me before.

I was just turning to leave, and the room was still absorbing my behavior, and I was still most definitely the center of all attention, when my cell phone rang. Which surprised even me, since almost everyone who called me was sitting right there in the same room.

But it could have been my dad. Or Dixie. It could have been Everett's mother, calling to offer me a job after all, which would have been a great climax to the moment. It could even have been my old roommate from New York, Bekka, calling to beg me to move back because the island of Manhattan just didn't function properly without me. All of these thoughts flashed through my head in milliseconds as my "Xanadu" ringtone revved up, and I tried to decide if I should answer.

In the end, the prospect of being able to close my tantrum with the declaration "And now, I'm moving back to New York" was so appealing, I answered it.

I rooted around in my purse for the phone, found it, checked the number on the screen—*212! The Big Apple!*—and then, with the entire table looking on, said, politely, "Hello?"

It wasn't Bekka, actually. It wasn't even close to Bekka. It was so far from Bekka that I couldn't even place the voice for a good while, as the whole room listened to me listening.

Here's what the voice said: "You Texas girls are going to kill me."

I said, "What?"

The voice went on. A grumbly, heavy, worn-out-sounding voice. "Get out of my state! Stay on your own goddamn side of the Mason-Dixon Line."

"Who is this?"

"Do you know how many beauties come from Houston?" the voice went on. "I Googled it. Jennifer Garner and Renée Zellweger and that brunette from *Charlie's Angels.*"

"Jaclyn Smith," I said. She had gone to my high school.

"You're like a line of ants, trudging north. Why can't you just stay in your mound?"

And that's when I recognized the voice. "J.J.?" I said. It was definitely J.J. Though perhaps a little less dy-no-mite than usual.

"What?" he shouted.

"Are you drunk?"

"Of course I am!"

This might have been a good moment for me to excuse myself and take my conversation outside by the pool. But I was so dumbfounded to hear his voice, and so curious about why on earth he would be calling me, that I just stood there. And every single person in the room listened to my end of the conversation. Even Everett was watching me openly.

"Why are you calling me?" I went on.

"I've got something to tell you about, ex-girlfriend. And it's not going to make me look like a very good guy. But I probably don't look like a very good guy to you, anyway. You hate me already, don't you?"

"I don't hate you," I said. Though I actually did.

"Yes, you do."

"No, I don't." Though, again, actually, yes. I did.

"Just tell me you do. I need you to hate me right now."

"Fine," I said. "I hate you."

"A lot?"

"Yes, okay? I hate you a lot."

"How much?"

"Come on."

"Tell me how much you hate me, goddamn it!"

"I hate you a huge, pulsating, blinding amount, you selfish, lying, job-stealing pig!"

"Good," J.J. said then. "Very good."

"And guess what else?" I added. "You are bad in bed." Here, I looked up to meet Everett's listening eyes. "Really terrible in bed." My eyes were locked on Everett's. "The worst."

"Okay," J.J. said. "That's enough."

"Want me to go on, Elton John?"

"That's plenty," he said.

"So what do you want?"

There was a long pause. I waited. We all waited. Then J.J. said, "It's about Veronica." And the word "Veronica" came out as a strangled, croaky whisper, as if he were physically wrestling his body into saying it. As if saying that name was going to change something that could never be changed back.

Clearly, a big moment for him. Except for one thing. I had no idea who Veronica was.

"Who's that?" I said.

"Veronica!" J.J. shouted.

I was quiet.

"Veronica! Veronica, Veronica, Veronica!" He was slamming his hand down on something with each word.

"Yeah," I said, with a little head-shake. "That's not really helping."

"You really don't know who I'm talking about? Are you kidding me?"

I shrugged. "I need a little more to work with here."

J.J. let out a frustrated growl. "I can't believe you're going to make me do this. The Tits. I'm talking about the Tits!"

"Oh," I said pleasantly, stretching out the sound and nodding my head. "The Tits! How is she?"

There was a long silence, and then J.J. said, "She just tried to kill herself."

I didn't know what to say to that. Finally, I came up with, "Please tell me you're not serious." But I already knew he was.

"I need you to drive somewhere for me," he said then. "Can you do that?" He sounded less drunk now, all of a sudden. Less drunk; more urgent.

"I can," I said, matching the urgency. "I absolutely can." I looked around the room, at all the dinner-date faces still turned toward me, the faint aroma of perfume and hair spray mixing with the smoky kitchen scents of Clive's cooking—all of them now desperately curious for me to finish my call and fill them in. And Mackie most of all. I knew she'd be asking me about every bit of this later, and I also knew I'd give her just the barest details and leave it at that.

"Just give me one second," I said to J.J. I still had their attention. It was not too late for a kick-ass ending.

Then I took a step closer to Everett's beer bottle, still waiting on the table. I picked it up by the neck and placed my eyes on Everett—and, without dropping his gaze, turned the bottle upside down and poured the entire thing on his lap.

Then I said, "Have a good date, folks," pointed my six-month belly toward the back door, and followed it out.

"Where am I going?" I asked J.J. as I started Mackie's car. My stomach touched the steering wheel, and I had to slide the driver's seat back.

"You hate me, right? You already hate me?"

"I already hate you. Where am I going?"

"It's a psychiatric hospital," he said, and he told me the name: the Rancho Verde Facility. He read directions to me, pronouncing the street names like he was speaking a foreign language. "Take Interstate 10? Past Brookshire? And then north on something called FM 2260? Past a rusty bridge? It says if you go past the Dairy Queen, you've gone too far."

So I headed for I-10. Brookshire was outside of town. It was going to take a while to get out there. Plenty of time for Kid Dynomite to fill me in.

"The Tits is from Houston?" I said.

"You have to stop calling her that."

"Sorry."

"How can you not know she's from Houston? It's like the first thing she ever said to me. Didn't you talk to her at all?"

"No." No, I hadn't talked to her at all. No. I ignored her, like everybody else did. Except the photographers and wardrobe and makeup—and also, from the looks of things, J.J.

"What were you doing talking to her?" I said. "You didn't even work on that campaign."

J.J. didn't say anything.

"I already hate you," I reminded him.

"Well," he said. "What do you want? She was gorgeous. It's not my fault she was gorgeous."

"J.J., she's fifteen!"

"She's nineteen."

"You were sleeping with her?"

No answer.

"Is this why she tried to kill herself?"

No answer.

"J.J., please don't tell me this girl tried to end it all over somebody like you."

"It wasn't just me," he finally said.

It was a convergence of things. All piling on top of each other, as bad things tend to do. J.J. had, as was now pretty clear, started up an affair with her during our Boob 'em shoots, and he'd kept things going for several months after.

"What about your wife and her picnic basket?" I asked.

"Let's not bring my wife into this," J.J. said, as if I were the person who'd done that.

The affair had been torrid. Some days, he couldn't get enough of Veronica. But other days, she bothered him. She kept making him mixes of her favorite music—Justin Timberlake, Jewel—and then cried when he didn't listen to them. She started texting him all the time and calling him at his house. One day she showed up during a client presentation in a trench coat and lingerie.

"Can you believe that?" J.J. paused to say. "During a client presentation?"

"I do actually hate you," I said. "I'm not just saying that."

"Good," J.J. said. "I hate myself."

"Actually," I continued, "*hate* isn't even the right word. *Hate* is too cute a word."

"Do you want me to finish?" he asked.

"Do I have a choice?"

He went on: Then his wife got pregnant, and she came down to the office to show him the little plus sign on the stick while he was "in the conference room" with Veronica. His secretary had stalled the wife by showing her online sites for baby names, but he'd been about an inch away from getting caught and watching his entire life crumble down around him. That, he explained, was the wake-up call he'd needed.

"*That* was the wake-up call you needed?" I said.

J.J. resolved to be a better man, to stop messing around, to settle down for real and become a well-behaved, dedicated, attentive husband and father. And, of course, to break things off with Veronica.

"Are you sure that's her name?" I said. "That doesn't sound like a real name."

"That's her name," J.J. said. "Veronica Locke."

Not a real name. Who had hired this girl?

Anyway, he did break up with her. He had hoped to give her a supportive hug and send her on her way, but she had gone "all *Fatal Attraction*" on him, crying and screaming and whatnot. Finally, he'd had to warn her that if she ever contacted him again, he'd have her thrown in jail.

"She bought that?" I asked.

"Sure," he said. "She's nineteen."

Then, the next day, she went to an audition for a bathing suit cat-alog and they told her she was too fat. And that night—dumped, alone, unemployed, and five pounds over the limit—she went home and swallowed the entire leftover bottle of codeine from when she'd had her wisdom teeth pulled. Her roommate found her on the kitchen floor next to a tumped-over three-liter bottle of Diet Coke.

"J.J.?" I said.

"What?"

"I'm going to need a stronger word for *hate*."

She spent a week in the hospital. Her parents flew up from Houston with her childhood teddy bear to bring her back home. She wrote it all to him in a letter.

"And you didn't visit her in the hospital," I guessed. "Did you?"

"I thought it would just make things worse."

"Worse for who?"

"Everybody, okay? Everybody!"

And who knew? He might have had a point. Married ex-boyfriends with pregnant wives might not be the best sources of comfort for their suicidal teenage mistresses after the big breakup. Kind of a gray area, though.

J.J. told me Veronica's parents had committed her to a rehab out-side of Houston.

"A rehab?" I said. "What kind of rehab?"

"Alcohol, drugs, and eating disorders," J.J. said.

"Which one does she have?" I asked.

"I don't know," J.J. said. "Maybe all of them."

We still hadn't quite covered why, exactly, he was calling me. "What am I supposed to do about all this?" I asked.

"Help her," he said. Plain and simple.

"How?"

"I don't know!" His voice was a shriek. "I don't know!"

And something about his anguish gave me comfort. He must have cared about her a little, at least, in his paltry way.

"I don't know if I can help her," I said. "She may be past the point of repair."

And then, just as I turned off the highway onto FM 2260, J.J.—selfish, stupid, horny J.J.—started to cry.

I just listened. To the sound of FM 2260 blurring under the tires, and to the sound of J.J.'s conscience rising to the surface.

And then I'd arrived.

Rancho Verde wasn't a *ranch* so much as it was *ranch-style*. A rambling, suburban building out in the country, surrounded by long grass and oak trees, with a little parking lot and a sign on the front door that said ALL FOOD AND DRINKS MUST BE LEFT IN CAR. OR CONFISCATED.

J.J. hadn't spoken for several minutes. Just as I rolled to a stop, he said, "I don't know what to do."

It was time for me to go in. I suddenly felt outraged, like if I had to spend one more second on that phone, I would crush it with my own hand.

"You don't know what to do?" I said. "For real? Here's a hint. Start by holding yourself to the minimum standards of common human decency."

"I swear, I didn't know she was so fragile when I met her."

And then I turned off the ignition and yanked up the brake. "All women are fragile," I said. "You goddamn stupid-ass motherfucker."

Chapter Nine

It was good that J.J. called when he did. I'd been getting confused. I'd been thinking that things like kisses in pools were important. But J.J.'s call reminded me that such things were the opposite of important. Kisses in pools, clandestine affairs, fixations on brothers-in-law—these were the things we did to distract ourselves from what actually mattered. These were the soap operas of life, the melodramas, the mini-crises that occupied our attention while famine, war, and death raged across the human experience.

I sat still in the quiet car for a minute and listened to myself breathe.

I didn't really have a plan of action for Veronica. I wasn't sure what, exactly, I was going to say to her when I walked in and signed the guest log. I was thinking that maybe I'd try to explain to her what a bad person J.J. was. It seemed important that she understand that he wasn't worth all the fuss she'd made over him. I thought I might even tell her that I had dated him, too, years back, and hold myself up as a person who had gone on to survive, and even thrive, without his company—though whether or not I was thriving was, of course, still up for debate. Whatever was going to happen, I clung to the idea that the truth would set her free. That once she realized he wasn't worth it, she'd feel better—like I could suture up her broken heart with a set of rational arguments.

I figured I'd work it out. I'd say something, whatever I could think of, and then go home.

But that was before I walked in and saw her.

Does it go without saying that I barely recognized her? Is it just a given that she was not the girl I remembered? I'd seen her. I'd spent more than a month with her not that long ago, handing her countless pieces of gum as I bustled around organizing things. I'd pored over her photos for weeks and weeks. Even now, her cleavage was on every bus in town. At the very least, she should have looked familiar.

I wasn't expecting her to be lounging around Rancho Verde in a Boob 'em bra, of course. In my mind, I had allowed for some clothes. But other than that, I was basically expecting the girl from the campaign. Though I knew on some level that the girl from the campaign didn't really exist. She had never existed. We made her up. We airbrushed and lit and posed and styled and Photoshopped her into existence. I should have known that better than anybody, but I was shocked to discover, when I stood across from Veronica in the foyer of the building, that I could barely see a resemblance between her and the bra girl. They were like two different people. They *were*.

Sitting cross-legged in one of the enormous living room chairs, she looked about the size of a throw pillow. She could not possibly have been five pounds over any weight limit. She had to be a size 0. Or even a negative size.

Still in my hot-pink self-defense garb, I leaned over what suddenly felt like an obscenely large six-month belly to put my face in her line of vision. "Veronica?" I said. "Do you remember me?"

She did, a little, when she looked up. "You're the boss. From Marston and Minx."

The Boss and the Tits. Together again.

"That's right," I said, pulling up a stool. "I was the boss. We did those bra ads, remember?"

"Sure," she said, taking me in. I was maybe four times her circumference. Maybe five. Then she said, "You look different."

It popped into my head to say, *So do you.* But instead, I said, "Well, I'm pregnant."

"Oh," she said, and nodded. Then, "Those ads we did are everywhere."

"Yep," I said. "They sure are."

"When I tell people that's me, they want to know if it hurt to be branded."

"What do you say?"

"I tell them it's all fake."

"And what do they say then?"

"They want to see the scar."

She seemed to brighten for a second at the memory of those days, but then, when she came back to the present, her face went sour again.

"I'm not the boss anymore," I said. "They fired me, actually. I live here now."

"You do?" She was trying to put it together.

"Not here." I gestured around the room, in case that wasn't clear. "But here in Texas."

"Isn't Texas the worst?" she said. "I have to stay for ten weeks before I can go back to New York."

And I heard that. I really heard that. Right then, I knew exactly what this tiny girl was feeling. I knew exactly what it meant to come home before you were ready—before whatever it was that had always scared you didn't scare you anymore.

"Texas rocks," I said, just to see if I could get her to believe it. "You're so lucky to get to come home."

She gave me a look. *Please.*

I was talking to her like she was a small child. Which she most certainly was not, as every photo I'd ever seen of her could affirm. But what can I tell you? At that moment, she looked like a very small child—and it wasn't so much that looks *could be* deceiving as that they *were always* deceiving. Which is why our Boob 'em campaign was selling bras faster than the stores could stock them. Which is why so many people asked Veronica what it felt like to be branded.

"How did you know I was here?" Her eyes were puffy, her lips chapped. She had Band-Aids on her hand, and I tried to figure out what they were from.

I wasn't sure what to say. I did not particularly want to align myself with J.J., or say anything about him that might cast him in a better light, or even mention his name. In fact, each passing minute made it clearer to me how little talking about him could help. She seemed far too fragile for a rousing discussion of J.J.'s shortcomings. My plan of arguing her into a better emotional place was disintegrating, and I didn't have another one. I really just wanted to show up like a fairy godmother—mysteriously, but right in the nick of time—and make everything all better.

Then she said, "Did Mr. Dynamite call you?"

For a second, all I could do was blink. "Please tell me you don't call him Mr. Dynamite."

She looked embarrassed, and then I felt bad for embarrassing her.

"He told you to call him that?" I asked.

"I just heard people calling him that." She shrugged. "I thought it was like a nickname or something."

J.J. had been sleeping with a girl who called him Mr. Dynamite, and he *hadn't realized how fragile she was*.

"Let's just call him by his regular name, okay?"

"What's that?"

"Dick," I said. "Let's just call him Dick."

And she agreed.

I wound up staying until the lights blinked for bedtime, getting all the dirt on the other girls at rehab. Once Veronica got going, she really could talk. She told me about the bloated spaghetti they served at lunch, and the chain-link yard for the smokers, and the group therapist who had tried to get them to sing "Somewhere Over the Rainbow."

"You're kidding, right?" I said.

"Nope," she said. "And I've only been here two days."

I couldn't be responsible for this girl. I wouldn't be. Even though J.J.'s words "Help her" kept brushing against my ears—and even though people like me were part of the reason girls like that wound up in places like this—I was having enough trouble keeping my own self afloat. Taking on a project like Veronica Locke's mental health was a surefire way to capsize everybody.

By the time I was heading back out, she had perked up so much, in fact, that I was starting to feel like I might not need to come back at all. Veronica seemed much better. This place seemed to function pretty well. And with that rumor going around that the guard dogs would maul anybody who tried to escape, Veronica certainly wasn't going anywhere. She was where she needed to be, I told myself, and now I could leave her to the professionals.

• • •

And yet, by Monday morning at breakfast, when Clive announced he'd be working from home that day, my first thought was that I could borrow his Prius. And my second thought was that he was smacking his cereal. And how unattractive that was. And how he looked sort of tubby this morning, in this slant of light—and was so obviously not crush material. And how, at the very least, I could thank Everett Thompson for the equivalent of a good, hard slap in the face.

"Can I borrow your car?" I asked Clive.

"Sure," he smacked.

"What for?" Mackie wanted to know. She had left her sugar spoon in her coffee, and every time she took a sip, I expected it to poke her in the eye.

"Just stuff to do," I said. At this point, after living together since December, I was telling her almost nothing about my life. In just over half a year, she'd gone from being a person I shared everything with to a person I shared almost nothing with. I knew it, I was aware of it every minute I was with her, but I didn't know how to change it. It just was how it was.

When I got back out to Rancho Verde, Veronica was not as easy to find as she had been the first time. The sitting room was empty, and I had to ask for her up at the desk.

"We don't have anyone here by that name," the receptionist said.

"Sure, you do," I told her. "I just saw her yesterday." But I felt a jolt of alarm. Had she suffocated herself with a pillow? Run off to Mexico with Mr. Dynamite? Been mauled by the guard dogs?

I pointed to the chair she'd sat in the day before. "I sat right there and talked with her for over two hours."

The receptionist peered over and squinted. Then she said, "You mean April? Weren't you talking with April?"

"Um," I said. "I thought I was talking to Veronica Locke."

"Twig of a girl?" the receptionist said. "Chapped lips?"

"That's her," I said with a nod.

"Well, that's April May Schneider."

The receptionist pulled up April May Schneider's Monday schedule on the computer and then directed me down toward the stables. Grateful for the lax security and the Texas hospitality, I gave a smile and said, "Thank you, ma'am."

The stables were a good walk down a gravel path from the main building. April and a group of other girls were getting an introductory tour of the place, and as I shadowed them I learned that they were all expected to help take care of the animals during their time at the facility. Duties they'd face included, but were not limited to, shoveling stalls, collecting eggs, and brushing, milking, and feeding a whole pop-up book full of barnyard animals.

I liked the philosophy of it: That hard work was its own reward. That spending time outdoors could steady the soul. That animals had a lot to teach humans about dignity. That taking care of others was just the same as taking care of oneself. This type of therapy seemed a lot wiser to me than just belting out Judy Garland songs.

As the group headed down toward the duck pond, April noticed me and waited for me to catch up.

"Hi, April," I said, wondering if she'd notice the name change.

"Hi," she said. Nope.

"Where are your parents?" I asked. I'd expected to see them.

"Working," April said. "Somebody's got to pay for this place."

"What about the money you earned modeling?"

"Oh, that," she said, waving her hand. "That's spent."

The duck pond was enormous, and stocked with catfish, and we stood by its shore as the guide informed the girls that they were welcome to catch, scale, gut, and eat as many as they liked. Then the guide took out a pole and did a casting demonstration.

"How are you doing today?" I asked April.

"Better," she said. "And guess what else?"

"What?"

"I joined the choir."

"You did?"

She nodded. "We're going to practice our song every night for a final show at the end."

"What's the song?"

" 'Somewhere Over the Rainbow.' "

I held still. "You're kidding me, right?"

She shook her head. Not kidding. "But not the one Kermit sings," she said.

"Oh," I said. "Good."

"Would you like me to sing it for you?"

What to say? "Yes, I would."

Then, by the catfish pond, as the other girls began to cast their bait, April took a deep breath and lifted her eyes to the clouds, and then the noises of rustling grass and buzzing dragonflies and lapping pond water were joined by her quiet, clear voice. She couldn't quite hit the high notes, but she took it slow and simple, singing "la, la" over the words she'd forgotten. If I'd expected the lyrics to have a special significance for the girls staying here at Rancho Verde, I was disappointed. But I was not disappointed by the melody, which I hadn't heard in years, and which seemed to rise into the air and whisper itself around everything near us. I'd forgotten the sweetness of the tune, and April looked positively angelic as the simple song rose out of her. Before I knew it, I felt tears in my eyes.

As she finished, she turned to me. "What do you think?" she asked.

I nodded and said, "Beautiful."

"It's a good song," she said. And then, "Do you have any gum?"

I couldn't save her. I couldn't. But at that moment something rose up in me, and I had to try. "You can't go back to New York after this, April," I said. "New York is not good for you."

She shrugged. "I have to go back," she said. "I'm getting married."

I had planned to never speak to J.J. again. But on the drive back, I called him. At the office.

"You proposed to her?" I demanded.

"Months ago!" he answered, as if the memory of a marriage proposal could fade with time. "Months ago!"

"You didn't ever take it back?"

"Well." The pitch of his voice was rising. "I broke up with her! Shouldn't that have covered it?"

"J.J.," I said. "She's not bright. At all."

No response.

I went on, "Or hadn't you noticed?"

"Dumb in some ways," he said. "But surprisingly brilliant in others."

"Well, she thinks she's about to become Mrs. Dynamite," I said. "Which of the two is that?"

And on that note, the connection went dead.

Clearly I'd given him too much benefit and far too little doubt. What on earth had he been thinking? What else had he said to this poor girl? What argument against a man, rational or otherwise, can take root when he has promised a girl the world? My mind started to race with other promises he could have made, gifts he could have given, vacations he could have planned, admiration he could have lavished— all ways of keeping her right there by his side, despite every other reason he'd give her to leave.

When he called back a second later, I was so livid that I didn't even say hello. I just picked up the conversation where I'd left off, saying: "And if you got this girl pregnant, too, you sick, pathetic son of a bitch, I will find you where you sleep and shoot you myself."

There was a long silence on the other end then, before it occurred to me to check the number on the caller ID. And I saw a Houston area code.

So I said, "Hello?"

Then, in that regal, unmistakable voice, I heard: "This is Barbara Tierney, and I am hoping against hope that I've dialed the wrong number."

Barbara Tierney was calling to offer me a job. And as soon as the words were out of her mouth, and without even asking her what the job was, I said, "I'll take it!" She could have been asking me to be the floor mopper. Or the rat catcher. Or the toilet plunger. I really didn't care.

At the moment she called, something big was happening down at the Preservation Society that she didn't have a minute to explain to me. In our brief time on the phone, she was interrupted several times by people who needed urgent answers to urgent questions. I could hear phones ringing in the background, and a general sizzle of activity. She asked if I could make it to an emergency press conference later that afternoon, and I said I could.

Just as we were about to hang up, I asked if she could tell me what was going on. She had to go, and the words had barely left her mouth before the line clicked dead: "They're tearing down the library."

Later, as I dressed and stretched my panty hose up over my belly, I wondered which library it was. Houston's a big city. It has a lot of libraries. It had just renovated its enormous downtown library a few years back. Could that be the one?

The Preservation Society was in frantic motion when I got there—its living room packed with people and reporters, the Xerox machine running full force. I saw Howard Hodgeman across the room, and he waved like we were old buddies. I saw Barbara Tierney up at a podium, testing the microphone. The living room overflowed with people, and I wasn't even sure where I would find a place to stand. I started to kneel down on the rug, but a reporter saw me— and my midsection—and gave up his seat.

When Barbara Tierney started speaking, the room fell silent. She had the kind of voice that did not need a microphone, but it was on anyway, which made her sound ever so slightly like the voice of God. She laid out the situation, and I was spellbound. We all were. I don't think anybody even scratched an itch the whole time.

"As you know," Barbara began, "Houston has the weakest preservation laws of any big city in the country. Those of us who care about preservation have had our hearts broken a million times. I've got a scar for every building we've lost: the Shamrock Hotel, the Gulf Publishing Company, the Ashland Tea House, the Cooley House. Everybody here knows the list."

She took a deep breath.

"Yesterday, I got some news. The background you already know: The city plans to sell one of our only two Carnegie public libraries to a developer, and will redistribute the books to other libraries around town. The developer who is buying the Carnegie building plans to demolish it, scrape the land clean, and build a high-rise."

The room murmured a little.

"Those of you who have seen this library don't need me to say that it's a breathtaking civic structure—a building that honors not just the city but the idea of buildings itself with its gracious presence. It is ninety-nine years old. It's in constant use—located just a few blocks over from an elementary school, and home to a thriving reading program."

The room was quiet.

Barbara went on. "It was a sneak attack. Plans for the sale came up so quickly that we haven't even had time to add the building to our endangered list. But two days ago this exceptional building got a second chance. A donor has offered to give half the funds to buy the building if the citizens will vote to pass a bond for the remainder of the sale price. City council has agreed to put the sale on hold and put the bond issue on the ballot for an upcoming referendum in November. The building is a treasure, and we can save it. But we have to get the word out and pass that bond."

After she'd finished, as people mulled around the room and had coffee and doughnuts, Howard came to find me. At the same time that he gave me a warm handshake, he said, "I'm all out of Kleenex today, Sniffles. Hope you can hold yourself together."

I stayed at the office late into that evening, filling out the forms they needed to make me an official part-time hire and enjoying the excitement. I sat at the big table in the conference room, and Howard came to sit next to me during a coffee break.

"You're getting the wrong idea about this place," he said, slurping a sip. "It's never this exciting."

I didn't look up from my forms. "No?"

He went on, "Mostly, it's just phone calls, and research, and community meetings. And one little historic building after another falling to the dozers."

"Sounds like a dream job."

"It is today," he said. "I can't remember the last time we had such a fighting chance."

I looked up then. "What is a 'Carnegie library' anyway?" I asked.

Howard choked on his coffee and then coughed for a while. Then he dabbed his mouth with his pocket hankie and said, "Tell me you didn't just say that."

I squinted a little, and ventured, "Is it like Carnegie Hall—except, you know, a library?"

But Howard had already walked out of the room, leaving his mug on the table.

"Howard?" I said. "Howard?"

When he came back, he had a picture book as thick as a dictionary in his hands. "Here," he said, setting it on top of my forms. "Educate yourself." The book was titled *Carnegie Public Libraries of America*.

I looked at the book, and without even opening it, I said, "Looks like there are quite a few of them."

Howard gave what I was starting to know as his signature eye-roll and started back toward the kitchen. "Yes. Quite a few." Then he called, "But they're going down like bowling pins."

I looked down at the enormous book full of a billion things I didn't know and said, "I am so not qualified for this job."

Howard leaned back through the doorway and said, "Tell me about it." Then he added, "But Barbara has always liked you, apparently, and she thinks you have 'leadership potential.' So here we are."

"She's the boss," I said with a shrug.

"She sure is."

The sun was down. I was almost done with my forms, and it was after supper time. Mackie had saved me some homemade pesto, and I was just thinking I would head home when Howard popped his head back into the room. "Don't go yet," he said. "Barbara wants to talk to you."

For half a second, I feared that Howard had just told her I didn't know what a Carnegie library was—and she was going to take back the job offer before I'd even turned in my paperwork.

But she didn't. Instead, she explained the reason that they'd hired me in the first place. It turned out they needed a little help with some advertising.

"What I didn't go into at the meeting," Barbara began as she took Howard's seat at the table, "was our plan for trying to save the library." Then she said again that everything rested on the voters.

"The argument we've been making all along," Barbara said, "is that this building is an irreplaceable asset to cultural life in our city." She paused. "But we say that about a lot of buildings."

In practical terms, Barbara's statement that Houston had "the weakest preservation laws of any big city in the country" meant that anybody could knock down pretty much any building at any time. Even famous buildings, or significant buildings, or beautiful buildings. Even buildings that were, as this library was, on the National Register of Historic Places. To knock down a building, Barbara explained to me, all you had to do was apply for a permit.

"What if the permit is denied?" I asked.

"If the permit is denied," Barbara told me, "you simply wait ninety days. And then you knock it down anyway."

"That's legal?" I asked.

"That's legal." Barbara gave a short sigh, and then she told me the only real way to save a building around here was to buy it. Which our donor would help us do—for more than the asking price. If we could pass that bond.

"What will the ballot question say?" I asked.

"We don't get to write the question," Barbara said. "But the wording we've suggested is 'Shall the city preserve its historic Carnegie library by passing a bond for funds to save it from demolition?' "

"I'd vote for that," I said.

"Be sure that you do," Barbara said.

Here's what the Preservation Society wanted from me: That same donor had allotted some funds for publicity, and they wanted me to design some billboards. "We need you to get the word out about the library," Barbara said. "We need you to get people excited. We need you to make the city fall in love with it."

"Love is not really my area," I said.

"But advertising is," Barbara countered.

"Put a bra on it if you have to," Howard called from the other room.

And then Barbara turned to me with a serious face and nodded yes: "Put a bra on it if you have to."

That night I lugged Howard's coffee table book home, rested it on my tummy, which had become a veritable table, and examined every single page. I stayed up until two in the morning, reading, learning, and taking notes. I wasn't sure who, exactly, I needed to impress, but I did not leave even one page of that book unturned. It felt good to be reading and thinking, and my thirsty brain gulped the words and pictures down until my eyes were falling closed on their own.

By the time I went to sleep, I'd learned just about everything a person awake after midnight could learn about Carnegie libraries: that more than sixteen hundred had been built in the United States in just about every architectural style you can think of— from Spanish colonial to Beaux Arts to neoclassical—all near the start of the twentieth century. Within fifty years many had been torn down, or turned into community centers, or "updated" beyond recognition.

The book was practically an encyclopedia. It listed everything known about every library built. Though the Carnegie Corporation had thrown away the plans to all the libraries, many had been vigorously documented and photographed. I saw more architectural styles than I ever knew existed, and more libraries than my eyes could believe. Except for one: In this exhaustively comprehensive book, the particular Carnegie library we were trying to save was missing. The book listed the other two—the one still flourishing up on Heights Boulevard, as well as the one the city demolished in 1954—but had completely forgotten our little endangered building. I had hoped to come in and dazzle everyone with my intricate knowledge of the structure. Instead, I had to content myself with random facts about others. I felt a little offended that the editors of this tome had overlooked it. And I hoped that wasn't a bad sign.

I told Howard about it in the morning—feeling a little proud of myself, like I'd really done some good sleuthing. A knocked-up Nancy Drew.

I'd hoped to impress him, but he was too busy to be impressed. Everybody was busy. Later I would learn that it was always like this on a site-visit day, that the people at the office just couldn't help but get giddy about seeing the buildings. Especially this morning, since this case was so high-profile, and since it involved—though nobody talked about it—so much hope.

When I saw Howard, I held up the book with both hands. "Our library's not in here," I said.

He was carrying two cameras, a tripod, a laptop, and a Starbucks venti. "So?" he said.

"They forgot us," I said plainly, waiting, really, for him to interpret what it meant and explain it to me. It felt like a big discovery somehow. Like at the very least it would register for him as interesting.

But it didn't. Howard didn't even slow his pace. He shouted his answer over his shoulder and continued out to his car. "So they missed one," he said. "It's not the phone book."

The truth is, by the end of the morning, I would be very grateful that I hadn't beheld the building for the first time in a tiny picture on a page. I don't know how I had managed to grow up in this town and never once visit this library, but until that morning, when we all drove over together to visit, I had never seen it. And as tired as I was after my late night, and as warm as I already felt in the morning sun, I will never forget the moment I lifted my eyes up to that building for the very first time.

I must have been the only person in the group who hadn't seen it before. Everyone else climbed out of the caravan of cars we'd driven, gathered up cell phones and BlackBerrys and notepads, and headed in, heads down. But me, I stopped still on the walkway. I leaned my head back and my mouth fell open a little. I felt a tickle, almost a shyness, in my chest, the way you might if you suddenly bumped into a movie star at a cocktail party—some mixture of surprise and delight and the self-consciousness that remarkable beauty inspires.

There is no question that the objects that surround us impact our experience of the world. Right? Sitting on the deck of an ocean liner is not the same experience as, say, taking a seat on the subway. Standing in a field of flowers is not the same thing as standing in line at the DMV. Sunlight is not the same thing as fluorescent light. Inside is not the same thing as outside. Beautiful is not the same as ugly. These statements aren't just opinion, right? They're facts.

I'm not sure if I can describe the building. I'm not sure a catalog of its details—the red brick, the balustrade, the limestone carvings, the stained glass—can do it justice. Later, Howard would describe it to me as a Classical Revival–style Greek cross plan with vaulted pavilions forming the arms. In fact, I'd collect all sorts of words to describe it, like *pediments* and *entablature* and *pilasters*. But really, in the face of something as solid and as heroic and as real as that building, words are just a little thin. It's like trying to sum up the Parthenon. What would you say? *It has tall white columns, and lots of carvings, and it's really, really big.*

One thing I can say: Seeing this library knocked the wind out of me. The way the look of it created the feel of it: The shine of that old wavy glass in the windows. How the bricks and trim and stone all came together and made it more than just what it was. The scale, which managed, impossibly, to tower over you and welcome you, to feel both enormous and cozy, both regal and kind. It rose up out of the little park of St. Augustine that surrounded it: its feet so firmly on the earth, but its octagonal dome and widow's walk railing brushing the sky.

That said, it did need some work. The paint was peeling, the gutters were sagging, and one of the massive stone ball finials had fallen off and was resting in two cracked pieces by the entrance.

Howard did not fail to notice me gaping.

"You've never even been here, have you?"

"Of course I have," I lied, falling in line behind him. And then, "A long, long time ago. So long ago I can barely remember."

Later, Howard would walk me through the photos we'd take that day and explain the architectural principles that made the building what it was. How the shapes and angles all played off each other and made relationships that were pleasing to the eye and soothing to the soul; how the arrangement of windows and columns and doors addressed primal human needs for safety and order and connection. By the end of the day, I would be starting to understand the psychology of the architecture—not just that it was beautiful, but why.

But at the time, all I knew was that the experience of standing before this grand, slightly neglected building somehow, in some way, made me want to be a better person.

Inside, we gathered around the librarians, who showed us little quirks and delights about the building. One set of shelves spun around into a secret door. A closet housed a stairway up to the widow's walk. There was a sunny alcove where children often reported seeing a ghost-lady reading.

"A ghost-lady?" someone asked.

The head librarian nodded. "She's famous among the children, but no adult has ever seen her."

I looked over at the window seat in the alcove. If I were a ghost-lady, that was exactly where I'd sit.

The head librarian had worked there for twenty-seven years. She was glad to meet us all, and she was especially glad to meet me when Howard introduced me as "our ad girl."

"She's in charge of the billboards," Howard said, and the head librarian raised her eyebrows in appreciation.

But I didn't want to be the ad girl. I had left that life behind, after all. I had renounced it. I was improving myself. Hadn't I just stayed up all night reading? Wasn't I trying to become a better person? In that instant, I had an impulse to show her—and everyone there—that I belonged, at least a little.

So I said, without realizing how stilted the words were going to sound until I heard myself saying them, "This is a beautiful Carnegie library you've got here."

And there was a weird silence after that. At first, I thought the silence was everybody shaking their heads at my off-key attempt to sound like a person who hadn't just, barely, the day before, discovered that Carnegie libraries existed. But the silence turned out to be the librarians looking at me, and then at all of us, like they couldn't believe their ears.

"A Carnegie library?" the head librarian asked. And I was this close to launching into all my new information and giving her a little crash course in her building's place in history when she said, "This isn't a Carnegie library."

I would have said, "It's not?" if Howard hadn't beaten me to it.

The librarians could not believe that we didn't know this. Weren't we the Preservation Society? Wasn't it our job to know what was what? The folks who built this library had applied for a Carnegie grant and been turned down. They had wanted a stage for plays, a "lyceum" (the head librarian pointed our attention to the stage at the front of the room), and Carnegie had been against it.

"Carnegie said no?" Howard asked.

"Carnegie said no," the head librarian confirmed.

"It's listed as a Carnegie," Howard said then.

"Well," the head librarian said, "it's listed wrong."

"If Carnegie didn't build it," somebody else asked, "who did?"

Here, the librarians paused to smile at each other in a way that let us know we were about to hear a good story: A young town doctor named Emmet Frost had fallen in love with a woman whose favorite thing to do was read. Her name was Minnie Sadler, and she was a charter member of the fourth-oldest book club in Texas, founded in 1909.

Howard and Barbara glanced at each other. This was news to both of them, I could tell.

The head librarian went on: Dr. Frost proposed to Minnie, but she turned him down, and he left town brokenhearted. Within a year, he'd contracted yellow fever and, knowing that he was dying, arranged for a gift of ten thousand dollars in his will to build the library. He appointed Minnie and the other ladies from the book club to the library board, and they oversaw its design and construction, complete with their lyceum and a special room upstairs for their book club. There was an old story that Dr. Frost had mailed the engagement ring he'd bought for Minnie to the brick mason to hide somewhere in the building's mortar. But there was another old story that the brick mason had given it, instead, to his own girl. Nobody knew which was true.

"Dr. Frost died lovesick in 1910, construction started in 1911, and Minnie married another man two years after that," the head librarian said. "And Andrew Carnegie had nothing to do with any of it."

. . .

Later, back at the office, after we'd brought in Vietnamese sandwiches for everyone, I asked Howard maybe one too many questions about his vocational choices.

It started off easily enough. I just wondered how he'd picked Houston, of all places, to do this work. "Seems like a recipe for disappointment."

"It's a tough town for preservation," Howard said. Then he held up his sandwich. "But it's a great town for restaurants."

We talked for a while about how Houston had always been so focused on progress and the future, it didn't often look around at itself and enjoy what it had right there. "We always want the next big thing," Howard said. "If a building is Beaux Arts, we want Art Deco. If it's Deco, we want modern. If it's modern, we want some hideous early-eighties office building. Newer is always better here. Even if it isn't."

"I hear that," I said, as Howard got up to start a new pot of coffee. There were a lot of great things about my hometown. It was a hot, friendly, helpful city full of energy and skyscrapers and cheap, delicious food. I had too much sense to take it for granted. But it's also as easy to criticize your hometown as it is to criticize yourself. It's a part of you, and you can't escape that fact, and so sometimes you have to rail against it. You have to prod it to do better. You love it and hate it at exactly the same time for exactly the same things.

Howard had grown up here, too, it turned out—and he claimed there was no other town he wanted to live in. Except New York.

I felt a prickle of nostalgia for my former life. "New York," I repeated, nodding as we paused the conversation to give the city its due. Nostalgia actually filled up that moment for me, and then spilled over. I started to wonder why I had ever left.

But then Howard saved me. "I adore this city," he said, with exactly the conviction I needed to pull me back home. "I'd stay here forever for the Tex-Mex alone."

We were in agreement. A great town and a frustrating town. And our role now, in our current jobs, was to nag it, and nag it, and nag it to become the best version of itself—which, when you boiled it down, was a gesture of love. Among other things.

And then, randomly, I said, "What's the point of saving old buildings, anyway?"

I was really just making conversation. But Howard squeezed his eyes shut tight and pushed his fingers up under his glasses to press on them. "Did we actually hire you?"

I watched him. "Yes."

"If you have to ask"—his voice was muffled through his hands—"you aren't going to get it."

"I already get it," I said. "But I want to hear you talk about it."

Howard took his glasses off. It had been a long day. We'd been publicizing the library's plight all afternoon, and the pace, which had been frantic before the site visit, went absolutely haywire after we'd all actually seen the building and learned the truth about who had built it. It was embarrassing, yes, that we hadn't known the full story about Emmet Frost, since it was our job to know these things. But it was also thrilling to have such a great story. We were already sending out press releases with the heading "Library of Love." Andrew Carnegie had given a lot of libraries to a lot of towns—in itself an amazing story. But Emmet Frost had built only one. And it was for the girl he loved.

Howard was rubbing his tired eyes now. We were going to be here until midnight, at least. "You want to know why we should save them?" he asked. Then he looked at me. "Because they're beautiful."

"All of them?" I asked.

"All of them," he said. "By definition."

Even the dilapidated ones, he went on. Even the ones with shutters missing or termite problems or sinking roofs. Even—God forbid—the ones that had been "modernized," "updated," and "improved" in the sixties.

"Why?" I asked.

"Because those buildings were made with care," he said. "Because back then they didn't know how to build them any other way. Because the materials used for those buildings came from the natural world instead of an assault of plastic and fiberglass and aluminum and asbestos. Things back then were built to last and to honor the space around them—the street, the square, the town."

"That's quite a mouthful," I said when he was done. And then, "Are you saying life was better then?"

"Architecture was better then," he said. "As for the rest of it, I'm still trying to decide."

Later I would learn that Howard lived with a boyfriend named Terry in a little Craftsman bungalow they'd restored inch by inch. The house itself was 1915 down to the hardware, but the furnishings inside were a whimsical potpourri of painted and reupholstered finds, many of them vintage modern, a spare, hip, totally eclectic look. Howard liked to preserve things. He liked to rescue. He liked to find the treasures among the trash, and his idea was to save and preserve the best of any era. He liked modernism, too—when it was done well.

"What I care about," Howard said, "is quality. A big box store with an acre of parking out front? Something like that annihilates every human experience except for shopping."

Howard cared about the psychology of the world around us. He believed that people were happier when they were surrounded by beauty. Or, at the very least, that people couldn't be happy without it. He wanted to apply good decorating principles to the whole country.

"If our cities met their potential," Howard insisted, "we could cut this country's Prozac bill in half."

Then Howard gave me the names of some websites to check out that were brimming with historic photos of local buildings that had been lost. "Go look at them," Howard said. "Look at them and try to imagine what kind of a marvel our city would be if we had taken care of them. It would be indescribable. It would be magical. There would be too much beauty to believe."

Chapter Ten

And that's how I came up with the billboards.

I started teaching myself about the history of architecture, and libraries, and Houston. They gave me a desk in the Preservation office where I could work, but I also wound up spending quite a bit of time in the Frost library itself, in part because it had books and old photographs and wise librarians who were happy to help me. Also because it was just a nice place to be: Even though some of the larger maintenance issues had been, shall we say, deferred, the place still felt good—the tall windows with tree leaves fluttering outside, the warm yellow on the walls, the archways, the rich stain on the wood floors, the books.

I also went there, at least a little, because I was hoping to catch a glimpse of the ghost-lady. Some part of me really wanted to believe that the past could echo its way into the present.

Was I still pregnant at this point? Yes, I clearly was. Had my body morphed into an enormous, flesh-colored beach ball? Yes. No question. And had I stopped looking in mirrors or even, really, glancing down below neck level? You betcha. At seven months, I had become a wobbly Weeble, and the only way I could think of to stay sane was to ignore the situation completely.

Except of course when the babies kicked, or got the hiccups. Or when I couldn't roll over in bed. Or when I saw the ultrasound pictures taped to the fridge. In fact, the more pregnant I got, the harder it was to think of the situation as temporary. That big belly encroached on every moment of my waking life, and even when I was winning the fight to pretend it wasn't there, I was still fighting.

You might have expected me to marvel a little bit over the situation. It's possible that if it had been a pregnancy that belonged to me, I might have done just that. Instead, I marveled at the way, when you lend your body to someone, your mind and heart have to go, too. And I waited until I could have them all back. By waited, I mean counted the days—and sometimes the hours—until that scheduled C-section. Until then, the plan was to think about absolutely anything else.

Like the library. I had two weeks to come up with something, get it mocked up, and then get it to the printers. There was some pressure, but I took my time. For a week or so, I just churned my thoughts around through my daily rotation of activities: mornings at the Preservation office, making Howard's coffee and cramming through a stack of essential reading he'd left on my desk; lunchtime and a little after at the library, doing research and soaking up the atmosphere; and afternoons making what turned into daily trips out to Rancho Verde. I was waiting for something brilliant to come to me and figured it was best to keep busy.

I hadn't intended to visit April every day, but I did. If I timed the drive right, it was only forty minutes each way. I got the feeling no one else was visiting her. It was also just a relief to have somewhere to get away to. I loved it out there at the Rancho. I'd have checked in myself if I could have.

And the car I wound up driving was the twenty-year-old Volvo that my dad had bought for my mom. It had occurred to me that he really didn't need it, because he rode his bike to work. Dixie was doing the grocery shopping now, and the Volvo was mostly stashed in the garage.

"Dad?" I had called him one night to ask. "Can I borrow your Volvo while I'm in town?"

"Sure!" he said, not paying much attention. "Of course." And then, as he thought about it, "What for?"

So I told him about the Rancho, making it sound a little less far away than it actually was. "I feel like I need to visit this girl, Dad," I concluded. "I feel responsible for her troubles."

"You aren't responsible for her troubles!" my dad said. "That's bananas!"

"Dixie says when we comfort others, we comfort ourselves."

"She's a wise lady," my dad said. And then, as an afterthought, "Do you need comforting?"

"Sure," I said. "Doesn't everybody?"

He thought for a minute. "I guess I can't see any harm in your visiting." I knew he was stroking his beard. "The Volvo's in pretty good shape for its age. Except there's a *Willie Nelson's Greatest Hits* stuck in the tape deck."

"Does it still play?" I asked.

"I can't get it to stop playing," he said.

"Thanks, Dad," I said.

"Of course, I'd hate for you to get a flat tire. Or go into labor."

"I'm sure it'll be fine," I said—though I wasn't, entirely.

"Tell you what," he said then. "I'll come with you."

"Come with me?" I asked. "What? You mean every afternoon?"

"Sure!" he said. "Why not?"

I could think of plenty of reasons why not. "What about teaching?"

"It's fine," he said. "That's what TAs are for."

"Won't you get in trouble?"

"What can they do to me?" my dad said. "I've got tenure." Then, after a pause: "Believe me, if there were a way to get fired, I'd have found it by now."

I didn't quite know how to answer.

Then he pushed on, "What if the car breaks down on the highway?"

"Dad!" I said. "You don't know how to fix a car."

"I can certainly call Triple A," he said.

"So can I."

"It's not safe," my dad insisted. "A pregnant girl alone."

"You're forgetting I've taken Dixie's class."

There, he paused. "She's really something, isn't she?"

I hummed in agreement. She absolutely was.

"Okay," I said finally. "Yes. If you'd like to come along, I'd love to have you."

"Good," my dad said.

And I followed that with "Great."

And part of it did seem kind of great. Although I really couldn't picture spending all that time alone in a car with my dad. I could not imagine what on earth the two of us would find to talk about.

But it turned out we didn't talk about anything at all. We both just sang along with Willie Nelson. My dad knew every single word to every single song—and he had a pretty good voice. Not only that, he could harmonize.

"Maybe I should take up the banjo," he said aloud at a stoplight once.

"Dad," I said. "You totally should."

It worked out. My dad was always happy to read, and as soon as we arrived, he'd stake out a chair under the pecan tree. I wanted to teach April that there were many important parts to life besides dates with people like J.J. I'd always bring something—like a cross-word puzzle book, or a copy of *Little Women*, or a newspaper clipping—and spend hours out on the patio with her, trying to stimulate her thoughts. Trying to get her to broaden her perspective. There were so many components of a rich life. Love was one, sure. But so was friendship, so was helping people. So was taking walks, and singing, and wondering about things. I wanted to convince her that a real love, a better love, would come to her if she took the time to enrich some other—any other—part of her life. I wanted to convince her that there are some things we can find only when we aren't looking.

"You mean like a hobby?" April asked.

"Yes!" I said. "Do you have any hobbies?"

"I like to read fashion magazines."

"That's a great one," I said with a big nod. "Now let's think of one where you make something. Or do something. Or learn something."

The words were too mean. Who was I to mock anyone at all? Just months before I had been as thoughtless and self-absorbed as the best of them, and my transformation certainly wasn't complete. She wasn't asking me to go out there. What was the point of making that long drive over and over if I wasn't going to do it with compassion?

I should have realized right then that I was mad at April for not being Mackie. Or that I was frustrated that she didn't quite fit into the empty place in my heart where my friendship with Mackie used to be. April never asked me to visit, and it's funny to think back on all the hours she tolerated me on the patio. I lectured her about global warming, gave her a little primer on feminism, confessed my fear of spiders, rhapsodized about the delights of reading poetry, and walked her through the steps of making a quiche. Sometimes, when I came to a pause, I could hear exactly what Mackie would have been saying if she'd been there.

But what I mostly got from April was "oh" and "wow." Sometimes she fell asleep.

Whenever I could, I slipped anti-J.J. propaganda into the conversation. At first, I tried to be subtle, but that didn't seem to work too well. Eventually, I wound up just interjecting random insults, like, "He's really terrible in bed, isn't he?" whenever his name came up.

To that one, April had shrugged. "I don't know."

Was it possible he'd improved?

But she went on, "I'm not really a fan of sex."

And I said, "I can think of about two thousand crosstown buses that might disagree with you."

"Oh," she said. "I look sexy, but I don't feel sexy."

I shouldn't have been surprised, but I was. "You don't like sex?" I asked.

She shook her head.

"Have you ever liked it?"

"Never," she said. "Not once."

"Because sometimes it can be fun," I offered. Then I had to point out: "Though never, ever with Mr. Dick Dynamite."

She shrugged. Then she said, "But I like to go shopping! He took me shopping all the time."

"Sure," I said, wanting to validate her. "Shopping is the best!" And then, regretting it even as I asked, "What did he take you shopping for?"

"Bras, mostly," she answered. "I must have a hundred bras."

Sometimes it's hard for me to remember exactly why I was avoiding Mackie. Clearly, something had come between us—something, say, about the size of a basketball. But it was all me. Mackie wanted me to run errands with her, but I said I was too tired. She wanted to stop by the office and see where I worked, but I said I was too busy. She wanted to hear about my new job, but I didn't want to talk to her. Instead, I talked to April.

One afternoon, as I balanced a bottle of water on the shelf of my stomach, I told April the story of Emmet and Minnie.

"That's so sad," she said at the end. "Good thing she didn't marry him, though—if he was just about to die."

Then I told her about saving the library. I tried to rouse her to the cause. Having something other than myself to worry about had done wonders for my outlook, and I wanted to give April a similar boost. "It's the most beautiful building in the city!" I said. "And they're going to tear it down! Unless I can convince everybody in town to save it!"

April had just painted her toenails and was blowing on them. "But if it's old," she said, "maybe it's time for a new one."

"But a new one could never be as good!" I said. "That wood doesn't exist anymore, and they don't even make that type of glass. Bricklayers don't have the same skills anymore, and neither do stonemasons. Plus, you could never afford a building like that now. All that stone? The slate roof? The copper gutters? Forget it! Now it's all plastic and particleboard and baby pine. Those old buildings were built to last."

"Until someone knocks them down," April added.

April turned out not to be a fan of old things. She listed several old things she did not care for, including the gym at her church that "smelled like catfish," the Captain and Tennille songs her parents played over and over, and her grandfather.

It bugged me that she didn't seem to have any sense of history—or maybe just that she would disparage the Captain and Tennille—and so I collected a stack of Howard's books from the trunk of the Volvo to show her. She sat very still at a picnic table while I flipped the pages of Howard's favorites, a collection of before-and-after photographs of the mansions that used to line the streets of midtown. April had sunglasses on, and I wasn't even sure she was looking, but I stabbed my fingers against the pages anyway, making my point over and over. *The Lucas house! Built: 1905. Demolished: 1961. The Sweeney house! Built: 1903. Demolished: 1968. The Carter house! Built: 1889. Demolished: 1965.* Page after page of mansions, châteaus, and castles, with spires, stonework, gingerbread trim, and, really, just to sum it up—splendor. All the houses so much more detailed and elaborate and fancy than anything around today. And almost all of them, one after the other, demolished for gas stations and mini-warehouses and parking lots.

On the drive home, my dad hanging his arm out the window, I felt a sadness pressing on my throat. I'd been trying to show April houses and gardens, but there had been people in the pictures, too. Children in white dresses with enormous bows. Mothers holding infants on porches. A birthday party scene. All these lives that had lived themselves out and been lost to time. All these people no one even remembered anymore. Built, demolished. Built, demolished. The buildings all dead, and the people, too. I wanted to save them all. I wanted to bring them all back.

And there in the Volvo, my dad belting out "To All the Girls I've Loved Before" to the wind, I got my brilliant idea for saving the library. Which was going to work great. If our donor would just kick in a little extra cash.

He did. Or she did. Whoever it was—and some in the office had speculated that it was Barbara herself, though we would never find out—approved the entire idea: a series of billboards along each of the three major freeways into town. Four billboards in each series spaced out in a sequence like Burma-Shave signs along the highways, and lucky for us this town had no shortage of them. The first three signs were the same format. A photo of one of those glorious mansions, and under it, the caption BUILT, 1889. Then, next to it, an image of what stood there now—say, a motel or a doughnut shop— with the caption DEMOLISHED, 1950. Or whenever. Then, the last billboard would have a gorgeous picture of the library, and under it, the caption BUILT, 1911. But next to it, instead of a doughnut shop, would be a big heart with the text SAVE IT! inside. And underneath, the caption VOTE TO SAVE THE LOVE LIBRARY!

We did it. I designed the billboards on my laptop and got the whole thing together. Howard loved it and was forced to revise his opinion of me. And after the billboards went up, they made big news. People were asking about them and blogging about them. The *Chronicle* ran a feature in the City section. The local TV stations did pieces. And somebody—not even us—started printing up bumper stickers that said: SAVE LOVE! SAVE THE LIBRARY! Then we made a batch, too. And T-shirts, which a local radio station agreed to give away. It seemed to be working, and bumper stickers started popping up all over town. It was, in a word, awesome.

That's how I spent my third trimester: working passionately on my two rescues, throwing all my worries and woes into situations that were largely out of my control. I had stumbled on not one but two all-consuming projects, and they kept me distracted and busy, much to Mackie's irritation.

I also now had weekly visits to Dr. Penthouse, which I dreaded. Mackie was keeping a chart of my weight, blood pressure, and urine stats. Dr. Penthouse would finish her exam and say to me, "Any questions?"

And I'd shake my head. "No."

Then she'd turn to Mackie and say, "How about you?"

And Mackie would pull out a typed sheet of them. Numbered.

In fact, Mackie had all the appointments in her planner and scheduled her work life around them. She'd drive us over, and I'd crank up the stereo so we didn't have to talk.

"You don't have to come to every appointment," I said one time, pretending that she was busy and might like an excuse not to go.

But it was I who wanted the excuse not to go. Every week seemed excessive. The doctors seemed so sure that something was going to go wrong with the babies. But nothing was wrong with them. They were fine. I was fine. Everything was fine. It seemed like—and I had this thought without any self-awareness about the broader issues in my life—being on disaster watch all the time couldn't be good for any of us. It could so easily become a self-fulfilling prophecy.

Mackie saw it as an attitude problem—like I didn't care, like I wasn't putting in my best effort. On the drive home once, she muttered, "Just because they aren't your babies doesn't mean you don't have to try."

But that was the best thing about this pregnancy. I didn't have to try. If it had required effort on top of everything else, I'd have quit halfway through. Honestly.

It made Mackie crazy that I, the queen of hypochondria, didn't worry more. But I worried only about imaginary things. This pregnancy was real. I could feel it. I was living it. And I just felt like things were okay in there.

So Mackie worried for me. What if I got preeclampsia? Gestational diabetes? Toxoplasmosis? A stroke? What if one of the babies wasn't growing right? Or died? Or they came too early? There were a million things that could go wrong, and Mackie had read about all of them, and printed out articles for me, stapled them, and left them in a stack on my bedside table.

It was a total role reversal. I was the one who was pregnant, but she was the one who was nuts.

The articles went unread. In the beginning, I'd made an effort, but now, I didn't even touch them. I don't want to say I was over the pregnancy, exactly. I did care about it, and I wanted things to go well, and I was interested in the changes in my body and the little people tumbling around inside it. In a theoretical way, it was really cool.

But in a real way, it was taking over my life. The bigger my belly got, the more I tried to ignore it. Even though I couldn't tie my shoes. Even though I'd gained forty pounds and my face looked like a flounder. Even though I had to be careful choosing parking spaces because there had been times when I literally couldn't get out of my car. I had never imagined how thoroughly this project was going to take over every single inch of my existence, and my strategy for self-defense was to pretend it simply wasn't happening.

Which put me at odds with every other delighted and fascinated person in my life. People looked at my belly more than my face. Howard loved to point at it and say, "Are you sure it's not triplets? A hundred bucks says there's a stowaway in there." Clive wanted to paint a face on it and take a picture for the Clacker website. And Mackie wanted to hold each and every one of the little newborn clothes she'd ordered off eBay up against it.

And there was one other problem. I was itchy. It started somewhere in the sixth month, when I'd gained eleven pounds in two weeks. At first, it was just patches, but as time went on it grew to cover my whole belly.

"I seem to have a rash," I told Dr. Penthouse at our next appointment.

She flipped on her exam light to take a gander.

"That's not a rash," she said. "That's your skin pulling apart." Then she warned me never to scratch it.

I burst out with a laugh. "Are you kidding me?" I said. "That's all I do all day."

But she had a cure for me, and she laid it out plain and simple.

She wanted me to rub my belly with a thick glaze of Crisco every morning, and then carefully wrap my midsection with Saran wrap, and then walk around like that all day long. Marinating in my own juices.

She had to be kidding. It was summer in Houston. It was 100 degrees and 98 percent humidity. I waited for her to crack a smile, but she didn't.

"Maybe just some hydrocortisone?" I asked.

"Not safe for the babies," she said, with a head-shake.

On the way home, we stopped for Saran wrap, and then, that night, I tried it. I wrapped myself up and put on my pajamas and sat down with a magazine. For exactly two pages. Then I cut the wrap off with scissors, wiped off the Crisco, and had a good, long scratch.

The rash was a metaphor. There was no solution. There was only the long wait until it was over. And so I waited. And endured, with a closed-lip smile, the photos, the pats, the inquiries, the jokes, the ultrasounds, the waddling, the sore back, and the belly serenades.

Plus, one more thing: the baby shower. Hosted by Dixie, at my dad's newly renovated house. A totally over-the-top New Orleans–style baby shower with streamers, Mardi Gras beads, balloons, gumbo, a jazz band, and gallons of champagne I was not allowed to drink.

I'm not sure exactly what the etiquette is for a baby shower in a situation like ours. It's hardly the norm for the mom to be on one side of the room opening gifts and the gestational carrier to be stuffing her face with crab fingers across the house.

I had excused myself after the first big chorus of "Surprise!" Dixie had invited every single person we'd ever met to this thing—from the looks of things, she'd stumbled upon my mom's old address book—and tricked us into coming over by saying she wanted to show us the house, which was all done but the kitchen. We had tried to weasel out of it, but she showed up at Mackie's with my dad one night right around supper time and they steered us into her car.

Before I knew it, I was standing in the newly painted mango living room with its new tropically themed furniture, surrounded by a group of at least a hundred women that included my third grade teacher, every cousin I had, some now-grown girls I hadn't seen since summer camp, and more than a handful of my mother's old friends.

Dixie had gone whole hog with the party, but it didn't quite come together. There was a lot of confusion. Who was Dixie? Which sister was I? What had happened to our house? Who, exactly, was the shower for? If it was Mackie's shower, why was I so pregnant? And, for some of the people I hadn't seen since grade school, where was my mother?

It might have been a good idea to bring all these folks up to speed with a quick announcement, but we didn't think to do it. Instead, we milled around with our little purple plates of hors d'oeuvres, hugging and squealing at the ladies we hadn't seen in years. Most everyone gathered around me, since I seemed like the obvious honoree, and even though I kept explaining over and over that these were not my babies, but Mackie's, it didn't seem to register. I could feel Mackie not watching me, as she sat with our great-aunt Lina on the couch. I knew she wanted all the hugs I was getting, all the "When are you due?" questions, all the excited eyebrows as people said, "Twins?" It didn't seem to matter who the babies belonged to. The person you fawn over at a shower is the one with the belly.

Even when it was time to open presents, as Mackie worked through gift bag after gift bag with little booties and angels on them, everyone was talking to me. How much weight had I gained? What was it like to have two in there kicking? How was I sleeping? How were my ankles? I couldn't help but feel guilty for stealing Mackie's attention. Even though I hadn't. Even though the last thing in the world I wanted to do was endure the birth story of every single woman in the room. To this day, I will never feel the need to hear the term "mucus plug" again.

There was one other topic of conversation that came up again and again: Dixie. Dixie in her skintight Wranglers, rhinestone cowgirl boots, and sequined baby-blue sleeveless top.

"Who's the stripper?" our old neighbor Bonnie asked me, nodding toward Dixie.

"She's not a stripper," I said. "She's a cowgirl."

"What's she doing here?"

"She's hosting," I said. "That's my dad's fiancée."

Bonnie glanced around like it was all coming together. "So that's who's responsible for the tiger-striped throw pillows."

"Her name is Dixie," I said. "And she's fantastic."

"She certainly is."

Bonnie, a divorcée, had been one of the ladies interested in my dad after my mom died. We had erased countless messages from her off our machine—offers to bring over dinner, offers to meet up at the movies, offers "just to chat."

Bonnie was horrified and delighted by Dixie at the same time, and took on the project of pointing her out to every single person who walked by, cackling each time and saying, "Can you believe it?"

The upside was that it took the focus off me. The downside was that it set the focus down hard on Dixie's sparkly shoulders. Before I knew it, a group of my mom's old friends had gathered in the corner to mock every single thing they could come up with about Dixie. I couldn't hear their words, but every now and then a hoot of laughter would break loose from the crowd and I'd glance over and know exactly what was going on.

But Dixie didn't know it. She was tidying up after guests and keeping the snack platters full. She was wiping up spills and setting out cocktail napkins. She was keeping an eye on Mackie and bringing her champagne. She bustled back and forth around the house, passing that group of women every few minutes, and every time she walked through the dining room, I felt my body tense up.

These women were generally polite enough to know better. But several of them had been rejected, ignored, or dodged by my father in the years after my mother died, and so brought a certain competitive spirit to a party hosted by the woman who had, at long last, won his affection. Plus, once they got going, they were having too much fun to keep themselves in check. They'd found a common topic and been swept up into a fit of cattiness. They tried to keep their voices down, but it seemed inevitable that Dixie would hear them at some point.

But she did not notice when she walked past just as Nancy Sowa said, "It's got to be a wig." And she did not notice when Joyce Novotny said, "What about the sequins?" I was just about to walk over and scold the entire group when Susan Marist shouted, way more loudly than she could possibly have intended, "It just looks like Kmart threw up in here!"

I froze. And so did the whole group, Susan Marist included. Too loud! Way too loud! What was this, middle school? I glanced around for Dixie. She wasn't in the room. I closed my eyes for a second and gave a little sigh of thanks, and then started over toward the group. I knew they'd had a few mint juleps. I knew it was fun to laugh with their old friends. But they were not going to talk that way about Dixie in my mother's house—hotel soaps in the guest bath or no.

As I got closer, something caught my eye. Down near the baseboard, just around the edge of the archway and out of sight, I could see the sparkly toes of Dixie's boots. And from their stillness, I knew that she'd overheard.

Maybe I should have given her some privacy. Maybe I should have kept to myself. But in that moment, I couldn't stop from stepping around to meet Dixie's eyes. And when I saw them, they had the exact expression I would have expected, though she shook it off the moment she saw me looking.

"Don't worry about it, darlin'," she said, giving me a smile. "It doesn't matter to me."

"I'm sorry, Dixie," I said.

"They're just jealous over this." She raised her engagement ring. "And this." She framed her face with her hands. "And these." She patted her sequin-covered boobs.

I couldn't understand all this fuss over my quiet, bespectacled, balding father. He was hardly Harrison Ford. He had the physique, quite rightly, of a man who spent his work hours in the library and his off-hours playing chess.

"I don't get it," I said to Dixie. "He couldn't possibly be a catch."

"But he is," she promised. "He is a catch."

I thought of the way my dad's crazy, untrimmed beard was so often flecked with sandwich crumbs, and how it made him look pretty close to homeless. "How can that be?" I asked.

"Sweetheart," she said, resting a hand on my arm. "He's not crazy, drunk, broke, or dead. And at our age that, by definition, makes him a catch."

I took that in.

"Plus, he dates women his own age," Dixie added. Then she leaned in. "I joined a singles group at church right after my divorce," she told me, "and there was only one man in it. Do you know why?"

"Why?"

"Because all the fifty-year-old men had signed up for the thirty-year-old group."

"There was only one man in your whole group?" I asked.

Dixie nodded. "And let's just say he had a very good year."

There was a noise from around the corner, and I could hear my mom's old friends tittering about something. I glanced over. "I'm going to tell them to leave," I said.

"Don't do that," Dixie said.

"My mother would have already kicked them out by now," I told her.

"Sweetheart," Dixie said then, "I'm from the backwoods of East Texas. There's not a group of mean ladies on this earth that can scare me."

The next time I saw Dixie was at the courthouse on the day she and my father were getting "hitched." She had on a skintight, lacy white bridal gown with a long train, and she leaned over my belly to kiss me on the cheek and then wiped the mark off with her thumb. "I bought it small," she said of her dress, "and then I took it in a little."

But it was my dad who stole the show. He had on a dowdy brown suit with a little stain on his tie—no surprise there. But something was different, and it took me a second to figure out what. Then it hit me.

"You shaved!" I said.

"Dixie wanted to get a look at my face before we made it official," he said. And then he smiled and ducked his head, just barely, like he felt shy. And then I noticed something else about my dad, something I must have always known but never thought about: He had dimples.

"You look just like the old you," I said.

He winked. "The old me. But older."

The ceremony was quick and small—just Mackie, Clive, and me there to witness—and I couldn't stop staring at my dad's face. It was like getting something back that I hadn't even remembered I'd lost.

Afterward, we drank champagne from plastic cups on the courthouse steps—Mackie allowed me three sips—and then drove down to a honky-tonk in Pearland where every single person knew Dixie. To my shock, every single person seemed to know my dad, too. Turns out—who knew?—Dixie and my dad went two-stepping every Saturday with a big crowd of her friends, who all loved my dad and called him "Professor." Watching the men congratulate him with slaps on the back and the ladies leave lipstick on his soft, new cheeks, I was amazed. My dad: smiling! Laughing with these big, beefy guys in cowboy hats and gimme caps. Tapping his toe to the music. Whisking Dixie off to dance, the two of them tearing up the floor.

Mackie and I met eyes across our table. "He seems really happy," Mackie shouted over the band.

"He sure does," I shouted back.

Seeing my dad so at ease, so cheerful, so *alive*, was the best feeling I'd had in weeks. It left me with a kind of contented glow that didn't disappear all night. Even when Clive took Mackie's hand and pulled her off to the dance floor, too. Even when I accidentally spilled my ginger ale all over my eight-month belly. Even when a big cowboy wouldn't take no for an answer and steered me like a heifer around the dance floor more times than I could count. I had a good feeling that night. I kept thinking about how even the most hopelessly lost people can sometimes get found.

If my father could come back to life, I kept thinking, anybody could.

Chapter Eleven

I carried that pleasant feeling with me for more than a week. It didn't fade, in fact, until the night of the hurricane.

Everybody I'd met in New York thought of cactuses and tumbleweeds when they thought of Texas, but that's not how Houston is. It's down near the Gulf of Mexico, and the air stays wet and sultry most of the time, hot and humid like a sauna. One summer, it rained seventy-five straight days. There's so much rain in Houston, and so much deep, reverberating thunder, that we take water and floods and even hurricane season for granted. With a few notable—and terrifying—exceptions, hurricanes in Houston are not usually that big a deal.

But the week after the wedding, a doozy of a hurricane named

Imelda started making the news. Mackie grumbled about newscasters being fearmongers, and she and Clive and I spent some time debating which was getting worse—the weather itself, or the news coverage of it—without ever reaching a conclusion.

We did not evacuate, as some other people were starting to do, mostly because most predictions had Imelda making landfall closer to New Orleans.

"Poor New Orleans," Mackie said every time we turned on the news. "They just can't catch a break."

Houston didn't seem likely to get hit, and I was too pregnant to fly, and I certainly didn't want to ride in a car all the way to Austin or Dallas. Plus, somehow, the idea of leaving just seemed a little dramatic. We'd lived in this town too long to get fussed by a little wind and rain. Even Clive decided to go ahead and take his business trip to Atlanta. We made a choice not to worry.

But as we got closer and closer to the big day, Houston began to look more and more like a target. With one day to impact, and the freeways out of town clogged with traffic, Mackie and I were alone in the house, keeping the TV news on day and night, and starting to wonder if we might actually wind up getting killed.

But it was too late now. Nervously, we decided to try to make it fun. Mackie popped popcorn and made virgin margaritas. We decided to sleep in her big storage closet, and talked about moving her TV in, too—to access important weather updates, but also to watch the *Masterpiece Theatre*s in her TiVo queue. The panic and excitement of the weather crisis somehow pushed back the clouds of our own personal storm and made it easy for the two of us to get along like we used to. For the first time in ages, I found myself enjoying Mackie's company—and missing her, too, even though she was right there, because I was reminded so strongly of how good things were when they were good.

We were halfway through our drinks, and it hadn't even started raining yet, when Mackie said, "I'm sorry it takes a hurricane to keep you home."

"Three cheers for the hurricane," I said, and we toasted to it.

Then we heard a key in the back door, and there, in a poncho, with a flashlight, a bathing suit, a blanket, a trauma kit, and wearing her scrubs, was Barni.

It was the first time I'd seen her in weeks, absent as I'd been, and when I saw her supplies and realized she'd be crashing our sister party, before I could stop myself, I said, "Why didn't you evacuate like everybody else?"

She pretended to think about it. "I don't know. I think I was saving lives at the hospital."

I nodded. "Emergency liposuction?"

She came right back with a false smile. "Oh, my God. That's so funny."

I didn't want her to spoil things. "Don't you have somewhere else you could go?"

But Barni was, in her own words, "freaking." She came on inside. "Haven't you guys seen the news?" she said. "The whole city's going to be blown off the map!"

"It won't be," Mackie said firmly.

But Barni wasn't listening. "I'm too young to die!" she said, still clutching her things. "I've never even been to Europe!"

"Nobody's going to die." Mackie made her voice a perfect blend of soothing and firm—and sounded, I noticed, exactly like our mother. "We're all going to be fine."

I stood up from the sofa, thinking I'd put on a kettle for tea, but the sight of my enormous eight-month belly made Barni worse. "Oh, God," she said. "You're going to go into labor during the storm, aren't you?"

I put my hand on my hip. "I thought you were supposed to be a doctor."

"Not yet!" she said, pointing at my belly. "I haven't done that yet."

"Look, nobody's going into labor," I told Barni, copying Mackie's tone. "Not you. Not Mackie. And most certainly not me." Dr. Penthouse had actually declared a while back that it could happen "any day now," but I figured I'd keep that to myself. "We have a scheduled C-section next week," I went on, emphasizing "scheduled."

Before Barni could say another word, the doorbell rang.

Mackie walked toward the door. "Who the hell could that be?"

"It's my boyfriend," Barni said, following. "I called him to come and save us."

Oh, God, I thought. Not that boyfriend. Please let it be another boyfriend. Anybody but Everett.

I squeezed my eyes closed while Mackie opened the door and then dropped my head into my hands when she said, "Hi, Everett."

Barni squealed and shouted, "We're saved!" and a few minutes later, they all showed up in the kitchen, Barni rubbing against Everett like a cat.

And then there we were, the four of us—the only people we knew still left in the city. Clive was in Atlanta. My dad and Dixie were on their honeymoon in "New York City," where Dixie had never been. Everett's mom had evacuated with a group from his stepfather's nursing home days before. Howard and Terry were taking a "hurrication" in Santa Fe. And Rancho Verde had just packed up April and all the girls on Greyhound buses and driven them to Dallas.

Everett seemed to deflate when he saw me, and I remembered it was the first time I'd seen him since pouring beer on his crotch. But I wasn't apologizing. I knew he'd deserved it, and so did he. Enough said.

Instead, Everett looked me up and down. "You're not going into labor, are you?"

"Not if I can help it."

He frowned at my belly. "How long till your due date?"

"A month still," I said. "I'm fine."

Then Mackie put her arm around me. "Don't worry. She's way too sensible to go into labor during a hurricane."

We all got into preparation mode, and Everett turned into Disaster Guy. He piled up batteries and flashlights, filled up the bathtubs as "reservoirs" in case we lost power, and talked about creating a "collapse zone" and making us all sleep under a table. He used terms like "Roger that," and "What's the status?" and tried to organize us into patrols. He wanted to nail boards to the windows, but Mackie drew a line there.

"Those are sustainably grown hardwood frames," she said.

So Everett scouted the area for danger, charged all our cell phones, and gave out assignments. Barni and Mackie had to fill jugs of water, find blankets, and collect first aid supplies. Everett had to cut down any ominous tree branches.

"What am I doing?" I asked.

"Nothing," he said.

"I can help somehow," I said.

"You're too pregnant to help," he said. "Go knit a bootie or something."

Dismissive. And rude! And a little misogynistic. As if cutting down tree branches was in any way more impressive than creating two human beings. Who exactly, besides Barni, had voted him the boss?

I started to pick up a water jug in defiance, but he grabbed it away from me, leaned into my face, and said, "At eight months with twins, you could pop any minute. Go. Sit. Down." When I didn't move, and just stared right back at him, he added, "Please."

He wasn't wrong. So I went. But with a not-because-you-told-me-to sashay. And still thinking to myself all those mean things from a second before. Plus: *Bossy. Pompous.* And, what the hell: *A little sexy.*

Following Everett's lead, we started calling the storage closet the "safe room." The bag of Band-Aids and Neosporin became the "trauma kit." The jugs of water and boxes of granola bars became the "rations."

I started teasing Everett a little, just to make sure he knew he wasn't really the boss—to make sure he knew he was in charge only because we were letting him be. For a while, I saluted, and called him "Sarge," and "G.I. Joe," and then "Gomer Pyle." I offered to pick up things from the "mess hall" and bring them back to the "barracks." After a bit, I decided it was funnier to treat him like a pirate, and he became "Cap'n," and I tried to get him to say "arrgh." Though I'm not sure anybody thought it was funny but me.

It started to rain while we were eating dinner—suddenly, even though we'd been expecting it all day. The sky got black in the time it took to toss the salad, and when the deluge finally came, it was so thick we couldn't see the back fence. We shifted our eyes between the window and the TV news like tennis spectators until Mackie stood up, tossed her napkin on the table, and suggested we hit the safe room.

"We can do the dishes in the morning," she said. "If the house is still standing."

Upstairs, Mackie arranged pillows and blankets into a big four-person bed in the center of the room. Then she found a deck of cards, and she'd just helped me ratchet myself down to the floor for a game of gin rummy when Barni noticed my mom's dresses hanging in the corner.

"Oh, my God! What are those?" Barni set her cards down immediately—faceup—to go investigate.

"Dresses," Mackie said. "They were our mother's."

"They're gorgeous," Barni said, touching the fabric. "Can I try one on?"

"I don't think it's a good idea to leave the safe room," Everett said.

But Barni had already pulled one of the dresses off the hanger. "Then I won't," she said, and started to take off her clothes right there. We all had to look away as she changed into dress after dress, prancing around us and running her fingers through Everett's hair while we played cards.

"Those dresses are enormous on you!" Mackie said to Barni at one point, just minutes after Barni made a joke about using my belly as a footstool.

Barni loved talking about the dresses. "Aren't they huge? I've just always been this way," she said, twirling a little. "Just born healthy, I guess."

Oh, God. I hated her so much.

Barni had a weird habit of calling Everett "Boyfriend," as if it were his name. Like, "Boyfriend, what do you think of this hat?" Or, "Boyfriend, did you hear that clap of thunder?" It grated on my ears, and every time she said it, I glanced over at Everett to see if he was cringing, too—if dating somebody that wacko was embarrassing to him. Though it didn't seem to be. He didn't really even seem to notice. Or hear her at all.

Somewhere around eleven o'clock, we agreed it was a good time for lights-out. We decided to sleep in our clothes in case we had to make a dash to safety. We all stretched out—the four of us, side by side like crayons in a box—with our pillows and blankets on the berber-carpeted floor.

And despite all my attempts to get a position in the lineup as far as possible from Everett, somehow the two of us wound up right next to each other in the middle. So I just held very still, extra pillow under my belly, eyes squeezed closed, and waited for sleep—listening to the rain on the roof and the occasional gongs of thunder that seemed to shake the whole house. I didn't even peek over when Barni started whispering to Everett.

Even though I couldn't really hear what Barni was saying, it sounded like that word again, over and over: "Boyfriend." "Boyfriend." "Boyfriend." I squeezed my eyes closed tighter. I'd have closed my ears, too, if I could have.

Hours later, when a boom of thunder woke me up, I was lying on my back, like Mackie had warned me I was never supposed to do because of something about the babies' blood flow. I was thinking I should roll to my side, but there was something heavy across my body, just below my collarbone, and I could not imagine what it was. It was so black in that windowless room that I couldn't see at all, and I had to reach up to investigate with my hand.

It was an arm. It was Everett's arm.

Soon after I discovered the arm, I realized that Everett's face was close by, too. He was curled on his side, turned as far away from Barni as a person could be, with that arm stretched across me and his face close enough to the crook of my neck that I could feel his breath making eddies of air against it. I blinked my eyes to try to see better before deciding that I didn't need to. There was nothing that I needed to see. All I had to do was hold still and feel.

I'd thought sleeping in a twin bed this pregnant was uncomfortable, but sleeping on the floor of a closet took things to a new level. My back hurt, my shoulders hurt, my hips hurt, my boobs hurt. But I didn't want to move. I had to pee, but I ignored it. My butt was numb, but I ignored that, too. I just lay there for the longest time, feeling the weight of Everett's arm across me and the tickle of his breath swirling past my neck. True, he was a bossy, militaristic, kiss-

'em-and-leave-'em jerk who had refused to say "landlubbers" even when I'd offered him fifty bucks, but I could easily have stayed like that until morning.

Except that right then one of the babies moved, or rolled, or did some kind of acrobatic thing, and then pressed some pointy body part into my bladder—making it very clear that if I did not get up right away I was going to wet my pants.

I moved Everett's arm and crawled away, hoisting my body up from the floor as quietly as I could.

After I'd peed, and washed my face, and gazed out the back window for a while, I couldn't bring myself to go back into that closet. The rain was sheeting down, and the pool had overflowed, and the sight of it, though a little terrifying, was also a little beautiful. I flipped on the TV news to see what was going on with the storm and was relieved to hear that it had spun off in yet another new direction, to the weatherman's surprise and delight, and was losing steam fast and headed off to the west—toward nowhere in particular. The rain we had now, he was concluding, was the worst of it we'd get. I watched for a few minutes, then snapped the set back off and sat on the sofa by the big windows, watching the rain for a while.

And then someone sat down next to me. Everett.

He sat close. Close enough that I knew if Barni could see her Boyfriend, Boyfriend, Boyfriend, she would not be too happy. He'd startled me, sneaking up like that, and I was just about to tell him so when I noticed the look on his face. He was staring at me very intently, like he was thinking about something important, or feeling something important, or about to do something important. I held myself still and waited for it and thought about how he always seemed to be shifting back and forth between interest and disinterest, between affection and anger, between hot and cold. I never quite knew what to expect.

But at this moment, when he finally spoke, after all that buildup, I knew what I expected. I expected something momentous.

Here's what I got instead: "Did you just flush?"

"What?"

"Nobody's supposed to flush, remember?"

I stared at him.

"We talked about it," he said. "No flushing! We have to conserve water in the lines."

We had talked about it—or, at least, he had.

"I forgot," I said.

"Well, you can't forget," Everett said.

"What are you, the potty police?"

"We could be trapped here for days with no water. Do you really want to flush it away?"

"Actually," I said, "the storm just shifted. It's headed out west."

He looked outside to check the weather itself against my statement.

"I just saw it on the news," I promised. Then I said, "That's why you came out here? To talk about flushing?"

"I came out here because you woke me up and I couldn't get back to sleep." His voice was a little accusatory, like I'd been inconsiderate. Like I'd been the one not following the etiquette of sleeping side by side.

"I woke you up?"

"Yes."

"I woke you up because I had tiny human beings poking my bladder, and I was about to pee all over the place, and you"—here, I pointed at him—"were practically sleeping on top of me." Then, to underscore the point: "I had to *excavate* myself out from under you."

Who knows where the conversation could have gone from there.

Things were certainly more out in the open than they had been. We were alone, in the rain, and we'd just been snuggling. If we'd had a little more time, we might have wound up talking, or fighting, about almost anything. But we didn't have more time. Because next, something happened: I felt a warm rush of fluid gush out of my body.

I stood right up. "Oh, my God!" I could feel the wetness running down the insides of my thighs.

"What?" Everett stood up, too.

"I think my water's breaking!"

Everett looked at the puddle collecting on the floor between my shoes. "I thought the babies were scheduled for next week."

I gave a short sigh. "A towel would be helpful," I said.

When he got back, he had this to offer: "Maybe you're just peeing on yourself."

"This is not peeing," I said. "Besides, I just peed. Remember, Potty Man? *I think I know what peeing feels like.*"

Although, when Dr. Penthouse answered her page minutes later, the first thing she said was "Maybe you're just peeing on yourself."

"What?"

"Sometimes that can happen, near the end."

"Is that what's happening?" I asked, looking for an answer from a person who was not even in the room, or even the city. A person who had evacuated to Martha's Vineyard days earlier.

"If it's your water breaking," she said, "it'll keep coming. If it's just pee, it'll stop."

Suffice it to say, it kept coming. A lot. And so, my labor had started. But not, as I've pointed out to many people many times, until after the hurricane was over.

"You said you weren't going to do this!" Mackie said after Everett woke her. She brought me some more towels and checked the sofa cushions.

"I'm sorry!" I said.

And that's how the four of us—Mackie, Barni, Everett, and I—wound up plowing through the flooded streets of Houston, in his Jeep, in the rain, at three in the morning, to the hospital.

That's also how Mackie became the mama, and I became the auntie, of two girls, just as Mackie had predicted—and I had known all along. Mackie and Clive named both for me: baby Sarah and baby Jane. Two perfect fraternal twins. Or, as the doctor on call that night put it, more accurately, using a word that was just as beautiful: Sisters.

I'm not going into too many details of the birth. It's enough to say it was horrible. And wonderful. Both in equal measure. And everyone says you forget the pain of childbirth. And I really, really hope that's true.

The babies came in three hours. Three hours total. I was fully dilated by the time we made it to the delivery room, and then the babies just tumbled out like groceries through a wet sack. They came too fast for a C-section. They came too fast for an epidural. The hospital staff was delighted with me. "It's like you were born to do this!" one nurse chirped.

"Please don't say that," I said.

Here's what I wanted: My C-section. I wanted to lie still and have this situation taken care of by professionals. I had never even entertained the thought of actually giving birth to those babies. I was simply going to check into the hospital and have them removed.

But it's amazing how often the universe gives you the opposite of what you want. That night, as the floodwaters were still rising outside, I did most of my laboring in the emergency waiting room in a wheelchair—as a dull-eyed receptionist who was completely unimpressed by the miracle of life taking place before her eyes noted every detail of my medical insurance and practically did my taxes before letting us through.

"Isn't this the *emergency* room?" Mackie kept saying to anyone in scrubs. "Can't you guys see we have an *emergency*?"

At one point, a gunshot victim cut in front of us in line. I remember Everett, who had been pacing mutely around like a guard on watch, turning to Mackie to say, "Who gets shot during a hurricane?"

To which Mackie replied, "Who has a baby during a hurricane?"

Barni took me on as her responsibility, checking my pulse and timing my contractions. But she wasn't much help, and she was even a little pouty because we hadn't gone to the hospital where she worked.

"It's not on her insurance list," Mackie kept explaining.

And Barni kept saying, "It's fine. It's totally fine."

We barely made it to the delivery room. I swear, I almost had the babies in the hallway just outside. As it was, we hadn't even had a chance to tie my gown. Barni and Everett were told to wait outside, and Barni was still trying to argue her way in as the door clicked shut.

Then it was just Mackie and me. And next, in less time than seemed possible after all these months of planning for the big day when I'd give birth, the whole thing was over, the babies were cleaned up and swaddled, and we were each holding one in our arms. I'd wanted them both to go to Mackie. I'd tried, actually, to wave the nurse away from me as she brought the baby over. But she held the little bundle out to me, and I didn't know how to deflect it without ruining what was supposed to be a beautiful moment that we'd all remember fondly forever. So I took it. Her.

Even before the baby was in my arms, I knew I shouldn't look. As curious as I was, I had this clear feeling that I should not, under any circumstances, do any of the things that mothers do. I was not this baby's mother, and nothing in the world at that moment seemed as important as staying clear on that one simple fact.

I closed my eyes and turned my head away.

Mackie was gazing down and cooing at hers, chattering away with questions like "Who's a bug? Who's a little bug?" and exclaiming like crazy over the little cowlick and the little eyebrows and the little earlobes. I felt so bad for the twin who had wound up with me.

After a minute, Mackie paused to look up and say, "I can't believe Clive missed this!" and then she noticed my closed eyes and my posture.

"What's wrong?" Mackie asked.

"Nothing," I said, still not looking. "I'm just so unbelievably tired."

"Oh—" Mackie said. "Of course."

"Could you take this one, too, for a minute?"

"Sure!" Mackie said, stepping over closer. "Isn't she beautiful, though?" Mackie asked, as the nurse made the transfer.

I nodded, eyes still closed, and said, "She absolutely is." And I wasn't lying, even though I'd never looked at her face. She was beautiful. I didn't need my eyes to know that.

Then I pretended to be asleep, listening to Mackie coo, until I finally really was.

The babies were a month early—technically, two days shy of full-term. But they were plenty big and healthy, and they didn't have to stay too long in the hospital, and neither did I. I did not face any complications, and Mackie, as she had promised, brought champagne later to the hospital room. Once the babies were dozing in the nursery, we celebrated. Though I didn't feel much like celebrating. I felt many other things. Dopey from the pain pills the nurses kept bringing. And relieved. And happy for Mackie. And glad to be finished. And also, honestly, on many different levels and in every sense of the word: *empty.*

So, I slept. Slept and slept. Once I got my strength back, I would turn my attention to other things. But in those fuzzy days in the hospital, I just dozed, comforting myself with the knowledge that my work, at least for the moment, was done.

Mackie's work, though, was just getting started.

I remember a whole host of nurses and residents tromping in and out of my room in the days after the babies came. A beautiful pot of hydrangeas arrived from the folks at the Preservation Society. Clive, who had raced back to town through all the post-hurricane pandemonium to join us, stopped to check on me a couple of times. He also brought me a big order of takeout sushi, which was something I had sorely missed. Dixie and my dad cut their honeymoon short to get home to us—and I remember my dad giving me a Statue of Liberty snow globe, and Dixie sitting by my bed almost every time I opened my eyes, sewing sequins onto a pink faux-fur throw pillow.

"Whatcha makin' there?" I asked one time.

"For the nursery," she said, and held it up.

I had plenty of visitors. Howard and Barbara and every single librarian. Barni even came, and brought the phone number of a personal trainer who could "help anyone." But after that first day, when we drank champagne, I didn't remember seeing Mackie even once.

It was okay, I told myself. She had her hands full. And no matter what kind of a challenge it was to be pregnant, it could be no match for the sudden ass-kicking of becoming a mother to twins.

But, as much as I could understand about Mackie in theory, I couldn't help but feel a windy hollowness behind my rib cage. In truth, I had been assuming that once the pregnancy was over, things would all go back to normal, and Mackie and I would find each other again.

Which could not have been further from what happened—and it took me a little while to understand that there was no Mackie to find. She was so absent from my life, with those babies, she might never have even been there at all. Once they arrived, Mackie just disappeared.

But, to be fair, so did I.

Chapter Twelve

By the time I left the hospital, the floodwaters had all drained and the sun was out. My dad and Dixie drove me back, detouring to take me past the big oak that had been struck by lightning in the storm.

We made the baby transfer official, and Mackie and Clive left the hospital with them as entirely new people—as parents.

I left the hospital, at best, as an old person: the old me.

"We're not going to Mackie's?" I asked, as we pulled up in my dad's driveway.

Dixie turned around from the front seat. "They'll have their hands full over there. And those babies do a lot of crying. We thought you might like to stay here for a couple of days."

I nodded. That sounded good. Better, at least, than crying babies. Though I did get the feeling the decision wasn't entirely up to me.

My dad got the bags while Dixie helped me up the walk and reminded me that I hadn't seen the new kitchen yet.

"Would you like the tour?" she asked, once we'd shuffled inside.

"I think I might just lie down," I said. I was a little off balance in many ways.

Dixie and my dad helped me up to my old room, which Dixie had made good on her promise not to touch, and there, while Dixie went down to get me a hot water bottle and some vegetable soup, I lay on my childhood bed, gazing up at a poster of Eddie Vedder I'd stapled to the underside of the canopy.

"Eddie," I said to him in a whisper. "What was I thinking?"

I wound up staying much longer than a couple of days at my dad's house—though from then on, I would really think of it as Dixie's house. Every few days, I'd ask Dixie if she thought I should go home, and she'd wrinkle her nose and say, "Maybe another day or two."

Instead, Dixie and I just got hooked on *Days of Our Lives*.

I had to hand it to Dixie. She rose to the occasion. She spent most of her days taking care of Mackie and the rest taking care of me. "I don't know who needs me worse," Dixie said one evening, and then, not unkindly, or at least not intentionally so, added, "But at least Mackie has a husband."

One afternoon when she was checking on me, Dixie decided my hands looked dry, and she sat by the bed and rubbed lotion on them while I closed my eyes. I thanked Dixie for all her help, and somehow I wound up telling her about how I'd rubbed my mother with lotion when she'd been sick in the hospital. I'd wanted to rub her hands, but her arms had IVs, so I'd pulled back the sheet and gone to work on her feet whenever I wanted to do something for her. I felt, in that strange, sterile room, like any human touch had to be a comfort. I felt like I was helping her, in however small a way.

Then Dixie and I got to talking about my mom, and I couldn't help but notice that I felt a little disloyal for liking Dixie so much. Part of me still saw her as the competition.

But Dixie didn't view it that way. "Your mother will always be your daddy's one true love," she said. Then she leaned in and winked at me. "But that's okay with me, because I have a true love of my own."

"You do?" I asked.

She nodded. Then she stood up and pulled the waist of her jeans down a little to expose her hip. And there, at least the width of a grapefruit, was a full-color tattoo—sideburns, sunglasses, and all—of Elvis, circa 1972.

Pretty soon, I was feeling good. I don't know if it was all that soup Dixie kept bringing me, or just sheer determination—but within a couple of weeks after the birth, I was a lot better. The emptiness I'd felt just after the babies were born went away, and I reverted pretty fast to my default setting of *just me*.

Early on, I made a list of things to do. First was to get my body back, and I studied several "new mom" websites to form a plan of attack. I wrote down a schedule of activities for the following weeks that involved walking, weight lifting, a spa day, a haircut, salads, a temporary tattoo of Rosie the Riveter, and hourly minisessions of Kegels. Ugh.

Websites—and common sense—told me that many women had trouble getting in shape after giving birth, especially to twins. But those women, most of them, anyway, had motherhood to contend with after the birth. I'd gained only about forty pounds during the pregnancy—not bad for twins—thanks to Mackie and her whole wheat spaghettini. Plus, I had done quite a bit of walking. I saw no reason I couldn't pull myself together lickety-split. I did not have sleep deprivation or lactating mammaries or the panic of tiny new lives depending entirely on me every second. I had no one but me, and as sad as that was, it was lucky, too.

Other postpregnancy projects included resting, sleeping, and oohing and aahing over Dixie's brand-new kitchen. It seemed like the least I could do.

"It's French Provincial," Dixie said, when I saw it. "They shipped everything over from France." Then she showed me the baguette drawer. "I don't care for them too much, myself," she added. "But the French do."

She had spared no expense with that ex-husband's money. She had taken the place down to its studs and even moved one of the windows. She'd custom-ordered wooden panels for the fridge doors, imported stone from Provence for the countertops, and bought a new set of copper pots to hang from a rack above the Viking range. The kitchen blinds had a remote control.

It was, to put it mildly, not my taste. In fact, the only way I could stand in the place without feeling dizzy was to pretend that we were in a different house, in a different neighborhood, in a different city. But, for Dixie's sake, I faked it like a champ.

And who was I to say that this ornate, self-conscious, over-the-top kitchen was not better than the one that had been there before? I had preferred my mother's kitchen, true—with its Formica counters, its trim little fridge covered in reminder notes, its wooden dinette table, its home-sewn café curtains. But maybe what I really had preferred was my mother. Or the idea of my mother. Or the not-even-possible possibility that one lucky day I might walk in and see her scrambling eggs in her blue terry cloth robe.

This kitchen, here, now, was not a place my mother would ever stand in. I couldn't see her there. I couldn't feel her there. The newness of the place made it seem like my mother had never even been there at all. And then, just like that, I'd really lost her. I didn't know much in the days after giving birth, but I knew that. My mother would never come home if she didn't have a home to come back to.

But I had to love Dixie. How could I not? She was a caretaker. Of laundry, of plants, of people. She liked to help things flourish. One of her two rescue shih tzus had even taken second place at the Shih Tzu Shindig in San Marcos—not six months after she'd found him "eating worms from the garbage" out behind her condo. Dixie clicked around in those little low heels and clip-on earrings with a zest that was positively contagious. I felt it, my dad felt it. Even Mackie felt it.

Dixie cooked warm and soothing meals, kept the place spotless, and had the television running day and night in the family room "just for company." She was always bustling with a project, on her way to something or on her way back from something. She did not hold still, or pause to worry about things, or mope. As much as I disliked her decor—and the tiki-hut shirts she kept buying my dad—there was no way to deny she could bring things back to life. At night, when my dad was home, we'd eat steak dinners and then watch TV in the living room while she made coffee and sliced pieces of cake.

Maybe she had turned the place into Dixiewood, but I could see what my dad was drawn to. He had lucked out when he found her, and I made sure to tell her so. And him, too.

The truth is, you can't have everything. You can't have the old and the new at the same time. And so I chose Dixie over longing for the past. Just like my dad did. As if there had been any choice there at all.

In theory, the plan was to recuperate from the birth and start working on moving back to New York. I would stay to help with the library project, of course, but then I'd be returning in good time to my old life. Because my sense of myself as a New Yorker was fading. And if I wanted to get it back, I needed to chase it down.

But I didn't feel like chasing it down. I was tired. And life in

Houston was pretty comfortable. I would have expected to be on the phone from the hospital, arranging with my old roommate the specifics of my return. But I wasn't.

Early on, I had a lot of visitors. Almost every person who worked at the Preservation Society either stopped by or called. They said they missed me at the office. Relatives and old friends came by with flowers and food. I'd meet them in the new living room while Dixie brought us coffee and cookies. Even after I went back to work in the mornings, I'd still let Dixie pamper me in the afternoons. She was impossible to resist.

For about a month, I lounged around and did nothing except sort my mother's things and organize them into keepsake boxes while listening to Peter, Paul and Mary. I had six weeks of maternity leave, and though I had not expected to take them all, I did not expect the time to fly like it did, either. I felt a distinct temptation to stay in that house forever, getting loved like one of Dixie's rescue animals. But then, right around the same time, three things happened to pull me back to my real life.

The first thing was a visitor. One afternoon, when I'd been there about a month, Dixie clicked along the hall, peeked in my room, where I'd fallen asleep with a book on my chest, and whispered from the doorway, "There's a handsome man here who says he used to be your boyfriend."

I hadn't seen Everett since the emergency waiting room, and I told Dixie to tell him I was in the shower while I got myself cleaned up. I hated him, yes. But I wasn't going downstairs without washing up, brushing, flossing, putting my hair back, and putting on some clean clothes, lipstick, and mascara.

In the end, he waited almost thirty minutes before I showed up. I'd have made him wait longer, but I got impatient.

By the time I arrived in the kitchen, Dixie was cooking up a late-afternoon snack of toasted English muffins and hotel-jar jam, and I was feeling a tingle of nervousness at seeing him again.

But the guy I found there was not Everett at all. It was J.J.

He looked up and said, "You look terrible."

And I just turned to go right back upstairs.

But J.J. ran over. "Wait!" he said.

He was disheveled—tie open, collar unbuttoned, five o'clock shadow. He looked like a person who'd truly come a long, long way.

I said, "What on earth could you possibly be doing here?" Maybe it was my tone of voice, but Dixie scuttled out of the room then, leaving a half-buttered muffin.

"She's gone," he told me.

"Who's gone?" The wife? The mistress? The cleaning lady?

"Veronica!"

"You know that's not her name, don't you?"

"I'm serious! She's escaped!"

His eyes looked bloodshot, and he'd been shredding his napkin. I handed him the unfinished muffin. "When?" I asked.

"You have to help me find her!"

And I did feel, at that moment, like I had to help him find her. Not for his sake, really, but for hers.

"Fine," I said. "But I'm driving." A few minutes later, as we walked to his rental car, I said, "How did you even find me?"

"My secretary." J.J. shrugged. "She said to tell you she's sorry."

"I still hate you," I said.

"Join the club."

As we drove, he laid it all out. "Veronica" had escaped during "some kind of tornado" as the facility was evacuating to Dallas. They'd stopped at a Whataburger, and she'd disappeared during a bathroom break—telling one of the girls that she was going to hitchhike back to New York, where love was waiting for her.

That had been a month ago! Funny that I'd been feeling so guilty since the babies for not visiting her, and she wasn't even there. Once I was no longer at Mackie and Clive's, I didn't feel such a strong compulsion to drive out to the country every day. And now that I had Dixie taking care of me, my need for company had receded, too. But if I'd even called to check in, I'd have known, at least, that April was missing. Now I felt even guiltier. I might have been able to help out in some way. Though I'm not sure what I could have done.

J.J. hadn't been notified because he wasn't family. He'd found out only because he happened to call, and that gracious receptionist had spilled the whole story.

It was bad. And J.J.'d had an entire plane ride to ruminate on just how bad it was. "She could be dead," he said. "She could be maimed. She could be lost, or hurt, or trapped." He put his head in his hands. "Anybody could have picked her up on that highway. Anybody."

Was this love or craziness? Charming or creepy? Passion or perversion? It was a tough call.

"So you called to talk to her?"

He nodded.

"And they said she'd gone missing?"

He nodded.

"And then you caught the next plane to Texas?"

He nodded again.

"Did you tell your wife where you were going?"

"She thinks I'm on a fishing trip."

"Maybe that's a blessing," I said. And then, "Is she still pregnant?"

He started tapping his head against the window.

"J.J.," I said then. "Even if you find this girl, you can't be with her."

"What do you mean?"

"She's a child," I said. "Or, at least, she's not a grown-up."

"I'm in love with her," J.J. said.

"You can't be. You just can't be," I said. "She's never even had an orgasm."

"She told you that?"

"She did. And it's not just because you're bad in bed, though I'm sure that doesn't help."

He put his head in his hands again.

"It's because she's *posing,* J.J., when she's in bed. She's so busy posing that she misses the whole point." I paused a minute before something hit me: "And that's not just sex. That's her whole life."

We went around and around about this topic on the drive out. Me trying to make him see the irony that the girl our agency had turned into a national sex symbol did not even like sex. Him refusing to see how that was relevant to the topic at hand.

"You need to leave this girl alone and go back to your wife," I said. "Be a grown-up!"

"But she loves me," he argued.

"She doesn't know what love is," I said. "And neither do you."

"I just need to see her again," he said.

"You don't even know her name!" I said. "And guess what, Mr. Dynamite? She doesn't know yours, either!"

When we arrived at Rancho Verde, J.J. gave the receptionist a piece of his mind. How could they have been so lax? Didn't they know she was a fragile person—and also a little sneaky? He stomped around. He banged on the desk. He threatened to sue. Finally, the receptionist called the director to come in from home.

The director arrived a few minutes later without his jacket or tie and stood motionless while J.J. did an encore. The sun was setting, and the director had the distinct look of a man who had been just about to take his first bite of supper when the phone rang. He flipped through April's file while J.J. stood tall and self-righteous, a little breathless, nostrils flared.

"Looks like Miss Schneider is home with her parents now," the director began.

"Miss Schneider?" J.J. started up. "That's not even the right file!"

But I poked him, and then nodded. "That's the right file," I said. "April May Schneider."

J.J. stared at me as the director said, "I can't give you the family's contact information. But I'm going to head back home to eat my supper. And I will thoughtlessly leave the file right here on the desk."

And he left. We wrote the number on a Post-it and walked back to the car.

I'd had hopes for April that she might wind up working at Rancho Verde and spend her life in the tall grass in jeans and sneakers, gathering eggs and brushing down horses. Perhaps becoming a naturalist or a bird-watcher. When I imagined a happy ending for her, that was what I saw. A simple, wholesome life on the land. But maybe I was reaching too far by creating a master plan of happiness for her, given that I couldn't even pull together my own.

Who knew? Maybe J.J. would find her in the morning and profess all kinds of love. And maybe J.J.'s wife would wind up with a better man and get a second chance at getting it right.

Or maybe they would all just barrel on through their lives, snatching at happiness when they could, stumbling through one incomprehensible moment just to stumble through another. Kind of like the rest of us.

The second thing that happened, right around that same time, was a talking-to. Dixie asked me to come with her to the grocery store one morning, and on the way, in her owl-eye sunglasses, she turned off

Reba McEntire and patted me on the knee. Then she said, "I know why you haven't visited your sister."

"I haven't *not* visited her," I said. "I just haven't happened to visit."

But I was covering. I hadn't visited, it was true. I'd tried to make myself go over several times, but each time, I found my stomach squeezed into a little fist at the idea, and I'd stop at the door.

With Mackie, it became just another thing we didn't talk about.

But Dixie was on to me. And there was almost nothing Dixie didn't talk about. "You're afraid of those babies," she said.

It's not often in life that a person you really don't know all that well tells you something true about yourself that you hadn't quite realized. But she was right. She was so right, I didn't even bother to argue. Or speak. I just tilted back against the headrest and listened all the way to the store while she told it like it was.

"You're afraid you're going to want them. You're afraid they're going to feel like yours. You're afraid it's going to tear you to pieces to see them. And it might. It just might." A guy in a Mini Cooper ran a red light, and Dixie leaned on the horn. "But you have to go anyway. Because sometimes you have to be brave for the people you love."

What was there to add to that? She'd pretty much said it all. Now we knew the truth. But knowing the truth is not always that useful. It's not like it changes anything.

I wasn't just afraid that seeing the babies might tear me to pieces, I knew for certain that it would. I knew I wasn't ready, and I knew I needed some time, just as surely as I knew Mackie was overwhelmed and desperate to see me. I could see Mackie's side of it, yes—but I could see my own so much more clearly.

"I'll go with you, if you like," Dixie said.

But I didn't want to go. Un-pregnant, I had a new sense of my possibilities. I wanted to go out. I wanted to feel good. Hanging out with Mackie seemed like the wrong direction. Now, after months and months, I could sleep on my stomach, I could roll over in bed, and I could touch my toes. Miracles! I was like a postpartum wondergirl and I amazed myself over and over with my skills. I still had a long way to go, but it seemed like there was nothing I couldn't face. Nothing, that is, except for Mackie.

The best I could do with Mackie was short spurts on the phone. Inevitably, she got called away by some spit-up crisis or exploding diaper catastrophe after a few minutes. Phone calls with her these days were only the most basic conversational transactions. They didn't much resemble talking:

"How are you doing?"

"Okay. Not too bad."

"Did you get any sleep?"

"Not really."

"What are you up to right now?"

"Eating cold pasta and a bag of chocolate chips."

That kind of thing.

They'd hired a baby nurse, but she didn't seem to do much good. Mackie slept while she was there, and as soon as she left, Mackie was alone again. Clive helped out, but he seemed to find a lot of reasons to need to go to the warehouse. The babies were on wildly different schedules, and as soon as Mackie finished putting one to sleep, the other would wake up.

Mackie was not herself. My cool cucumber sister, who was almost never flustered, sounded frantic most of the time. She burst into tears at the craziest things. She hung up on me constantly to go deal with those babies without even saying good-bye. Sometimes she didn't even hang up, actually. She'd just set the phone down and walk away, and it was a sentence or two before I figured out there was no one on the other end. She said the house was a mess—diapers and spit-up cloths and bottles—both washed and unwashed—littering every surface, and Dixie verified it.

"Maybe you should see more of the baby nurse," I suggested.

But Mackie shouted, "No!" Then she gave a sigh that was half growl. "I'm trying to bond."

Mackie's perfect life was a little bit in shambles, and I did have sympathy for her. More than once, when a baby screeched into the phone, I made the joke, "Is that Clive?" But it never made Mackie laugh—and one time it made her cry.

I knew she wanted me to come help her and keep her company and warm up bottles for the girls while she took a shower. But I couldn't help but think that was Clive's job. Right? I'd seen a little feature on Dixie's TV about how men often disappeared after a new baby came. They felt overwhelmed and unsure of themselves. They missed their wives. They felt out of control. And so they threw themselves into work or chores or golf until they figured it out—even though sometimes it took months, or years, or never happened at all.

But that didn't seem to fit Clive. He was a good guy. He'd bought a camcorder to capture the moments, and put a bumper sticker on his car that said, WHO'S YOUR DADDY? Even if Mackie wasn't exaggerating about how busy he'd become, I was sure he'd snap out of it soon. Here was his chance to benefit from that fantastic paternity-leave package he'd set up and take his full six weeks. If I swooped in and did everything for him, he'd never have to figure out how to help. I told myself it was tough love. But what can I say? I also really, really, really didn't want to go over there.

One time on the phone, Mackie said, "Can you have postpartum depression if you never gave birth?"

"Sure!" I said. "Depression is for everybody."

As awful as it sounds, she was bringing me down. I'd felt bad long enough. I wanted to feel better. It's embarrassing to confess it, but sometimes I avoided her calls. I know I sounded a lot more magnanimous back in the beginning, when I was offering up my womb so graciously. I was a great sister then. Hell, I was a great *person*! Now I was a little less great. But that didn't change anything. Guilt could make me answer the phone, but nothing on earth could make me visit.

I wished them well, but I was kind of done. For now, at least.

Besides, I had a new project. Because then a third thing happened to pull me back into the world. I went back to work.

Almost as soon as I was out of the hospital, Howard was calling me. Time was getting shorter—as of the girls' birthday, September 17, there were only two months left before the referendum. My second day at Dixie's, Howard called to ask, "When do you think you'll be in?"

"Don't I get like six weeks off?" I asked.

"We don't have six weeks," Howard said. "We need you back *pronto*. And you're missing all the fun."

It still took me a month to go back, and by the time I did Howard had already planned our prereferendum awareness-raising event without me. I missed the first two meetings—"due to childbirth," Howard had written in the minutes—but the third one was scheduled for the very morning of my return, and they waited to start it until I got there.

I almost didn't go. I almost stayed at Dixie's and spent the day in front of the *Sex and the City* marathon playing on cable. But if I hadn't gone, Howard would not have had the chance to tell me that everybody in the office had "taken a shine" to me and wanted me to come work there full-time. If I hadn't gone, I wouldn't have been offered the fancy position of Endangered Structure Coordinator. And, most important, if I hadn't gone, Howard might not have talked me into the brilliant, earth-shattering idea he'd had for publicizing the library. An idea so great, it couldn't fail. An idea so great, we might as well have moved the library from "endangered" to "saved" on our website right then and there.

An idea, also, that had the potential to get me killed.

"But that's why it's so brilliant," Howard said, and I believed him.

• • •

At the meeting, folks were crowded around the table, and the room was too warm. Everyone hushed as I walked in—at that point I was four weeks postpartum—and stared at me with shy smiles. I still didn't fit into my prepregnancy clothes, and I'd considered wearing one of my maternity suits back to work. In the end, I'd decided on a black T-shirt, which Dixie ironed for me, and some stretchy black sweats. If I'd realized what a splash my arrival was going to make, I'd have accessorized more.

But then I started to detect a kind of nervousness to their attention, and then, when Howard began the meeting, I noticed that half the people in the room were watching him speak, and the other half were staring at me.

Howard started by welcoming me back, and I noticed that he was watching me, too. Speaking only to me and flashing big, un-Howard smiles that came across more like grimaces. I sat up a little straighter and listened closely.

"As you know, Sarah," Howard began, "we've had two planning meetings that you've had to miss because of your"—he searched for the word—"condition."

I nodded.

"Those meetings were very productive. We really had some great ideas."

I nodded again.

"In fact, we had one idea that is so exciting and headline-grabbing and unprecedented that it may just work."

He was taking too long. "What was it, Howard?" I asked.

But Howard wouldn't be rushed. He wanted to set the scene: They'd been throwing out ideas for a pre-referendum rally, some way to get everybody jazzed up before voting day—and someone threw out the idea of doing a read-in on the library lawn, with the librarians bringing books out. Then Ryan the fall intern had suggested that people bring picnic blankets and read to their kids, and Tom the bookkeeper tossed out the name of a Western swing band. Before they knew it, the whole room was calling it the "Read-In at the Love Library," and Mimi the bookkeeper was suggesting releasing a flock of ninety-nine heart-shaped balloons—one balloon for each year the library had stood. Then Barbara suggested a kissing booth.

Here, Howard paused, and said, "I don't know how ideas happen, Sarah. But the next one was brilliant."

All the faces in the room were watching me now.

"These are great ideas so far," I said, and I meant it.

Then Howard went on. "But this is a big city full of people. A cute little neighborhood party wasn't going to cut it. We needed something big. We needed something totally insane."

"And you were just the guy to come up with it," I said.

Howard nodded, so serious. "You know the widow's walk balcony on top of the library's dome?"

I nodded.

"It's pretty wide across," Howard said. "Maybe seven feet or so."

I nodded again.

"And it has a railing around it. And you can get up there. It has a trapdoor with some iron steps leading up from inside."

"You want to do something crazy on that roof," I guessed.

Howard couldn't not smile. "I do," he said. "I want to send someone to stay up there. One hour for every year since the library was built."

"That's ninety-nine hours!" I said.

"Yep," Howard said.

"That's four days!" I said.

"Yep," Howard said.

And then, in a flash of certainty, I knew that it was the perfect thing to do.

"Howard," I said. "That's absolutely brilliant."

The room let out a group sigh.

"Good," Howard said. "I'm glad you think so." And then he kneeled down to where I was sitting, so his face was right in front of mine. "We really hoped you'd love the plan," he said. "Because you're the one who's going up."

Over the next hour, Howard explained to me why I was really and truly the only person in the office who could make it work. I was young, I was single, I was "telegenic" (though, he said with a wink, his cousin swore by apples and Greek olives for losing baby weight). We still had four weeks before I had to go up. "You'll be normal by then," he said with confidence. "Right?"

"I think so," I said. "I'll sure try to be."

"Well, you'll have to be," Howard said. Then he ran through his list of why all the women in the office were ineligible. "Mimi's married, and so is Carmen. Anna is afraid of heights. Maggie's a single mom. And Barbara"—he whispered this last part, double-checking that she wasn't still in the room—"is too old."

"Why does it have to be a woman?" I asked.

"Because it's a Kiss-a-Thon," Howard explained. "At the end of your vigil, you'll give one lucky winner ninety-nine kisses. Except we're going to rig it so that Ryan the intern actually does the kisses with you."

I looked around. Ryan raised his hand. I'd seen him before. He had straight, white teeth and plump, college-kid lips. Definitely kissable.

"It's a raffle," Ryan offered.

"Great," I said back.

"So, are you in?" Howard asked, and I could feel every eye in the room on me.

But I had a billion questions. Wouldn't I harm the roof? What if

I rolled off while I was sleeping? What if it rained? What about lightning? How would I shower? How would I go to the bathroom? How would I eat? Wouldn't I be so bored? What if I got attacked by a bird? And who on earth would want to kiss a girl who'd been up on a roof for four straight days?

But Howard had already worked everything out. I would take a tent, which we'd tether to the railing around the dome's roof, and a sleeping bag and a pillow and little air mattress. I'd have a cell phone and a laptop—and I'd blog the whole thing. I'd be allowed to come down for bathroom breaks, teeth brushing, and face washing, but we'd keep a big stop-clock at the scene and pause it whenever I left the dome. Barbara would be in charge of the meal delivery schedule, and she'd also recommend books to read. I'd also have a bucket of essential supplies, like water balloons, paper airplanes, and a slingshot.

We'd have a big rally on the last day, with cotton candy and a swing band playing out on the library lawn. We'd advertise the heck out of it and get all the media coverage we could. We'd bring library books out and let the librarians read to the kids. We'd let Barbara tell the story of Dr. Emmet Frost and his lady to the crowd in front of a banner that read SAVE THE LOVE LIBRARY!

And then, as a grand finale, we'd have the Kiss-a-Thon. A raffle drawing where guys in the audience could pay a dollar—which seemed awfully cheap, but Howard said we weren't in it for the money—for the chance to come up on the roof and kiss me. "Ninety-nine times?" I asked.

"Ninety-nine times," Howard confirmed.

We decided we'd put a big flip chart by the podium with numbers up to ninety-nine, and after each kiss, Ryan and I would shout out the number, and Barbara would flip it. Then, at the end of kiss ninety-nine, we'd release a flock of ninety-nine balloons and send me home for a shower.

I loved it.

Barbara, when she rejoined the meeting, was less convinced. "It's a suicide mission," she said. "A hundred dollars says whoever goes up gets struck by lightning or falls to their death."

"Barbara," I said. "This is going to work."

And there it was.

Howard knew a guy who could take a publicity photo for me that we could plaster all over town. "She'll need a stylist," Howard said to Barbara, as if I weren't standing right there. He gestured toward my curls. "Maybe straighten those things out. And some very good lighting." He paused then to study my face, his own squeezed into a worried frown. Then he relaxed. "It'll be fine," he said. "This guy can make anybody gorgeous."

The next day, Barbara and Howard's semicareful evaluation of the roof proclaimed it "in pretty good shape," though at this point, we were all so gung ho about my going up that there wasn't much point in even checking it out. They made me promise I'd wear a safety harness at all times, even while sleeping, and stay hooked to the railing, which seemed sturdy, and I promised I would. Though I'd have promised anything.

The more I imagined it, the more delighted I felt. Maybe I just needed a new adventure. Maybe things down on the ground weren't working out for me the way I had hoped. Maybe I just wanted to see something go right for a change. But the more I thought about spending four days up on that roof, the more I couldn't wait. I'd have gone up even if it had been rotten, even if it had been rusted, even if it had been full of holes.

"I knew you'd do it," Howard said, giving me an air-hug. "Just like I knew you'd take the job with us."

"Am I taking the job?" I asked. In all the commotion, I'd almost forgotten about it.

"Aren't you?" Howard said. "You'd be crazy not to. You're not worth half that salary."

"Well," I said, frowning. "I'm supposed to move back to New York. That's the plan."

"You can move back to New York anytime," Howard said. "Jobs this great are once in a lifetime."

"Why do you want me to take this job?" I asked. "You don't even like me."

"But I don't hate you," Howard said, raising an eyebrow. "And I hate everybody."

We had a month to stir up a frenzy, and we set to work publicizing. I went on radio talk shows and public television. We printed up a new set of bumper stickers that said just: 99 KISSES, with "www.savethe lovelibrary.org" underneath. Howard's friend took my photo, after putting so much makeup on me that I was unrecognizable. We changed our billboards to feature my glamour shot. There I was, all glammed up, all over town: KISS THIS GIRL AND SAVE THE LOVE LIBRARY!

And in the meantime, I started looking for an apartment. That's how I wound up moving home to Houston: by accident. By walking backward while telling myself I was walking forward. By planning to want one thing, and then actually wanting another. It was a big decision to move home, and even as I was making it, I fully expected to change my mind.

I started circling ads in the paper and driving around to look at apartments. The central part of Houston has a hearty selection of cute little duplexes from the twenties and thirties and forties. I ruled out anything without central air-conditioning and anything that wasn't straight-up adorable from the curb. I figured, if a landlord didn't know how to take care of the outside of a building, there was no hope for the inside. Officially, I was not in a rush. I had a place to stay already, after all. Two, really.

I wanted to find something amazing, and amazing can be a tall order. But I also felt antsy to get started on my real life. I'd been in limbo for too long. I wanted to nest, and decorate, and liberate all my furniture from the storage facility in New Jersey where I'd left it. I arranged to have everything shipped down to Texas, which was going to take a while, and then hoped I'd find something before the truck arrived.

But nothing was quite right. My standards were too high, maybe. Some apartments were too shady. Others were too sunny. Some had been updated too much and lost all their character. Others had not been updated at all and felt grimy. I'd find a cute place on a bad street, or a bad place on a cute street. Something was always off.

And then Howard overheard me talking about it with Ryan the intern—who'd gotten a little flirty with me now that we were kissing partners—over lunch one day. He came over and grabbed me by the shoulders. "Did you just say you're looking for an apartment?" he said.

I nodded. "That's right."

"Oh, my God. Come with me." And he dragged me out of my chair at the conference table so fast that I left behind half a tuna salad sandwich and a full bottle of Evian.

Howard pulled me out to the parking lot and pointed at his car. "Get in," he said, and I did. On the drive, he made a call.

"I have someone for you," he said. "She's perfect! Can you meet us?"

After he hung up, he turned to me and said he had a friend who was moving to Paris and had six months left on the lease for his apartment. Then Howard said, "You are the luckiest person I know."

"I don't feel lucky," I said.

"Sweetheart," Howard said. "First: You need to get better at counting your blessings. And second: You haven't seen this apartment yet."

Five minutes later we were pulling up to a white stucco Spanish-style 1920s building in midtown called the Isabella Courts. The bottom floor was shops—a little art gallery, a café—and off on a side street was an enormous archway with an iron gate. A woman let us in and gave Howard the key. We were about to go up a wide set of steps to the second floor when Howard turned to me and said, "You're going to kiss me with gratitude when you see this place."

"I'm saving all my kisses for Ryan," I said.

But I could tell already it was going to be good.

We climbed the stairs. And when we got to the top, I froze in my tracks. "Oh. My. God."

"That's right," Howard said, looking around. "That's right."

Again, words can't describe it. But I'll throw out a few: a two-story courtyard filled with enormous palm trees, mosaic tiles, arches, and iron tables and chairs, with adorable little apartments looking down on it from all sides.

Howard had to jab me with his elbow. "Breathe," he said, and then he led me up a second set of steps and let me into a tall, bright apartment with cinnamon-colored hardwoods, white plaster walls, enormous windows, archways, a fireplace, French doors, and little casement kitchen windows overlooking the courtyard. Even empty— the furnishings were already on their way to France—it was gorgeous.

I stood in the middle of the room, breathless from the sight. Howard watched me look around for about sixty seconds before he flipped open his cell phone and hit Redial. And he didn't even wait for me to speak before he said into the phone, "She'll take it."

•••

Three weeks later, I was in. I took over the lease, the moving company delivered my furniture, and I spent a full day at Target getting everything else.

My own space. My own things. A sense of myself and my preferences and my colors everywhere I looked: my chocolate-milk-colored sofa, my red ceramic lamp with the drum shade, my Craftsman rocking chair and the folk-art chicken painted in reds and browns with the big words "These eggs are golden to me" across the body in funky, hand-done letters. It wasn't that I needed these things to know who I was, but it was nice to have reminders.

I wanted Mackie to come and see the place—I could think of no person I wanted to share it with more, actually—but she never left the house anymore, unless she was putting on a jogging outfit and walking one block with the double stroller before giving in to the babies' crying and going home. The situation with Mackie had been way too close for comfort for way too long, but the tensions were starting to recede—at least for me.

And the irony was not lost on me that now that I had my body back, it felt solitary. Now that I had my own apartment, it felt quiet. Now that Mackie wasn't making me crazy, she felt far away. Now that I had all the things I'd been longing for, I longed for other things.

I thought about what Dixie had said about comfort, and I wondered what things were comforting to me. I sat in my little kitchenette, there on the third night in my fabulous new place, and made a list:

THINGS THAT ARE COMFORTING:

Tea.
Warm water on your skin.
Thick socks.
Humming.
Laughter.

Fireplaces.
Taking walks with your sister.
Talking to your sister on the phone.
Having someone arrange your fruit in a smiley face.
Having someone refuse to examine your imaginary tumors.

I couldn't deny that I liked my new apartment. But looking at my list, I also couldn't deny that, for the first time in ages, I longed to see my sister again.

Chapter Thirteen

But it was time to go up on the roof.

The morning of, we met the press on the library steps. And by "press," I mean three reporters and a blogger taking pictures with her camera phone.

We'd had to work backward for the timing. The Kiss-a-Thon was slated for four o'clock on Saturday, and so I was heading up on Tuesday morning at ten. That gave me 102 hours, exactly—three hours of padding for bathroom breaks and teeth brushing. "What if I don't use all three of those hours?" I asked Howard.

"That's fine," Howard said. The only thing he cared about was that I put in my official ninety-nine before the rally at four. "If you have to put in an extra hour or two of waiting, who cares?"

"I care," I said.

But he was right enough, and at ten on Tuesday morning, we snapped a picture of me with my backpack and tent, in my "Love the Library!" T-shirt and as clean as I'd be for a long time, for the morning's press release. Then Howard gave me a quick hug, said "Don't get killed," and sent me on my way. The head librarian led me to the staircase, and then pointed me up.

At the second-floor balcony, I paused to look around and make a wish for a good outcome—that the stunt would work, that people would take notice, that we'd manage to save the building. That I wouldn't get struck by lightning.

Then I started on the second set of steps, which led up to the top of the dome. These were maintenance stairs, much narrower, hidden inside a closet door. Each step clanked. The latch at the top was padlocked, but I had the combination. Soon, I was through the trapdoor and up on top of what felt like the tallest building ever.

It was about three stories high, maybe—two stories and a dome. I had planned to stand tall and wave down to Howard to start the clock timer, but instead I crouched down and stuck my hand through the railing. Howard waved back and turned on the stopclock. I watched it run for almost two minutes before I turned my attention back to my new rooftop life.

First thing was to set up the tent, but I had too much vertigo to do it yet. Instead, I sat cross-legged in a corner and just looked around at the treetops and the sidewalks below and the cars that went by. Howard took a few pictures of me and then went back to the office. Then I was alone.

My first impulse was to call Mackie, but she had a screaming baby in the other ear and kept shouting "What? What?" as I tried to talk.

"Why even bother to answer the phone when the baby is screaming like that?" I asked.

"What?" Mackie said.

Next, I tried to get online. But though Howard had sworn up and down that there would be a wireless signal up there, I never could connect. So much for blogging the whole thing. I took a few pictures of the view. I made up stories about the people I saw down below. I put my hair back in a ponytail. I forced myself to stand at the railing and look down. And, mostly, I wondered what on earth could possibly have made coming up on this roof seem like a good idea.

I needed a project, so I set up the tent. I was supposed to tether it to each corner, but Howard had suggested I do a few extra "just in case." I hung a banner that said, WE LOVE THE LOVE LIBRARY! over the railing. I blew up my little air mattress. I unpacked my backpack: notebook, pens, colored markers, a deck of cards, two packs of granola bars, three packs of bubble gum, breath mints (for the Big Day), some knitting supplies and *The Total Knucklehead's Guide to Knitting,* clean clothes, toothbrush and toothpaste, bottles of water, my iPod, a photo of my mom with a pansy tucked behind her ear, a photo of Mackie and me at the rodeo as kids, some nail polish, six different books on the history of architecture, a biography of a trick-roping cowgirl, sunglasses, sunscreen, a baseball cap for when my hair got too dirty to see the light of day, some bottled water, and a Rubik's Cube.

By the time I was all set up, it was time for lunch.

At noon on the dot, Barbara rapped on the hatch door. "I've got food!" she shouted, and pushed it open. "How are you doing?"

"I'm good," I said. "I'm great. They should rent this place out for events."

Barbara was not supposed to stay. We didn't want to distract from the image of me alone—the crazy library lover on the rooftop. Barbara checked her watch before she left. "Two down!" she said, with an encouraging wink.

"Ninety-seven to go," I added, wondering what on earth I was going to do with them all.

But I got into a nice rhythm. I read my architecture books and took notes. I wrote in the notebook about anything that crossed my mind that seemed important. Barbara brought me novels she'd found in the stacks. The librarians stopped the clock for my bathroom breaks during the day, and Howard, because he lived close by, took the evenings. The first night I was there, I lay awake for hours, listening to the leaves in the trees and the traffic going by, wondering if the lump on the back of my neck was some kind of neck cancer, wondering who would come to my funeral. Even after I fell asleep, little things—car horns, screeching tires, the flapping of the tent—woke me up.

By the second night, I slept better. It was a pretty nice spot up there.

And, yes—I got stir crazy with only seven square feet to move around in. And, yes—I got terribly lonely. And, yes—I started talking to myself: "Now, that bird looks a lot like the other one that just flew past. I wonder if they're friends. Hey, birdie! Was that your friend?" I sang to myself, too, and accompanied myself by drumming on the roof. Selections of Beatles songs, Joan Baez, show tunes. I found that "She'll Be Comin' Round the Mountain" took on a mournful allegorical significance when sung like Bob Dylan, and it sounded kind of bawdy when done like Ethel Merman. In the end, I sang every song I could possibly think of, stringing one after another into the longest, weirdest medley ever. And of course, I did multiple versions—more than of any other tune—of "Somewhere Over the Rainbow," including the Kermit version and the real one, as a little shout-out to the Rancho.

One thing I can say about spending ninety-nine hours, give or take, up on a roof is that it gives you plenty of time to think. I thought about everybody I knew while I was up there. I thought about my old roommate Bekka, and J.J. and his wife, and April, and my dad, and Dixie, and my mother, and Everett, and the new babies, and Clive, and, most of all, Mackie. And how I was missing her. Now that the babies were with her and she wasn't pumping me full of organic couscous. Now that I had an apartment of my own, and my stuff, and my (altered, but recognizable) waist back. Now that I'd had a little time to clear my head. I missed her. I kept thinking of things I wanted to say to her, and I started keeping them on a list. And I resolved that after I got down, I would go and visit her very first thing, and it would be a long visit, full of baby cuddling and bottle washing. So what if it broke my heart?

But then, on my last night on the roof, when the librarians had gone home and the stars were all out, there was a knock on the trapdoor. Barbara had already brought my last meal of the day, so the sound scared the hell out of me. I'd been so alone for so long. My first crazy thought was that it was a robber. A very polite robber. I held still, unsure if I should answer—as if whoever it was might decide I wasn't home—and then I heard Mackie's voice. "Open up. It's me."

I was so delighted to see her. Of course, I'd have been delighted to see anybody. But I was especially delighted it was Mackie.

"How did you get past the guard?" I asked.

She said, "It turns out, he likes redheads." He'd taken one look at her and asked if we were twins, and then she gave him a box of doughnuts. Then she added, "He thinks you're cute, and he's going to enter the kiss raffle."

"Great," I said.

Mackie and I did look like twins tonight. Her hair, for the first time I could remember, was curly like mine. "What happened to your flatiron?" I asked.

"It's under a pile of something," she said. "Somewhere."

"No time for hairstyling?" I asked.

Mackie shook her head.

Then I said, "Lucky for you it looks better curly."

Mackie smiled. "So you say."

I wasn't supposed to have visitors, so I whisked her into the tent, and when we were all zipped up, she looked around. "They're doing constant updates on you on the news," she said.

"Barbara's been telling me."

"The last one had footage of you trying to juggle an apple, an orange, and your tube of toothpaste."

I shrugged. "I'm very bored."

"When I saw it," she went on, "I called Dixie right away to come and babysit." Then she stared me right in the eyes. "I know what it's like to really, really, really need a visit from your sister." She waited.

"I'm sorry," I said at last, "that I haven't visited."

She was waiting for more.

"I'm terrified of the babies," I offered.

"Dixie has that same theory," Mackie said.

"I got it from Dixie, actually," I said. "But it's true."

"It may be true," Mackie said, "but that doesn't make it okay."

"Okay."

"I'm drowning over there! I really need you!"

"It's been two months!" I said. "You don't have the hang of it yet?"

And then Mackie gave me a look she'd perfected at least twenty years before. It was a *Give me a break* look that also managed to ask *Are you the stupidest person on the earth?* and *How can we possibly be related?* at the same time.

"I just really needed a break," I said, with a shrug. And then I looked her straight in the eyes back. "Really, really, really."

But sometimes a perfectly good explanation isn't good enough.

"I'm sorry," I said again. And then I thought about how, short of offering to move back in and help her, there wasn't much more I could say.

"We'll just have to agree to disagree," Mackie said at last.

And I said, "Fine."

Then, outside the tent, we heard a noise.

"What's that?" Mackie asked.

"News helicopter," I said. There'd been a few before.

I started to unzip the tent.

"Where are you going?"

"Well," I said. "I kind of have to make the most of the media moment."

Mackie looked nervous. "You aren't going to get naked or anything, are you?"

"No, no," I said. "Not naked."

But Howard and I had come up with an idea for them, and I was all ready, I'd been hoping a helicopter might swing by tonight. I was wearing a pink T-shirt with the words KISS ME! across it, and underneath I had on a tank top with a big red heart. I crawled out and stood up in the spotlight as tall as I could. Then I waved at the helicopter, and then peeled off the top T-shirt and swung it around over my head before flinging it over the balcony and blowing kisses up toward the reporters.

It's safe to say I'd never done anything like that before in my life. But for the Love Library, I'd do anything.

Mackie had been peeking through the tent. "You've lost your mind," she said.

But Howard, later, after he saw it on the eleven o'clock news, would call to tell me he loved me. "If I weren't gay, I'd propose," he'd say.

And I'd say, "If I weren't straight, I'd accept."

As I crawled back into the tent right then, Mackie said, "You really want to save this library, huh?"

I nodded. "And if I have to do a faux striptease to do it, I will."

"Isn't there a better way to get people's attention?" Mackie asked. "One that doesn't involve acting like a Girl Gone Wild?"

But I just shrugged. "Probably not."

She'd brought a Scrabble board in her bag. Without saying too much more, we set it up and started playing. Then, for the first time in a long time, things felt a little more like normal. After four days of talking to birds, and airplanes, and the wind, talking to Mackie didn't seem so hard. I started to chatter away a little at her the way I used to, going on and on about life on the rooftop. And then, somehow, I worked my way over to how nice it was that Mackie had come to visit me, and then I asked this question: "How great is Dixie to babysit for you tonight?"

And then Mackie, my sister who had seemed fine just a minute before, and who had just snagged a Triple Word Score with *cleavage*, and who never, ever cried, started crying.

"What?" I asked.

But Mackie just cried. She cried for so long, I finally stopped waiting for an explanation and just tumped her over into my lap. She stayed there with her head on my leg, and I stroked her hair. I didn't have to push for an answer. I could guess pretty well what it was.

After a while, Mackie said, "Dixie isn't Mom." And then she started crying again.

I combed through Mackie's curls with my fingers, and said, "You miss Mom?"

Very quietly, like she was hoping I might not even hear her at all, Mackie said, "I just don't think that she's ever going to come back."

It took a while for us to pull ourselves back together. After a bit, we each ate a handful of M&M's. It was ten thirty, and Mackie was worried that she needed to get home, but she didn't really want to go. We decided to put all the Scrabble tiles in alphabetical order before she left, and while we worked, she said, "The babies are awesome, but oh, wow—are they loud. And they cry all the time. I don't think you'd want them."

Then Mackie thanked me for having them for her, and I thanked her for giving me a chance to do something meaningful with my life. Then she apologized for being bossy and controlling, and I apologized for being grouchy and withdrawn. And she apologized for shoving Everett Thompson at me and I apologized for resisting.

"I shouldn't have pushed so hard," Mackie said.

"I should have given him a chance," I said.

And then Mackie dropped this bomb: "I was just nervous about that crush you had on Clive."

What? "What?"

"It just made me a little nervous, that's all."

"Who had a crush on Clive?"

"You did."

"I did not!"

"Sarah," she said. "Once I figured it out, it was so obvious. You turned beet red every time he walked into the room. Don't worry. It was just hormones. No big deal."

Now, sometimes, when faced with the truth, you just toss up your hands and admit it. And other times, when faced with the truth, you lie like hell. And then, if you're lucky, you find your way to a different truth. Maybe even a truer truth.

"The person I had a crush on," I said, "was Everett."

"That's not true," Mackie said. "You were dead-set against him."

"I was dead-set against you setting me up with him," I said.

"Why?"

"I didn't want you to mess it up."

"I would not have messed it up!" Mackie said.

"You always mess everything up!"

Mackie ignored that. "If you liked him," she said, "why did you tell me you were going to set yourself on fire?"

"Because!" I said. "I wanted to be left alone!" Then I met her eyes. "On so many levels, I wanted to be left alone."

Mackie thought this over. "Or maybe," she said, "because you knew in some deep place that he was the one. And so you had to thrash like an alligator to get away."

It was a heck of a theory. "I guess that's possible," I said.

Then I went on: "And then Everett gave me this great kiss in your pool, and I was so sure he was going to call me—and I had a few crazy minutes when I was convinced my whole life was going to change—but then he didn't call. He never called. And then he started dating Barni. The tenant!"

As Mackie took this in, she made a little frown. "I hate to say this," she said, "but I think I might have messed something up."

I met her eyes. "What?"

"There was a day when Everett told me he was going to ask you out. And I advised him against it."

"You advised him against it?"

"Actually, I told him exactly what you had just told me. That you'd rather"—and here, she used air quotes—" 'douse yourself with gasoline and set yourself on fire' than go on a date with him."

I stared at her. "You didn't."

She shrugged. "I did."

I squeezed my eyes shut. "Mackie!"

"You're the one who said it."

"But I didn't *mean* it."

"Sure fooled me."

And then I just stared at her. For so long that she finally started saying, "What?" And then, "*What?*"

"Mackie," I finally said. "You messed something up."

She walked me through what actually happened. The day after the pool kiss, when Mackie brought lunch to Clive and Everett at the warehouse, working on that lawsuit, Mackie had asked him how his date went with Barni.

"I carried her home after the party," Everett had told Mackie. "And then she tripped on the stereo cord, clonked her head hard against the coffee table, and passed out." He'd taken her to her own ER, and they'd waited six hours before being told she was fine.

Mackie had tried to make excuses for Barni, saying she was young and naïve. But Everett had interrupted her to say that he really wasn't interested in Barni, anyway. The person he was interested in, he said, was me.

But Mackie had shaken her head and said, "I'm sorry." My temper tantrum two nights before had finally convinced her. "It's never going to happen," she told him. "It's completely hopeless." And then, to sum up: "She absolutely hates you."

And so, Barni the tenant.

"I talked him into that, too," Mackie said.

I smacked myself on the head. "You told him I hated him."

"But I thought you did hate him!"

"But I didn't!"

Then Mackie smacked herself on the head—with each word: "But! Why! Didn't! You! Tell! Me!"

I shrugged. "I don't know. Bad timing?" Then I looked at Mackie's face, all puffy from tears and sleep deprivation, and I felt such a wave of tenderness for her. "Don't blame yourself, okay?"

"I won't," she said. "You don't blame yourself, either."

"I won't."

Then Mackie said, "Who can we blame?"

"Barni," I said. "Let's blame her."

Then Mackie drew in a quick breath. "Oh! I forgot to tell you!"

"What?"

"Barni's moving out. She's getting married."

I felt a prickle of adrenaline shoot through my body as I heard the words, and then formed the question, "Who is she marrying?"

Mackie heard the intensity in my voice and looked up. Then she realized what I was worried about and put her hands out to stop me. "Not Everett!" she said. "Sorry! Not Everett! One of her other boyfriends."

"Barni has other boyfriends?"

Mackie nodded. "A bunch. You know—she doesn't want to be tied down."

"What about Everett?" I asked.

Mackie shook her head. "Over. Long over. Not a good match."

I looked up at the ceiling of the tent in exasperation. "Duh!" I said.

"Yeah," Mackie agreed. "Duh."

It was looking like it was time for me to give Everett Thompson a call and straighten a few things out. But first Mackie and I had to agree to a no-fault pregnancy. Also, I had to promise to come visit her and the babies as soon as I came off the roof.

It was the first real conversation we'd had in months and months. And while it didn't exactly fix everything, it was a very decent start.

Of course, I didn't have Everett's phone number. And it wasn't listed. But when Howard called to congratulate me on my striptease, I had him find it.

It was 11:42 when I got off the phone with Howard, and I had to decide if it was too late to call Everett.

I decided it was. But then I called him anyway.

But he wasn't home, and so I left a message. Very likely the worst message in the entire history of answering machines:

"Hey there, Everett. This is Sarah. Harper. And, um, I'm just calling you now, at almost midnight, to tell you I just had a very weird conversation with Mackie about a chat she had with you a while back about me dousing myself with gasoline. Yeah. I was kind of horrified to hear about her telling you that, because the thing is, I didn't mean it. At all. Obviously. What I mean to say is, I think she may have given you a false impression about my opinion of you. I'm on top of a building right now and can't get down, but I'd love to discuss this over coffee or something sometime. If that sounds good to you."

And then I left my number, but—surprise—Everett did not call me. Not that night, and not the next morning. Which was fine. I didn't care. But I did tuck the phone in my bra strap so I'd have it handy if it rang.

By the time my last hour on the rooftop was almost up, I was resting in my tent and speeding through the last chapter of *Persuasion*, trying to reach the end before I ran out of time. The plan was to hide from the news helicopters that had been circling, on and off, since six in the morning, and the enormous crowd (we'd later estimate two thousand people) gathering on the lawn below, so that when the big moment came I could make a dramatic appearance.

I'd already washed my face, as much of the rest of my body as the library bathroom allowed for, and put on extra deodorant and a squirt of perfume called Heaven. I'd brushed and flossed and put on a fresh "Save Love! Save the Library!" T-shirt, and I was sucking on a breath mint, too, in anticipation of the ninety-nine kisses I was just about to share with Ryan, college hottie and almost–total stranger. And I was just thinking how weird it was to know in advance that I was about to be kissed, how usually kisses were not things you could anticipate down to the minute, when I got a call from Howard.

"We've got a problem," Howard said. "Ryan just threw up."

"Threw up?"

"It seems he's been throwing up all morning, and has a fever and some other 'intestinal issues.' But he didn't want to miss his chance to kiss you," Howard said. "That's a nice compliment, right?"

"Sort of," I said.

Now Ryan's mom was on her way to pick him up and a frantic search was on for a replacement.

"Don't worry," Howard said. "You're not that bad. We'll find somebody."

Howard hung up, and I commando-crawled out of the tent to peek around the banner and scan the crowd for anybody halfway decent to take Ryan's place.

But they were all strangers. I had been ready to kiss Ryan. We'd been flirting and working up to it for weeks in the office. He wasn't a dream-man or anything, but I had a good sense of his basic hygiene and I was fairly sure he wasn't insane. For one quick kiss at a kissing booth, I could probably have kissed a total stranger. But this was ninety-nine kisses. This was a lot of kisses.

I flipped open the phone and called Howard back. "Howard," I said. "I don't want to kiss a stranger."

"That's just about all we've got down here, babe," Howard said.

"Then, you do it."

Howard pretended he hadn't heard me. "Who?"

"You, Howard. You."

"I don't want to do it," Howard said.

"Howard," I said. "I don't care. I don't want some gross guy with bird flu and a porn garage coming up here."

"I can't," Howard said. "I haven't kissed a girl since ninth grade."

"Too bad."

"The idea of it turns my stomach just a bit, actually," Howard went on.

"I'm right there with you, Howard," I said. And then I decided to channel Dixie from self-defense class. Howard needed a pep talk, and I gave it all I had: "Somebody's got to do it, Howard! The show must go on! Do it for the Love Library! Do it for Emmet Frost and Minnie! Do it for all the buildings that have laid themselves down to the bulldozers! You can save this building, Howard! But we've only got five minutes! So go brush your teeth, grab a breath mint, and get your ass up here!"

It worked, but not really. Howard just let out a slow sigh. "Put some extra deodorant on," he said. "I'll be up in five."

In the time that elapsed, I tried to psych myself up to kiss Howard, with his walrus mustache, and his coffee-stained teeth, and his paunchy belly. He was wearing my favorite tie today, so that was a bright side.

I crawled back into my tent, popped another Tic Tac, and waited. We'd be fine. We'd just fake it. We were sacrificing ten minutes of our lives in service to the greater good. If Hollywood could do it, so could we. For the sake of the building, I could do anything. And I felt pretty sure Howard could, too. Someday we'd look back on it and laugh. Or, I thought, as I heard Howard's feet on the metal staircase below, maybe we'd just feel awkward and uncomfortable about it for the rest of our lives. Either way, it was the right thing to do.

At four o'clock, it was time. The band had stopped playing, and Barbara had begun her speech at the podium. People were gathering around her and starting to peer up at me. Three news helicopters were circling. I was ready. I could rise above everything, even my own limitations, and kiss the heck out of Howard. But I had this crazy feeling of dread. The ninety-nine kisses were supposed to be a spectacular grand finale, but I felt certain, all of a sudden, that the folks down below would be able to tell that Howard and I were just going through the motions. Even if they couldn't actually see Howard's face all squeezed up into a sour-lemon pucker. They'd just know, somehow, that we were faking. All these hours up here on the roof, and the grand finale was going to fall flat.

Then I heard a drumroll. It was time to come out, and so I did. The crowd cheered, and I did my best to channel Miss America. I think I even cupped my hand when I waved. But all the while, I was thinking, *This is going to bomb*.

When I heard the squeak of the hatch door opening, I had half a mind to just call it all off.

But then the person who pushed through the hatch wasn't Howard, after all. Or the security guard. Or any of the men down at the rally who'd bought a ticket for the raffle. It was Everett Thompson. In faded Levi's and a T-shirt. Looking so good, the crowd went crazy. Looking so good, I thought for a second I was having a hallucination.

Everett gave a little wave. "Hey."

Then I said, "Howard made you come up?" And without waiting for his answer, I said, "He totally chickened out!"

But Everett said, "I volunteered, actually."

"Did Howard tell you what you were volunteering for? Because now that you're up here, you're going to have to give me ninety-nine kisses."

"That's a lot of kisses."

"And you can't get out of it. There are news helicopters." Now there were four.

"I know. I've seen you on the news. They're doing constant updates about what you're up to. They're calling you 'crazy preservationist' like it's your title: 'Crazy preservationist Sarah Harper just finished her tuna sandwich.' " He paused, then said, "How's the knitting coming?"

"Terrible," I said. "It turns out I can't count."

Everett was hooking his harness to the railing. "Some of the commentators think another handicraft might suit you better. Jewelry making or potholders."

I said, "What are you doing here, Everett?"

"I was down on the lawn just now, talking with Howard about how the last girl he kissed was Martha Cimarelli in 1973, when your sister came up with a stroller full of babies and said she had something she couldn't tell me."

Mackie was here. I looked down, and she was holding one of the babies and waving. Clive had the other one, and he was waving, too. I took a second to admire the babies and their pink faces and matching sun bonnets. And then I saw Dixie, and my dad, and everybody good in my life, all down below, waving and watching.

"Did she say what it was she couldn't tell you?" I asked.

"No," Everett said. "But she said it was good. Then she told me to climb up here right away and ask you. And Howard graciously stepped aside."

I was trying to collect my thoughts. The people down on the lawn were starting to chant, "Kiss her! Kiss her!"

"So, what is it she can't tell me?" Everett asked.

"It's kind of a long story," I said.

"Also," Everett added, "I just checked my messages." Then he made a little wrinkled-nose smile.

"Right," I said. "What did I say on that message, again?"

"You said that the thought of me did not actually make you want to light yourself on fire."

I nodded. "It doesn't," I said.

"Okay." He was waiting for more.

"And I'm just really sorry," I went on. "I'm sorry for all of it."

He crossed his arms over his chest.

"Kiss her! Kiss her!" had turned to "Zip it! Lip it!"

But I wasn't ready.

"I'm sorry," I went on, "for high school, the way I broke your heart and killed your magnolia tree. And I'm sorry that I didn't appreciate you then. That I wasn't more grateful for your affection."

Then he shrugged. "I'm sorry I called you old," he said. "It was just the first mean thing I could think of."

"I'm sorry I poured beer on your crotch," I said.

"I'm sorry I dated Barni," he said.

"I'm sorry I made you talk like a pirate," I said.

"I'm sorry I snuggled you in the storage closet," he said.

"I'm not."

"I'm sorry your water broke before I could kiss you."

"You were dating Barni then!"

"Actually, I wasn't."

"But she kept calling you 'Boyfriend, Boyfriend, Boyfriend.'"

"Yeah," Everett said. "That was weird."

"Why didn't you stop her?"

Everett shrugged. "I figured there was a chance it was making you jealous."

"Mean!" I said.

"Yep."

"I'm sorry I pretended not to like you," I went on.

"Mean yourself," he said.

"That wasn't about you being unlikable. That was really about you being—you know—too likable."

"I was so into you right before Mackie told me what you said."

"You were?"

"Yep."

"But you're not anymore?"

Everett shook his head. "Nope. Not anymore." But his face looked like maybe he still was. A little.

"Oh," I said.

And then I noticed that the crowd had fallen silent. Then I heard someone on the lawn shout, "One! Two! Three!" And then the entire lawn, in unison, shouted, "Kiss her!"

And so Everett took a step forward, and just as he did, somewhere down below, another drumroll started. He put an arm around my waist and pulled me right up to him, belly-to-belly, like we had been on the plane, and for one deliciously agonizing second he did not kiss me, but instead just looked down into my eyes like he was waiting for something. The crowd was holding its breath, waiting.

And so I said, "That night? In the swimming pool?"

He didn't take his eyes off mine. "Yeah?"

"I melted."

And that's when Everett leaned his tall self down and pressed his mouth against mine, the two of us against the backdrop of the sky, the crowd cheering beneath—and it was a gentle, lingering thing, his mouth slightly open, his nose against my cheek.

When he pulled back, he said, "Was that one kiss, or two?"

I said, "That was one. You've got ninety-eight to go."

I turned and pointed at the crowd, and they shouted, "One!" And then Howard flipped the chart to "1." And then we were off, the crowd counting for us in delighted shouts, and we got into a great rhythm. I can still hear the sound of them now: "Two!" and then Everett turning back to me with a soft, economical, but by no means platonic, kiss. "Three!" And another. "Four!" And another. Their turn, our turn—them, then us. I was glad Everett was holding me because the height and the wind and the kisses and the warmth of his lips were all making me dizzy.

When we got to ninety-four, Everett shifted down and kissed my hand, which elicited delighted squeals. On ninety-five, he kissed my shoulder. Ninety-six was my elbow. Ninety-seven was the dip between my collarbones. Ninety-eight was my chin. And then, at ninety-nine, he paused to look at me. We were both a little breath-less. The crowd started chanting, "Do it! Do it!" but he just squinted his eyes at me for a second.

Finally I lifted my hands, put them behind his neck, and pulled his face to mine, and even though we'd just finished ninety-eight other kisses, this kiss, here, in that moment, stands out from all of them—because even as the crowd went bananas, and the Western band started to play a two-step rendition of "Love Will Keep Us To-gether," and ninety-nine heart-shaped balloons floated past us into the sky, everything seemed to fall away, and the goofiness and show-manship of the whole stunt disappeared, and it was just the two of us, kissing the sort of kiss that turns touch into a form of talking, as we spoke all the kind and hopeful things that are too tender for ac-tual words.

We kissed for so long, people started to lose interest. By the time we looked down, people had started reading to their kids again or were dancing to the band or waiting in line to buy cotton candy. Some were heading back to their cars to beat the traffic. Life had ambled on.

Though when we made it back to ground level and emerged from the library doors, a crowd gathered around us and cheered and clapped. People took our photo. A TV news reporter put a micro-phone up to me and said, "So? Is he a good kisser?"

I looked at Everett. "He could win a medal," I said. And then, "He should go to the Olympics."

So she turned to Everett. "What do you think of that?"

He was looking at me. "I don't need to compete at that level," he said. "I'm just glad to have a hobby."

And that's how we had our last first kiss. Which I count as our first real kiss. Even though there were ninety-nine of them.

Chapter Fourteen

So was it a just-plain-perfect happy ending? Hell, no. There's no such thing.

But did Everett and I get married two years later, barefoot on a Hawaiian beach as the sun went down? And did Dixie wear a hot-pink fringe jacket with a rhinestone pin in the shape of the Great State of Texas? And had she found my mom's wedding ring at last—in my dad's sock drawer—so he could give it to us? And did Mackie's black-haired toddlers strip down naked and splash in the ocean throughout the ceremony? And did we hire an Elvis impersonator to sing at the reception? Yes, yes—all yes.

But did Everett turn out to be totally dreamy in every way? Of course not.

I won't deny the cute things we do now, like make pancakes, and go on road trips to Austin, and make out at the movies. We go to the bookstore and then come home and read side by side on the sofa. We sleep in, and eat Häagen-Dazs and Italian food. We go on bike rides and drive down to Galveston and cook out on the beach. We talk and talk. But he also forgets to write down phone messages, and leaves his sweaty running clothes on the bathroom floor, and has no understanding of how to put dishes in the dishwasher. He scoffs at decorating magazines, leaves the seat up, and thinks all wine is "girlie." He doesn't understand the big deal with Tina Fey, and he once flat-out refused to watch *On Golden Pond* with me. And don't get me started on what it's like to watch a grown man play video games for hours on end. He's not perfect, but he's real. He listens when I read him lists of names for the babies we might have for ourselves some-day, when the time is right. And he thinks I'm delectable, and he makes me laugh. The longer I know him, the more things about him drive me crazy. Both bad crazy and very, very good.

And something about him reminds me of Mackie, as strange as that sounds. Or maybe I should say something about the way I am with him reminds me of the way I've always been with her. The way I want to tell him everything. The way I have to talk to him at least once a day. The way, for whatever reason, the person I am with him is my truest, easiest self. With other boyfriends, I managed the idea of closeness, or the appearance of it. With Everett, for the first time ever, it's the real thing. We like to get fancy and go out to eat, but I am just as happy with him in shorts and a T-shirt. Or in pajamas. Or, actually, in nothing at all.

I'd like to be able to say that those ninety-nine kisses more than two years ago changed everything for me. But even after they happened, I was still just the same person I'd always been. I still Googled diseases and made lists of symptoms. I still wondered with each hamburger I ate if that would be the one that gave me mad cow. I still made mistakes, and slept with a light on, and shouted Dixie's curses whenever I was alone in the car. I still missed things about New York and didn't quite know how to feel totally at home in my hometown. I still acted too tough sometimes and worked too hard a lot.

Of course. Kisses can't change your personality. Or anesthetize life's pains. Or bring your mother back to you. Life is always a struggle between who you are and who you'd like to be. It's always a negotiation between how you want it and how it is. There's no changing that.

The Monday after the rally, the city held its referendum about the library. And of all the people in the fourth largest city in the country, 12 percent turned out to vote. And that 12 percent, despite all the bumper stickers and billboards and news helicopters and the famous Kiss 99, did not pass the bond.

We had been certain it would pass. Nobody even had a doubt. When I came down from the roof, folks from the office hugged each other and slapped high fives until long after everyone else had gone home. We'd done it! The city had gone nuts that day. "You have no idea what a media darling you are," Howard told me. "I haven't turned on the TV once since Tuesday without seeing your face."

We had done our very best, but it wasn't good enough.

We knew it as soon as we went to the polls. Everett and I went together—after pancakes and coffee at a nearby diner—and had kissed for the cameras before going in. Then he'd squeezed my hand before we parted for our separate booths, and I'd gone in ready to rock the vote, but when I actually read the question on the ballot, this is what it said:

Shall the city uphold its citizens' right to purchase any available properties as they wish, without interference from the City Council, the Mayor, or other Interested Parties?

Not, in short, the question Barbara Tierney had suggested. There was no mention of the library, or historic preservation. It's possible that lots of people thought it was a hypothetical question. It's possible that folks voted against the bond without even knowing what they were doing. Barbara said, in an email to everyone that night after the results were in, that the library had probably been doomed from the start. "There were a lot of good people on our side," she wrote. "But some even craftier ones on the side of the high-rise. It's a good lesson for us. If you're going to do this work, you've got to gear up for heartbreak as a way of life."

Within a few weeks, the sale to the developers went through, and the librarians packed up the books. Then, in shorter order than seemed possible, the developers applied for their demolition permit, were denied, waited ninety days, and then knocked the library down anyway. On day ninety-one, the bulldozers rolled up on the lawn, and on day ninety-two the entire lot was dirt. They even took the sidewalk. They even took the trees.

That morning, I'd told myself not to go down there. I'd told myself to keep cool, to let it go, to move on to the next thing. But on my way to work, as carefully as I tried to steer toward the office, the Volvo wanted to go in a different direction. By the time the demolition started, I was clutching the fence and begging the dozer drivers for mercy with a small group of dedicated protesters that included each and every one of the librarians. I might have stayed there all day, but, before long, Howard showed up at the scene and cut his way into the group to find me. He pried my fingers off, put his arm around my shoulder, turned me tenderly away, and walked me back to the car.

"We don't watch them go down," he told me. "We never watch them go down."

I still can't drive by the spot where the library stood. I avert my eyes from the high-rise that stands forty-seven stories tall there now. I've seen it, of course—its asymmetrical aluminum windows scattered around the façade, its cheap brick, the fiberglass Greek statues scattered around the landscaping. It takes up every square inch of the lot and looms over the neighborhood like a McMansion on steroids. You can't pretend it's not there.

But I do my best. Out of respect for Emmet Frost, if nothing else. And the ghost-lady's sunny alcove. And the way everything eventually disappears. Out of respect for love. And loss. And heartbreak as a way of life.

But long before any of that, back on the same day as the referendum, I went to visit Mackie and the babies—as promised. A day or so tardy, but still.

She hadn't been kidding. The house was a wreck, the babies were both wailing, infant paraphernalia was everywhere. Mackie had the girls swaddled like papooses, one on her shoulder and one wailing in a vibrating bassinet, when she opened the door.

Mackie didn't even try to speak over the crying—she just turned and led me to the sofa, sat me down, wedged the babies into my arms one on each side, and fixed some bottles while I tried to reason the girls into a better mood: "We don't have to fuss like this! The bottles are coming! Let's everybody just chill!"

Once they'd had a good meal, they dozed off, and it was only then that I got a good look at them. This moment right here was exactly what I'd been afraid of all along—the moment when I held them for the first time with nothing to distract me, the moment when they could so easily have felt like stolen things ripped from my body. I braced myself for the pain of it, but it didn't come. When I finally felt them in my arms, they just felt like any other sleeping babies. Except these were Mackie's sleeping babies. One of whom needed a diaper change, though I couldn't tell who.

"They both look totally different," I said. "And they both look exactly like Clive."

"Don't they?" Mackie said. She had leaned her head back and closed her eyes. "Tiny, raven-haired mini Clives."

Mackie fell asleep within seconds, and so I just sat very still and watched them all dozing, letting my eyes drift from face to face to face—all of them so familiar, even the new ones.

All this time later, I am glad Mackie got what she wanted, and I'm happy I was able to help her, and I know it was the right thing to do. But I still can't shake the feeling that I've lost her. The weirdness from the pregnancy has fallen away, but the babies did change everything. For one, for the first time ever, Mackie has something in her life that's more important to her than me.

When the babies were first born, I was afraid that I would want them. But the problem turned out to be that they want Mackie. Every single minute of the day and night. And she wants them back.

I know it makes me sound selfish. But for so long, it was really just the two of us. Even with boyfriends or husbands around, in some way, we knew we came first for each other. But now, for Mackie, the babies are first—and everyone else is a distant, blurry second. She's more than two years into parenting now, and even though she's got the hang of baby life pretty well, those girls manage to keep her to themselves. I don't want to say that I'm jealous of them, but I am, just a little.

Especially when I have to wave my hand in front of Mackie's distracted face and say, "Hello! Can you listen for two minutes?"

Then she shakes to attention and says, "Sorry! Yes." And she turns her eyes straight to mine and focuses, just like I asked, on whatever I'm saying. For exactly two minutes. If we're lucky.

I thank her for managing it. But two minutes, of course, is nowhere even close to enough.

That's where friends come in, I guess, and I've made a bunch since I've been home. I've bonded with a girl in my building who works at the butterfly museum. I go walking a couple of times a week with a woman I met at the gym. I carpool to work every day in the Volvo with Mimi from the office, and we sing along with Willie and harmonize. I'm even friends on Facebook with April, who's back in Houston, working as a hairdresser, and dating a new guy whose first name is John Wayne.

These friends are all great. But they're not Mackie.

Here's what I tell myself: It's a good thing Mackie's not my friend. If she were a friend, she'd be gone by now. She'd have become one of those people with kids that you never see, and then years would go by and one day we'd bump into each other at the movie theater and give each other an enormous hug to overcompensate and say, "How are you? You look terrific!"

But she's not a friend. She's my sister, and I have no choice but to keep hanging on to her the best I can.

Dixie has promised me that it won't always be this way, that babies grow up and need less from their mamas, that Mackie will come back to me. "And when you have your own babies," she said on the plane flight to Hawaii, "you'll do the same thing right back to her." And something about the way she said it, as was often true of Dixie, made everything seem okay.

Dixie also told me something else about Mackie on that plane flight: something I didn't know. In the hospital, after the babies came, when I was sleeping like crazy, Mackie had come to visit me a bunch of times. Dixie watched Mackie shuffle between the nursery and my room, back and forth for a day and a half, before she finally took some time to go home to rest. "You were always sleeping," Dixie said. "And she didn't want to wake you. But she'd pull a chair up to the end of the bed, lift back the covers, and rub your feet with lotion." Then she leaned in. "You can ask Everett if you don't believe me."

"Everett was there?"

"Sure," Dixie said. "You had a whole room full of people keeping an eye on you."

"Why didn't you wake me up?"

"Well." Dixie thought about it. "You needed your rest."

On the night of those ninety-nine kisses, Everett and I helped clean up after the rally and then joined the folks from the office at a Honduran restaurant on the back patio—where we ignored each other above the table and held hands underneath it.

Then he came to my apartment and waited politely while I took the longest, steamiest, most optimistic shower of my entire life. I can still close my eyes and remember what it felt like to stand under the water on that particular night. It's such a sweet thing about people: that when we are truly happy, we can't imagine ever being unhappy again.

I dressed in the bathroom, and tied my wet hair back, and I had barely made it out and down the little hallway before Everett found me. We kissed up against the wall for a good while, and then we made our way to the bedroom. "It's okay for me to kiss you like this," he said somewhere along the way, "right?"

But I didn't say anything back. I just kissed him some more.

And then I had a thought I'd never had before. *This is love,* I thought. *That's exactly what this is.*

He stayed over that night. With me. On my bed, in his clothes, under a throw blanket. Spooning me unabashedly and waking up from time to time to make sure I was still there. I lay awake for hours while he slept, thinking about how much everything had changed, and about how heartbreaks and joys in life are all tangled together. You have to be good at one to be good at the other. In New York, I'd been careful to avoid all the sadnesses I possibly could. But coming home, without ever meaning to, I had plunged neck-deep into an ocean of them. I think it was good for me, in the end.

I can never lie awake at night without my mind drifting over to the memory of my mother, that image I've carried so long of her on her ship, standing at the railing, hair in the wind. But on that night, my notion of her changed. When I pictured her then, it was the roof of my library she was standing on—much closer than I'd ever realized, and, of course, infinitely farther away. She is not ever coming back. But I can sense her better now. I know what it's like to feel that same breeze as you loom above every familiar thing you know. I know what it's like to stand terrified at the railing and force yourself to look down. I have done the very same thing on my own sinking ship.

Here's what I tell myself now: That it's vital to learn how to make the best of things. That there is no tenderness without bravery. That if things hadn't been so bad, they could never have gotten so good. And that it's always better to have what you have than to get what you wanted. Except for this: Every now and then, when you are impossibly lucky, you rise above yourself—and get both.

A Note About the Library

The fictional Dr. Emmet Frost Library in this story is based closely on the real-life Dr. Eugene Clark Library in Lockhart, Texas. The character of Emmet Frost is based on the real historic figure Dr. Eugene Clark—who did give ten thousand dollars on his deathbed to build a library in his hometown; who was rejected by the woman he loved, Mamie Steele; and who did appoint her and members of her book club, the Irving Club, to the board of the new library. As in the story, the ladies designed a room within the library for their book club meetings. But unlike the Frost Library, the Lockhart library has not been demolished. It is a thriving, beloved, and essential part of the community of Lockhart. And the Irving Club still meets once a month in the building it has called home since 1900.

Acknowledgments

I'm tempted to just thank everyone I've ever met. But maybe that's too broad.

The problem with seriously trying to thank everyone who helped me bring this book to fruition is that I have a terrible memory. And maybe it's worse to try to name everybody and leave out just a few—say, for example, our pediatrician, Alex Injac, whom I left out the first two times around—than to just send out a broad thank-you to the universe. Then everyone can feel included! Which, if you're reading these acknowledgments, you absolutely are.

That said, I have a small list of people I cannot resist naming:

My agent, Helen Breitwieser, for being so smart and savvy, as well as my awesome publicist, Jynne Martin.

My old editor, Laura Ford, who had so many brilliant things to say about this story, and my new editor, Jen Smith, who I am delighted to be working with. Also, in general, the great folks at Ballantine, including Janet Wygal and Libby McGuire.

My friend Laura Mayes for introducing me to her childhood library, and the librarians of Lockhart, Texas, for taking such great care of it—and, in particular, Rose Aleta Laurell, whose antics inspired parts of this book.

Our family friend Gene Graham, for lending me her beautiful country house for a writing retreat.

The book *The Geography of Nowhere* by James Howard Kunstler, which really got me thinking about the built environment.

My friends Brené Brown, Karen Walrond, Jenny Lawson, and Lucy Chambers, for helping me get the word out about my books—and for being awesome. And other friends I love so much—you know who you are!

My phenomenal husband, Gordon, and my rock-star mom, Deborah Detering, who are like a dream team of child care, and who go above and beyond to support, nurture, and put up with me in very different but vital ways. And other great members of my family: Bill Pannill, Lizzie Pannill, and Shelley, Matt, and Yasmin Stein.

And, the best for last: my children, Anna and Thomas, who are a zillion times better than the best kids I could ever possibly have wished for.

ABOUT THE AUTHOR

KATHERINE CENTER is the author of *Everyone Is Beautiful* and *The Bright Side of Disaster*. She graduated from Vassar College, where she won the Vassar College Fiction Prize, and received an MA in fiction from the University of Houston. She's published essays in *Real Simple Family* and the anthology *Because I Love Her: 34 Women Writers Reflect on the Mother-Daughter Bond*. A former freelance writer and teacher, Center lives in Houston with her husband and two young children. Visit her website at www.katherinecenter.com.

ABOUT THE TYPE

This book was set in Fairfield, the first typeface from the hand of the distinguished American artist and engraver Rudolph Ruzicka (1883–1978). Ruzicka was born in Bohemia and came to America in 1894. He set up his own shop, devoted to wood engraving and printing, in New York in 1913 after a varied career working as a wood engraver, in photoengraving and banknote printing plants, and as an art director and freelance artist. He designed and illustrated many books, and was the creator of a considerable list of individual prints—wood engravings, line engravings on copper, and aquatints.